All the darkest corners

Dom Knowlson

First published by Morganfield Consulting Ltd.

Copyright © Dominic Knowlson 2023

Dominic Knowlson asserts the moral right to be identified as the author of this work.

This novel is a work of fiction. All names, places, characters and incidents portrayed in it are the work of the author's imagination. Any resemblance to actual persons, living or dead, events or locations is entirely coincidental.

Being made up, it contains technical, historical and geographical impossibilities the author is well aware of, so if you spot any, you don't need to let him know.

All rights reserved. No part of this publication may be reproduced, stored in a retrieval system, or transmitted in any form or by any means, electronic, mechanical, photocopying, recording or otherwise, without the prior permission of the copyright owner and the publisher.

Cover design and illustration by Fernando Cassani.

ISBN: 9798393097004

Thanks

To my editor, Sara Polecat, for making me look a better writer than I am.
To my wife, another Sara, and to my sons for making me look a better person than I am.
To all my family and friends for putting up with me being a bit crap sometimes.
To all the dogs, especially best dogs ever Goldie and Bailey, a pair of Jack Russells (a clue there) for their listening skills on the many long walks. At least I think they were listening.
To Curtis, Hook, Sumner & Morris for providing the soundtrack to my life.

1. Kitty

She had the sort of money that money couldn't buy, and from the moment Kitty Conlon walked into my office on that warm October day, I could tell she was used to getting her own way.

Of course, I didn't know her name then or about the money, just that wherever it was she came from, she'd stopped by the looks department on the way over. Brunette and bordering on petite, she was certainly my type, if a man can truly be said to have such a thing.

She wouldn't be considered beautiful in a classical sense (although I've never been entirely sure what that means) but was far over on the right side of pretty and well-polished, which can count for a lot. Particularly on a quiet Friday afternoon, which this just happened to be.

Let's not get ahead of ourselves though and back up to that money for a minute. After all, it's not altogether unknown in my line of work but it is still a rarity and worthy of consideration. Most of my customers weren't usually what you'd call well-heeled.

I found out later that her fortune wasn't the kind that is all crumbling mansions with threadbare carpets and bad plumbing: not old money but not exactly new either, it was somewhere in between. Whenever it was, somewhere along the line, one of Kitty's ancestors had made a pile: as usual on account of being bigger rascals and more successful thieves than yours or mine ever managed.

Like the money, this inconvenient fact had been thoroughly rinsed across generations of refined dinner parties and polished at cocktail soirees, resulting in the picture of elegance standing before me.

When she knocked and entered, I'd been looking over

the file on the Maddison case for the umpteenth time and had just put the familiar photograph back in the manilla folder and was transferring the whole lot back in the desk drawer for safekeeping. It could wait.

Surprising myself with an unusual display of gallantry, I stood up.

"Can I help you, Miss?" I asked in a voice that came out about a full octave lower than my usual speaking one.

"You can stop with the Miss for starters. The name's Kitty – Kitty Conlon – and technically speaking, I'm a Mrs. You are Mr. Morgan, I take it?"

"Sure, I'm Morgan. Generally speaking, I prefer it without the Mr. unless you happen to be from the police department, which I don't suppose you do. In their case I insist on it".

I offered her my paw and we shook.

"Shall we?"

Gesturing to the pair of well-worn Chesterfields and walnut veneer coffee table in the corner of my spartan office, I came out from behind my desk and went over, which gave me the chance to study her close up.

She had a kind of upfront, good-humoured sexuality that you could almost reach out and touch and might get you in a lot of trouble if you did. Her body spoke unmistakably of languid afternoons spent in a king-sized bed with the finest silk sheets. At least, that's what I thought I heard it say.

I was finding it difficult to concentrate.

She sat down, elegantly. Me less so.

"In what way do you mean 'technically speaking'?"

"You're the detective, aren't you? I'm sure you can fill in the gaps."

She had a point.

"You're not wearing a wedding ring, of course -

they taught us to look out for that sort of thing on day one at detective school, but that could be for one of a number of reasons."

She didn't take me up on the invitation, so I pondered what said reasons might be while the conversation paused. The pause grew up all by itself and before long had become downright pregnant.

"So are you..."

"I should really...."

We both began at the same time.

"Ladies first."

"Thank you. I'm not sure how this works. I've never had to engage a private detective before. I'm a bit nervous – do you have a cigarette?"

I'd have to watch Kitty: the shenanigans may not have been all that far back in her family's past after all. She was being coy, using a little girl lost routine designed to sucker me in.

I wasn't sure how I felt about her act, but decided that I didn't mind, under the circumstances. The circumstances being that I hadn't had a real case in weeks, or a pay cheque to go with it. Here was a well-heeled, good-looking woman in front of me and about to pour out her troubles, so I let myself play along.

"Sure. Here."

I offered her a cigarette from the burr walnut box on the coffee table and reached behind me for the desk lighter, a silver affair, which I held out for her. I had an idea the reason she was here might shed some light on those technicalities she mentioned but needed to hear it from her.

"Take your time. Start wherever you feel like it but try not to leave anything out".

"My husband, Jack is missing. We are separated and it's happened before, but this time is different...."

She didn't strike me as a smoker and took a tentative

puff on her cigarette, then changed her mind and put it out, confirming my suspicions.

"Go on."

"It might be easiest to start from the beginning".

"Okay then." I sat back.

"I met Jack when he came back from overseas. He'd been discharged from the army and was very dashing, with a man's world of experience more than me. He was handsome and a charmer - still is in many ways - and we were very much in love, even though my family had reservations.

We got married and have two beautiful boys – Victor and Frank - and for while things were just fine. Daddy even got over his huffiness when the boys came along and helped to set Jack up in a furniture business over in Wilmington, out there by the port.

Jack drank more than was good for him, but we were young, and it never turned nasty or seemed to really matter that much. Most people like a drink, don't they, Morgan?"

It was a rhetorical question, but I nodded encouragingly in any case.

"We were all enjoying ourselves back then, after that dreary war business was over."

I'd heard the war described in many ways before, but never in those terms.

"He has a wide circle of friends and was always out at the track or off playing cards with his army buddies or whoever. There'd be trips to Vegas with the guys or sometimes with a client; there was always some excuse or other for a drink.

Then he started disappearing for a few days at a time on unscheduled stop-outs. Drinking and getting into scrapes gradually became the pattern. I thought it would get better over time, but it doesn't work that way with people who drink, does it?"

I shook my head.

"Not always, no."

"Eventually I got fed up with it all. Just couldn't live with the lying and the uncertainty of not knowing where he was or when he was coming back and what state he might be in when he did.

I'd heard the excuses, the apologies and the pleas that he would change too many times. Drunks are liars, you know Morgan. Eventually for the sake of the children and for my own health, I threw him out.

In the end, it doesn't matter what people say or convince themselves they feel in their hearts, it's what they do that counts. You can only go by their actions".

"Amen to that."

"Daddy says that subconsciously I married a weak man to get back at him, but it wasn't always like that. Like I said, things were different at the start, and we were very much in love."

I made a mental note to look up who daddy was.

Kitty Conlon made men nervous, and she knew it. She was starting to get to me, and I knew it, so tried to focus back in on what she was saying while it was still tumbling out so obligingly.

There seemed to be a fair amount of make believe in her story, but it would have been rude not to play along, at least for a bit. I had nothing better to do and apart from anything else, wanted to see where she was going with it.

"So, what's different this time?"

"Different?"

"Your husband has been missing before. Why don't you just sit tight and wait for him to show up? Forgive me, but if you're separated, are you even sure you want him to come back?"

"It's true we're not close anymore, but I asked around and nobody's seen him for over a week now, which is unusual, even for him."

She was shaking her head now.

"It's not just that. There must be something seriously wrong this time – more than just the usual sort of situations he gets himself into. Yesterday was what finally convinced me to do something about it."

"Yesterday?"

"Our son Victor's birthday. He's he older of the two and turned nine yesterday, but there was nothing from his father. No present or telephone call and most especially, no visit. That's how I know there must be something really wrong and what made me ask around about him."

"Couldn't he have just forgotten, or still be off on a drunk somewhere?"

The headshaking was emphatic now.

"Jack may be a pretty lousy father by a lot of people's standards, but he is fanatical about remembering. Maybe it is his way of making up for the times he hasn't been there for them, but he always goes over the top on their birthdays. Toys, trips out, all that sort of thing.

I just know it wouldn't have slipped his mind. There must be something else stopping him."

"Did you go to the police?"

"I did, but they said that it wasn't much to go on. They took down the details, but they weren't really interested. Jack's been a bit of a nuisance to them in the past and my guess is they figure he'll probably show up when he sobers up."

"Yah, I can see why they might be inclined to think that way. How did you end up knocking on my door?"

"Daddy has a friend over at the D.A.'s office, who asked around for him. The word is that you are a pretty good operator – competent I think it was."

"Gee, I've always wanted to be seen as competent. Sounds like I've got some friends over there myself. They say anything else nice about me?"

"That underneath that gruff exterior you are pretty honest and reliable and that you see a job through."

"Here I was thinking I was all charm. Gruff, huh?"

"Actually, I think the word they used was surly, but I softened it a little".

"Much obliged.

Back to your husband. Is there anything else which makes you think that his disappearance is more serious this time? I have no wish to be impertinent and tell me to go to hell if you like, but your husband's disappearances – were they all drinking and horseplay, or were there other women involved?"

She became suddenly serious and immensely sad.

"It might seem strange to you, Morgan, but I never really chose to find out. I'm sure there was never anything *serious*, but I'm realistic enough to know there have probably been some casual acquaintances along the way. He is a man, after all, and a good-looking one at that.

I'm not sure how to put this best, but it never seemed that important to me. What used to eat away at me wasn't the thought of who Jack might be running to, but what he was running from. That's what I could never understand."

"How do you mean?"

"He would never talk about it, but I felt that his drinking was probably down to something in his past. Something he had seen or done in the war maybe. He was quite the hero, you know."

She was changing the subject and we both knew it.

In my line of work, I'm used to seeing people agitated; distressed about whatever impossible situation has driven them to my door. There wasn't any one thing about how she acted, or in what she said; it was just that I wasn't quite buying the sum of all the parts.

As if she could tell what I was thinking, a flicker of

concern went across Kitty's lovely features, there just for a split second. It might have been the only genuine emotion she'd shown since we started talking.

"I don't know your husband of course, but I have some experience in these matters. You need to know that sometimes difficult or unpleasant details emerge. Does he have any other bad habits to be taken into consideration? If there is anything like that, it will save time for me to know about it up front."

She paused, possibly making a play of thinking hard for a minute.

"There's really nothing that I'm aware of, Morgan."

"Okay then. If you're quite sure... For the avoidance of doubt: I take it you'd like me to find your husband?"

"Yes."

"What then?"

"I just need to know that he is safe and for him to get in touch. For the sake of the boys."

"OK. I'll need his address and a list of his friends and business associates, that sort of thing. Details of his hangouts and favourite haunts too. It will save me a lot of shoe leather."

I was reaching behind me for a pen and some paper from the desk, when she delved purposefully into an expensive looking black leather shoulder bag.

"I thought you might ask, so put a list together before coming over. There's a photograph too. Here."

She handed me two sheets of beautiful magnolia writing paper, folded together inside an envelope. I took them out saw that the lists were of names in one column, with contact details in the next and a brief note of the nature of the relationship in the next. Smart lady.

The handwriting was elegant copperplate, naturally, and the envelope itself was padded, presumably to stop any money that might find itself inside from bruising.

There was also a glossy black and white print of Jack Conlon, which might have been one of those publicity shots for a movie star with rugged good looks, all the way down to the dimple on his chin.

"Thank you. You'll want to know my terms and will need to sign a letter of engagement. I have one in the desk over there.

My rate is fifty dollars a day, plus expenses. A job like this, I reckon on it taking no more than about two weeks if I've got nothing else on."

People either showed up or they didn't, and if I couldn't track them down by then, it was usually because they didn't want to be found.

"Do you?"

"What?"

"Have anything else on?"

I shook my head sheepishly.

"Normally I'd ask for an advance, but you look like you're good for it."

She didn't miss a beat:

"Don't be so sure what I am and am not good for, Morgan".

I didn't know what this meant, but her mood seemed to have lightened, so gave her my bashful smile: the one designed to work on old ladies, small children and ice maidens.

She took an alligator clutch purse from inside the bag, which was obviously expensive, but I wasn't crazy about. My guess was that neither was the alligator. Then she counted out five one-hundred-dollar bills, which looked so crisp and new that she might well have had her own printing press at home to mint the things.

"Here's an advance. I'd like you to start straight away, please."

We moved over to the desk, where I fished out one of

my standard letters, which she signed in the same beautiful hand that I'd seen on the list and using a fountain pen that looked like it cost at least a month's salary for most people.

"We'll need two copies – one is for you and one for the file here".

She obliged and I wrote her out a receipt for the money, then in an act of generosity, gave her one of my cards having only about five hundred to spare. This was because I'd had a job lot printed up in a wave of misguided optimism when starting out although for some deeply flawed psychological reason I didn't care to delve into, was still pretty stingy about handing the things out.

"Oh, one last thing, Mrs. Conlon..."

"Kitty."

"Now that you're my client, I'd like to keep things on a formal footing, if it's all the same to you. Helps me to remember my place."

"You don't strike me as the kind of man to have a problem with that, Morgan, but if that's how you'd prefer it."

I let the remark slip by for now.

"Who exactly is your father? You've mentioned him a couple of times and it feels like I ought to know who he is. Should I?"

She looked amused and held my gaze for slightly longer than was strictly necessary before replying.

"My maiden name is Thornton, and my father is Earl Thornton. He's your standard pillar of the community type, Morgan. The family is in banking and he's big in the business world. Chairman of the country club, as well as various charities and the like. Oh, and he's a pretty big mason of some sort too."

I'd heard of Earl Thornton, of course. So, this was his daughter.

"Thank you. I think I get the picture."

Although I'd been around the block enough times to know that the public image was only ever half the story with a man like that.

"You've got my number now - call me day or night if there's anything that occurs to you – you can leave a note with my messaging service if I'm not around."

"Day or night?"

Like everything else she wore, the wry smile fitted her nicely.

It was my turn to be coy, but I stood there awkwardly and may even have blushed, instead of using one of the many great lines that I thought of about fifteen minutes after she'd left.

The French have a term for it; for those witty sayings that come to you after the moment has passed and you are on your way home from the party. It's *l'esprit d'escalier*: the wit of the staircase.

I was clearly getting ideas above my station and wouldn't have been considered much of a wit in downtown Paris, assuming that I had been invited to any society parties in the first place, which seemed unlikely. All of which daydreaming was getting me nowhere.

For the first time in a little while I had a client and a case to work on. Uncharacteristically, I got going right away, even though it was nearly the weekend. In my line of work, a foot in the door is worth two on the desk every time.

2. Agnes

Looking for people who don't necessarily want to be found is the stock in trade of the private detective, but can still be dangerous. A man could get in plenty of trouble in this town, get himself killed even, in the paid service of the rich and indifferent.

It being late Friday afternoon, and not knowing if it would be open over the weekend, I decided to start with the business premises and flicked through the pages Kitty had given me for the address. I figured I should just be able to catch them if I gunned it over there, so locked up hurriedly and made my way down to the street to fetch the Plymouth.

It was a '56 Fury with a couple of years on it I had picked up about eighteen months before, when the Olds 88 had finally gotten too tired. The salesman tried to sell me the new model, but they'd gone too far with the styling and this one was there. It was used, but cheaper and although I still wasn't entirely sure how I felt about the thing, it had redeeming qualities: namely that it had a big block and was fast.

I made it to Wilmington in record time and found the address without too much trouble. The business was called Elegance and the premises turned out to be a furniture show room, with what looked to be a warehouse at the back, housed in an old red brick building out by the docks.

This area had been pretty down on its luck in the years immediately after the war, but now it seemed like things were on the up again over here.

Kitty's notes told me Jack had gone into business with a couple of old army buddies, importing high end furniture from Europe - mainly France and Italy. Evidently this was for the affluent and aspiring middle classes, of which there were a lot in this city now that times were booming.

As I knew it must be, Jack's role in the business was taking care of sales. He had the looks and easy charm to win over the rich wives, who would no doubt be impressed by the family he'd married into. From what Kitty had told me, he also had the bonhomie and banter to schmooze their husbands, as well as his service record, which couldn't do any harm.

Not wanting to advertise my arrival, mainly out of instinct, I parked about half a block further up the street and doubled back on foot, working my way around to the entrance, situated at the side of the building next to the parking lot.

I might as well have not bothered, for all the good it did me. The look on the face of the woman I took to be the receptionist was a picture. She was on the way out of the door, walking backwards and with her key already in the lock, about to shut up, as I rounded the corner of the building behind her.

She turned and froze, frowning at me, unsure whether to come out or jump back inside, if needs be.

"You always go around sneaking up on people like that, Mister?"

"I'm sorry. I didn't mean to startle you Miss...?"

"Miss will do just fine for now."

I couldn't help smiling. Not for the first time that day, I wondered what it was about the women in this town.

"The name's Morgan and I'm a private detective. Forgive me, but it doesn't always pay to advertise your approach in my line of work."

"You might want to practice not making so much noise clattering around in your size nines then, Morgan. The racket you were making, I heard you coming around the corner, I figured you couldn't be a sneak artist, at least not an anyways half decent one."

I grinned outright.

"So, you're a PI huh? You got some kind of a licence I can look at?"

"Sure. I've been hired by Mr. Conlon's wife to look for him. Here."

Moving slowly towards her I removed my wallet, opened it, and held out the licence from the police department allowing me to operate as a private detective in the city. I gave her an apologetic sort of half smile. At least, that's how I hoped she would interpret my goofy expression.

To her credit, she had a close look at the licence before she shot me a little smile and a nod and handed it back. Her shoulders relaxed and she visibly eased up a little.

"It's Agnes; Agnes Moreno. Sorry about earlier. A girl has to be a bit careful these days and Mr. Conlon disappearing has got me a little on edge."

"So, do you think we could maybe step inside and talk about Mr. Conlon for a bit, Agnes?"

"Well, I was just about to lock up. We usually close a little early on a Friday and I have to catch my bus home."

"I appreciate that, but I'd really like to ask you a few questions and take a look around Mr. Conlon's office if that'd be okay? My car's around the corner and I could run you home afterwards?"

The frown again.

"Well, I don't know. I mean, I know that you're a private detective and I think you're probably on the level, but how do I know for sure that you're working for Mrs. Conlon?"

"I have a letter here and a list in her hand of people and places to help me start looking for her husband. Or we could go inside and call her if that'd make you feel more comfortable?"

"Let me see."

It might have been a ruse, but it would have had to have

been an elaborate one and I could feel her scepticism start to wane. Although there was still the cautious inspection followed by another little nod. This was a sharp lady.

"I guess that'd be okay. I've seen that handwriting before: it's pretty distinctive."

"Thank you, Agnes. Shall we?"

I gestured to the door.

"Alright then, but not for long. I have a date and need to get home before seven."

And why wouldn't she, I thought.

"I promise I'll have you home before then, otherwise my car might turn into a pumpkin, and we wouldn't want that".

It was a lame joke, but she smiled encouragingly in any case, which I was grateful for, then turned back towards the door.

Once inside, she hit a light switch and we crossed the floor of the showroom, which was double height and carried on past the reception desk, making for a single-story staircase on the right-hand side wall.

By the looks of the showroom, whoever was buying this stuff couldn't get enough of it. The place was packed with all manner of museum quality furniture with exquisite inlay and marquetry work, all honey coloured and smelling of beeswax. It might have been the parliament building of a particularly industrious race of bees.

There were exotic woods I didn't recognise and furniture I didn't even know the function of. These were statement pieces on a grand scale designed for equally grand houses and no doubt with the price tag to match.

There is a lot to be said in this life for good luck and timing, especially in business, and if the showroom was anything to go by, Elegance furniture had both.

"How did you know they were size nines?" I asked by way of making conversation, as Agnes led the way, a couple of steps ahead. She spoke over her shoulder to me as we climbed the stairs.

"Easy. I used to work downtown in Lanegans department store. You're what we used to call a regular guy. I bet you're about five feet ten or eleven and weigh in at around a hundred and seventy to a hundred and eighty pounds?"

Subconsciously, I pulled in my stomach.

"Something like that."

"A 40 regular with about a 34 inch waist and a 32 inch leg. I bet clothes fit you right off the peg without any alterations. Like I said, a regular guy. Mr. Medium."

Impressive, although I couldn't help but pull a face at my new name.

"Handy for everyday shopping but no good for the sales. Unless you can get there on the first day, you'll never find anything discounted in your size".

This was certainly the case. I let her carry on.

"That's how I first met him - Mr. Conlon. He used to buy some of his clothes there at Lanegans. He got to know me a little and one day he said that he was opening this place and looking to hire somebody to meet and greet and also to look after the office. He said he thought I'd be good at it."

I nodded sagely, agreeing with him.

"I liked him well enough, but I wasn't sure at first. Then I came and saw the place and thought, well why not? The money was better and it's closer to home too."

We'd reached the top of the staircase, it led up to a mezzanine level at the back of the store, where we turned left on to a corridor with a balcony overlooking the showroom, down to our left. There were doors leading off the passage on the right, towards the back of the building.

"This is Mr. Conlon's office here. First door."

"What are these other ones up here?"

"Meeting room in the middle there and the door at the end is Mr. Jenner's office. He's the other director and looks after the accounts and the import side of things. He's away over in Italy at the moment."

"Do you happen to know when Mr. Jenner will be back, Agnes. I may need to speak to him too".

Again, the little frown.

"I'm pretty sure he said next Tuesday, that'd be the thirteenth".

"Thanks."

I gestured to the door.

"Is it locked?"

"It shouldn't be."

I turned the handle, went through, and stepped out into the middle of a large corner office, making room for Agnes to come on in behind me, as I knew she would do. There was no chance I was going to get a look over Conlon's office on my own on her watch.

In contrast to the furniture that he sold, his office was quite plain, although on the large side. I wondered whether the simplicity was more reflective of his own tastes. It was also extremely neat and tidy; orderly even.

The inventory comprised a desk and chair; a couple of filing cabinets; an informal seating area with a couple of couches and coffee table bearing smoking materials; what looked to be a Boston fern in a pot in one corner and a drinks cabinet in the other.

One entire wall was taken up with the window at the back, throwing late afternoon sunshine into the room, although there wasn't much of a view to speak of, unless you happen to like dockyards and warehouses.

The other walls were mainly bare, except for a couple of photographs and some fine art prints, which were modern, abstract affairs, but neutral and inoffensive.

The desk lacked ornamentation and would be my starting place. It was a solid looking pedestal affair rather like my own, but in mahogany instead of teak and with a green leather insert, where mine had none. There was a matching upholstered captain's chair behind it, which I sat in.

On the desk were two walnut trays over on the left; an overly full one marked in and an empty one marked out. A Bell system model five hundred telephone, identical to mine, stood over on the right.

Sitting in the middle was a jotter pad and a perpetual desk calendar and penholder offset slightly behind that. This was of a more modernist design, with a heavy black glass base and gold effect metal and I noted that the date was set for September twenty fifth, which would have been about two weeks before.

"When was Mr. Conlon last here?"

"I've been thinking about that and I'm pretty sure it was the Friday before last."

Which tallied.

The only other item on the desk was a photograph in an understated silver frame sitting right in the middle, between the telephone and the calendar, which I picked up and studied.

It looked like a professional job, a studio shot of Kitty looking more youthful and with two young boys, who I judged to be aged about six and four in the picture. They were all smiling and looking happy.

I put the picture back.

"What are Mr. Conlon's work habits? Does he like to get in early, or stay late? What is he like with his paperwork, that sort of thing?"

As I asked this, I was discretely checking out the pedestal drawers on either side of the desk. The question was in part to deflect Agnes, who I thought might disapprove of me going through them.

"Mr. Conlon works hard. He likes to get in early but leave on time: he is very insistent that we all leave on time."

I made a mental note to ask who else worked there.

"When he isn't with clients in the showroom or meeting them here in his office, he spends a lot of time on the telephone or out visiting, mainly in the afternoons.

He's good with his paperwork. Conscientious and likes to keep a clean desk. He'll hate it piling up like it is now."

This seemed to be at odds with the little I knew of the man, but who knew? Maybe he was a high-functioning sort of drinker. Or maybe he didn't indulge every day, but just went off on one every now and then.

While she was talking, I'd been subtly jiggling the desk drawers, trying to shift them, especially the long one above my knees, not that it did me any good. They wouldn't budge.

"I don't suppose you have keys to these drawers, do you, Agnes?"

"No, and I don't think we should be looking through Mr. Conlon's things in any case."

I nodded. It wouldn't take long to force these locks if needs be, and it mightn't be necessary. It could wait for now, and I wanted Agnes on my side.

"Would you happen to know what he keeps in here?"

"I've never looked, but I suppose there might be some personal things. I mean, most people do, don't they – keep things like that in their desk?"

"What about the paperwork, that sort of thing?"

"The big drawers at the bottom are designed for drop files, I know that much, so he might keep personal documents in there.

Client records and sales invoices are over there in those filing cabinets. I'm in and out of those all the time looking for files or putting them away. Those are locked, but I have a key".

I stood up and went over to the drinks cabinet, another mahogany affair, and tried it. It had a mechanism I was familiar with which swung up and out when opened to reveal a mirrored interior, with a couple of decanters and cut glasses. Ingenious.

It looked like one of the decanters held whiskey or bourbon and the other slightly darker one maybe brandy: no doubt good stuff, to help seal the deal. Opening the doors to the bottle store underneath confirmed this to be the case as it contained some high-end looking hooch with impressive labels.

I took the short walk over to get a closer look at the photographs on the wall.

The first was of a younger looking Jack and Kitty with some other people seated at a table at some kind of a black tie do. She was in the middle of the shot, framed on either side by Jack on her right and an older man on her left. I recognised Jack from the snapshot she'd given me, but the older guy looked somehow familiar too.

Looking more closely, I could see that her right hand was interlaced with Jack's left on the tablecloth and her left hand was resting lightly on the right hand of the other man. The penny dropped: it was her father, Earl Thornton.

There were other glamorous looking people at the table, at least one of whom I recognised as a famous actor. They were all smiling and looking like they were having a good time.

Except for Thornton. His mouth was smiling, but he's eyes definitely were not, but you had to look very closely to see it.

It reminded me of a picture I'd once seen in a magazine of an old portrait of Henry VIII. You could just tell from the picture that he was evil, and Thornton had those same eyes. He looked a total bastard. A grade a, gold standard one, with oak leaf cluster.

The picture gave me goose bumps and I began to feel sorry for Jack Conlon, having this guy for a father-in-law. You just knew that whatever he did, it was never going to be good enough for Thornton.

It was off to one side over by the occasional seating and I guessed that Jack would sit on one side with this framed above his shoulder, in shot for whoever was sitting on the other couch. It wouldn't do his business any harm. After all, he was selling a kind of lifestyle, not just furniture.

There was another photograph over on the back wall by the filing cabinets which I wandered over to inspect.

It was of three men in full army dress uniform, obviously taken at some kind of a reunion do. A young Jack Conlon was in the middle, flanked by the two other guys. I couldn't make out their insignia, but they had a whole bunch of medals between them, so must have seen some action.

I turned and looked over at Agnes enquiringly.

"That's Mr. Conlon with Mr. Jenner on the left and Mr. Battaglia on the right. He's over in Italy and helps with buying and shipping. They were all in the army together – I think that's how they met."

I nodded my thanks for the explanation and studied the picture some more but couldn't glean any special insight from it. Just three regular guys looking relaxed and happy to have made it through the war. The three amigos.

The visit to Jack Conlon's office hadn't yielded a great deal so far, although maybe I was being a bit hard on myself, as I thought I understood his situation a little better now.

I decided to cut my losses and run Agnes home: she'd been helpful, and I didn't want to ruin her evening. Besides, I might be able to learn something on the journey over.

"Thanks for showing me around, Agnes and answering my dumb questions. How about I give you that lift home?"

"Well, if it's not too much trouble... I've missed my bus and its's a half hour wait for the next one."

We retraced our route back down the stairs and across the showroom, and I waited for her outside as she turned out the lights and locked up. Then we rounded the corner, me stepping aside off the sidewalk like the gentleman I'm not, since it wasn't wide enough for both of us, and I gestured to the Fury up the road at the kerbside.

"My ride."

I opened the door for her and held it open although there was no need and I felt a bit ridiculous even as I was doing it. It turned out her neighbourhood was only about fifteen minutes away, although it would take longer by bus of course.

On the way I probed some more.

"So how is the business doing? I mean financially – are sales good?"

She hesitated, thinking.

"I don't get to see the accounts as a matter of course: like I said, Mr. Jenner sees to all that. I'd say we have more customers than ever phoning up or in the showroom, and there are always lots of invoices to file.

I got a raise back at Easter time, so things must be good, I guess."

"So, there are no problems that you are aware of. You haven't heard Mr. Conlon and Mr. Jenner talking about money problems? No disagreements or arguments, anything like that?"

She shook her head, as I thought some more.

"Who else works at the showroom and in the office, Agnes? You said earlier that Mr. Conlon was keen for you *all* to leave on time."

"Well, there's the cleaner, but she comes in after we leave, and the maintenance man, but he tends to come in the evenings or on weekends.

The only other people around are the warehouse guys. There are two of them who stop by in the van sometimes, when there are deliveries to be made. We go over the inventory details, make sure what is going out is what the customer ordered, that sort of thing.

Mr. Conlon's friendly with those guys and he's always keen to check the details."

"So, there's another warehouse, not just this place? I didn't know that. Whereabouts?"

I wondered why Kitty hadn't mentioned it. It was like Agnes had read my mind.

"It's a bonded warehouse, there at the wharf. Mrs. Conlon probably wouldn't even know about it."

I'd heard of the term for imported liquor and the like but had only a vague idea what it meant.

"Do you know how it all works?"

"As I said, Mr. Jenner takes care of all the imports, so I don't really understand it all, but it's something to do with the stock having to clear customs and the point at which the company has to pay to import it.

Clients come in and choose what they want from the showroom or from catalogues – you know, those big glossy ones. It's high-quality stuff, made in Europe and they can order a particular piece or style in a different wood or whatever."

"It's made to order then; they're not buying the pieces in the showroom?"

"No. Those don't usually get sold unless we're short on stock or opening up a new line. It's mainly there for sales purposes.

The furniture comes in on ships, gets unloaded on the quay into the warehouse and we fulfil the orders from there."

"And that's the whole business?"

"Mostly, yes. There's a line in antique furniture too, for a few wealthy clients, but I don't really have anything to do with that."

"How does that work"?

"It comes in the same way, but it doesn't come through

the showroom. Mr. Conlon and Mr. Jenner handle that bit themselves."

As we got to her neighbourhood, Agnes said I could drop her on the corner just past her regular bus stop and she'd walk the rest of the way from there. I protested that it was just as easy to run her to home, but she said she lived with her folks and didn't want to have to explain why a stranger was dropping her off.

It also meant that I didn't get to see where she lived, either. Smart lady.

I pulled over, thanked her for her help and wished her a pleasant evening as she stepped out with a little wave. Then I sat there mulling it all over and got nothing other than a dull ache behind my eyes.

What next? I'd have to visit the warehouse of course, but that was back over at the docks and probably wouldn't be open now.

I dug out Kitty's list and took another look. Conlon's apartment was the next logical port of call, and I knew roughly where it was. There was also a bar he frequented which I could take in en route.

It was only around six thirty, so a little early for bar hopping, but it was a Friday, and the joint was between his office and where he lived, so it was possible he'd stop by there on the way home from work, making it around the right sort of time.

Then again, if he was a drinker, he might have gone there any time. Who knew?

3. Dutch's Bar

Downtown on West Fifth Street, the appearance of the place caused me to raise my eyebrows slightly as I passed it and looked for a place to park a couple of blocks up. It looked a dive, which might have been being unfair to dives.

Dutch's was a cellar bar, with a vertical neon sign spelling out the name within an arrow pointing down a broad flight of steps to what would undoubtedly be some new circle of hell.

I nearly didn't go in, figuring that this would be a late-night watering hole and one of last resort at that, but the sun was setting, and I was there, so braced myself and set off down below.

Pushing open the double doors revealed a long bar off to the left and I stood just inside trying to look unobtrusive, to let my eyes adjust to the light before venturing further.

The bar was lit more brightly than the booths set off to the right-hand side, stretching back underneath the street side and dimly lit with candle fittings on the walls. These might as well have been fitted with black light bulbs for all the illumination they provided, and I could just about make out an old couple sitting in silence at the booth at the far end.

There was the muffled, slightly menacing clack of pool balls coming from a further room at the back on the left-hand side, through a door slightly ajar and framed in a halo of light spilling into the relative darkness of the bar.

The décor was mock Tudor meets gothic revival, making it difficult to figure out what kind of clientele they were looking to attract unless it was passing knights errant, which this neighbourhood was probably short on. Evidently, the clientele hadn't been able to work out who they were meant to be either, as they had stayed away in their droves. The place was deserted.

I padded across a floor sticky with the residue of spilt drink over to the bar.

"What'll it be, copper?"

"Close, but no cigar. I'm a PI. The name's Morgan. You Dutch?"

"Not so's you'd notice. That was the guy before me. I'm Irish. Kelly."

"I like what you've done with the place."

He grinned.

"His taste, not mine. You drinking, or just sightseeing?"

"What's the beer like in here? No, don't answer that. I'll take one anyway."

It was against my better judgement, but I figured I'd better show willing. As he was pouring, I asked:

"I'm looking for a guy named Jack Conlon. You know him?"

"Why? What's he done?"

"Nothing that I know of. He's just not been seen for a while and his wife wants him found."

Kelly passed me my beer and gestured over to a solitary, crumpled figure about three quarters of the way along the bar, off to the right, far enough away not to hear us.

"He comes in sometimes. Marty over there knows him better."

I nodded and wandered along the bar with my beer, gesturing to Kelly to send a drink over to him. I stopped near the end of the bar, a couple of bar stools over, turned in Marty's direction and nodded.

"This spot taken?"

He looked at me with sleepy eyes and half shrugged. I made him for about seventy, but it can be difficult to tell with drinkers, and he could have been ten or more years younger.

Judging by his dishevelled appearance, he might have been on the hooch for some time, and he had a deep tan, which could have been an alcoholic flush, or something else altogether.

He didn't seem too intoxicated though and had been aware enough to glance over at me on my arrival. Other than that he was fixed, looking straight ahead at a point behind the bar somewhere.

"Help yourself."

I sipped my beer, which was surprisingly good. Marty's drink, which looked like bourbon, was set down in front of him and Kelly jerked his chin towards me:

"This guy's buying, Marty. His name's Morgan and he's looking for Jack Conlon".

"Jack's a friend of mine and I don't know you from Adam. What do you want with him?"

Marty hadn't picked up his drink and his eyes came alive more quickly than I expected. They were a piercing light blue.

I got my buzzer out of my pocket and held it out to Marty, explaining there was nothing wrong, but that Kitty had hired me to find her husband. I spoke slowly and clearly in what I hoped was a relaxing tone.

He didn't look at me as I spoke and showed no interest in my licence, preferring to stare straight ahead instead.

At the end of my spiel, he nodded once and said:

"Okay."

As we were talking, two guys had come out of the poolroom at the back and approached the bar. One was big, the other smaller. They looked like trouble and exuded a casual arrogance, like they owned the place. They were the kind who you took an immediate dislike to, largely because it saved time.

The shorter of the two, who was nasty looking and in an equally nasty suit, banged on the countertop unnecessarily and made a show of asking for two beers. Kelly's shoulders tensed, but he fetched two glasses anyway. I could tell he didn't like them any more than I did but guessed he wasn't in a position to be fussy.

The big guy carried on behind me round to the end of the bar and I heard the door to the restrooms swing open.

The shorter one had edged along the bar slightly and was now standing a couple of bar stools along behind Marty's shoulder. Not too close, but near enough to eavesdrop on the last bit of our conversation and I couldn't be sure what he had heard.

"Why don't you leave the man alone? He don't want your drink, and we don't want you in here poking around."

"It's Okay. He's on the level. It's nothing." Said Marty.

"Why don't you mind your own business?" This directed at me.

I didn't like where this was going.

I studied him more carefully. He looked small time to me but probably didn't know it, which made him and his partner dangerous enough in their own right.

"I am minding my business.
Besides, I like it here. I'm thinking of making this my local".

Kelly, who had been pouring two beers further down the bar, but keeping a watchful eye on proceedings, turned back slightly towards us. As his eyes were scanning back around, he glanced behind me, over my right shoulder.

His look told me everything I needed to know.

The big guy hadn't gone to the restroom after all but had let the door swing and then doubled back and was making his way along the bar, approaching silently from behind. He wasn't about to tap me on the shoulder and ask for a dance.

Experience has taught me that a bad situation only gets worse, so I had to act immediately and decisively, before the big guy braced me.

Glancing to one side but without moving my head, I checked the mirror behind the bar using my peripheral vision. There was the slightest of movements back there.

I brought my hands up in front of me, in a placatory gesture saying:

"Relax. It was just a joke. We don't want any trouble here..."

As I was saying this, I was calculating my next move and doing a silent countdown, judging his arrival. Three. Two. One...

On one I took half a step back with my right foot, which brought me close in, bumping into the big man and catching him by surprise. I had already lifted my left foot and stamped down hard, aiming for the instep of his left foot. My aim was a little off, but I connected well enough, and he yelled, pitching over to his left, away from the bar and into the room.

Dropping my hand, I stepped out into the bar slightly and swung around back over my right shoulder to throw the point of my elbow down hard at about where I figured his head would be. Even though he was off balance as he went down, he blocked the move easily with a meaty paw, catching me across the shoulders and spinning me back along the bar like a bowling pin.

The bar stopped me from going down, but I was winded and holding on to the rail. I'd damaged the big man, who had gone over and was lying half on his side and half on his back, clutching at his left foot in obvious pain and out of the fight for now.

Good.

My glance came up to his partner who had stepped out from behind Marty's stool into the bar and was in the process of reaching his right hand inside the jacket of that nasty suit, going for what would be an even nastier surprise for me.

Not so good.

I don't care much for guns in general, or gunplay in particular, although they are a fact of life sometimes. I was extremely grateful to see the business end of Kelly's bar piece, a 12-gauge, swing up and out from behind the counter, a beautiful gift horse, with a great big gaping mouth.

He racked one up noisily, which got everybody's attention and the mean looking guy got the message and dropped his right hand, turning from me to look over at the barman.

Kelly took a couple steps across to bring them in his sights and aimed the short-barrelled shotgun at both men, one standing and the other on the floor nursing his foot.

"Not in here. You've had your fun, now get out."

He gestured with the barrel to the exit.

With some difficulty the smaller one helped his fellow goon up and the pair shuffled across the bar to the door. He looked back at me with evil intent and either couldn't find the right words or thought better of saying anything.

Maybe it was the French thing again, *l'esprit d'escalier*, or just hard to come up with a suitable riposte to a pump action shotgun.

Marty hadn't moved an inch during it all but remained frozen at the bar.

"Thanks Kelly, I owe you one." I said after watching them leave.

"Nah that's OK. I wanted them gone anyway. They've been hanging around here for a couple of afternoons now, annoying everybody."

I wondered who they could possibly have been upsetting in the deserted bar, but didn't want to appear ungrateful, so nodded my thanks instead.

It was time to get going and I remembered another reason I don't like cellar bars.

"There a back way out of here?"

"Through the bar here, then right down the corridor to the fire door on the left at the end: it's not locked. There's an alley at the back."

"Come on Marty, let's go before they figure it out."

He snatched up the drink and downed it as I left a few dollars on the bar, and we made our escape out through the fire door, which led to a short flight of steps up to an alleyway. It ran along behind the buildings, parallel to the street at the front, but we went in the other direction and made a right at the end instead of a left. The plan was to make a wide circuit back to the car, keeping off the more obvious main route.

Staying close to the buildings for cover, I led Marty two blocks back, then turned left and made our way a couple of blocks across and then left again, heading back up towards the street, which I figured should bring us out about where I'd parked.

We maintained a strict military medium pace until the Plymouth appeared in front of us, me with the keys already in my hand as we got close. I scanned quickly up and down, surveying the street before encouraging him:

"In we get, Marty, quick as you like."

I popped his door and hopped around to the driver's seat. He was still getting settled as we peeled off into the traffic and I drove fast for about fifteen minutes, all the while heading broadly north but making a random series of turns and checking the rear-view mirror to see if we were being followed.

After a while I relaxed a little and thought about what had happened back at the bar. I had made them for small time: petty mobsters and reasoned that Kelly must have thought the same. If they'd been connected, he wouldn't have been so inclined to pull the gun from under the bar, before seeing how things played out.

I asked Marty what he knew about Tweedledum and

Tweedledee.

"They're from out of town but have been coming around for a couple of days. The big guy's called Louis and the mean looking one is Al.

They're looking for Jack too. They bought me drinks and asked about him, but I didn't like them so didn't tell them anything."

Nothing wrong with Marty's instincts. I drove in silence and reflected. These guys looking for Jack Conlon had to be more than a coincidence. It was a lead of sorts, but who were they and what did they want with him?

"If that's your watering hole of choice, it might be wise to avoid it for a while, Marty."

"I was thinking the same thing. It's not a problem. There's plenty of other places."

Speaking of which, I was hungry and wanted to have a proper conversation, ideally somewhere familiar and where they knew how to mix a decent drink.

I asked Marty if he'd eaten and he told me he'd skipped lunch, which I guessed might happen quite often. I had the money from Kitty in my pocket, so was feeling flush, and suggested I buy us both dinner, since we'd earned it. He agreed enthusiastically.

Checking my watch, I learned that it was a little after seven thirty, a respectable hour and just in time to beat the eight o'clock rush. My belly must have been directing proceedings subconsciously, as we were close by one of my regular spots over in West Hollywood.

4. Vincenzo's

Vincenzo's was a small, family run neighbourhood restaurant which I had been frequenting for a few years. With a standard bar and grill room set up, there was nothing particularly special about the place but that was one of the things I liked about it most. It was good, reliable and a well-kept secret.

I stuck the Plymouth in one of the parking spaces out front and we made our way to the entrance, Marty doing his best to smooth down the crumples in his suit and straighten his shirt collar, with partial success.

They were used to me turning up with all sorts of waifs and strays, usually damsels in distress or suchlike and never batted an eyelid.

Salvatore, the Maître d' (if that is the correct term in an Italian place) and the owner's brother, was on hand to greet us.

"Mr. Morgan, always a pleasure to see you. Your usual booth is free. Will you be dining with us tonight?"

I'd long since given up trying to get them to drop the Mr. bit and didn't mind it so much since they applied the term to all male guests. I nodded.

"Please, Salvatore and this is my friend Marty."

"Nice to meet you, Mr. Marty. This way please, gentlemen."

He led the way and presented us with menus at the booth, both formalities in my case, as I knew where I was going, and the menu hadn't changed in all the time I'd been there. As I said - reliable.

The particular booth I favoured was much the same as all the others, but towards the back of the room and off to one side. A combination of the positioning and lighting gave a good view of the door and anyone who might come through it, without it being easy to be spotted in return.

We sat.

"Something to drink, gentlemen?"

"I'd like a whisky sour with a beer chaser please. Marty here will have the same. Trust me."

This last directed at Marty, who nodded, a little uncertainly.

"Thank you, gentlemen. I'll have your drinks sent over and be back to take your order shortly."

Salvatore went to speak to the barman and to answer the ringing telephone. There followed a silent contemplation of the menu, again a formality on my part, since I knew what I wanted. A waiter came over and set down our drinks, then Salvatore returned.

"Have you decided, gentlemen?"

I gestured for Marty to go first.

"I'd like the prime rib, medium well, with shoestring potatoes and a side of tossed salad with Russian dressing."

Marty said this confidently, whilst looking over at me seeking approval and I chuckled. I've always preferred dining partners who are uninhibited and don't hold back.

"Excellent choice, Mr. Marty. For you, Mr. Morgan?"

"I'll take the ham and eggs, Salvatore. Eggs over easy, with French fries and a tossed salad with white dressing, please."

A regular choice and one I could even have knocked up myself, but inexplicably so much nicer when they made it here.

He gave a half bow and turned away.

I picked my whiskey sour up and Marty didn't wait for an invitation to follow suit.

"What will we drink to?" I asked.

"True hearts and sound bottoms." He replied. A sailor's toast.

I returned the familiar salute and took a hit from my drink, which seldom failed to hit the mark and gave a particularly good account of itself on this occasion.

Marty sipped his own drink and nodded his approval back at me.

When the food arrived, we ate a most convivial and meal in near silence, like an old married couple. I figured we could talk afterwards over coffee.

Being grown-ups, neither of us opted for a desert, and coffee turned up in due course. Black for me, white and with a large brandy on the side for Marty.

"Were you a sailor then, Marty?"

"Merchant Marine. Worked cargo ships before but went over when the war came. What about you, Morgan? You recognised the toast."

"Regular navy. Strictly for the duration, though."

"You see any action?"

"A little. South Pacific. You?"

"Convoys."

He'd uttered a single word, but it told me all that needed to be said and made us both quiet for a minute.

"So, how is it you know Jack Conlon?"

Marty thought for a bit, sipping his brandy.

"I stopped going to sea after the war and worked down at the docks. I ended up in the warehouse at his firm, you know Elegance, up until two maybe three years back. Liked it there."

"How come you left"?

"I got fired. By Mr. Jenner, the other partner. I was drinking back then and turned up late for my shift one too many times. He said I was still drunk, but I wasn't, and that he could smell it on my breath. That bit might have been true."

I waited for him to carry on.

"He's a real piece of work. From back East; New York, I think. He'd always had it in for me. He never liked it that me and Jack were friendly.

   Jack spoke to him afterwards to try and get my job back, but it didn't make any difference."

      "So, you worked there, but how'd you and Jack end up being friends?"

      "I'd been there a few years by then, so knew Jack from doing deliveries and stopping in at the office. I knew him as Mr. Conlon back then though. He's a real nice guy; always makes time for people.

   We didn't get friendly until about 1955 though. It was Veterans Day and I remember the year because it was ten years after the war ended."

      "What happened?"

      "There was a ceremony there over at the port, just a short distance along the quay from the warehouse. I went along and Jack ended up there too. It was a small service and he spotted me there and spoke to me afterwards. He'd been in the office doing paperwork or something, I forget what.

   It's a lost sort of day, but neither of us felt like going to a bar, or home even. He suggested we go back up there to his office for a drink.

   We sat and talked for a long time. We drank too, but not to get drunk. Not that time. He needed company and seemed very sad, like there was something really troubling him."

      "He had quite a war record, didn't he?"

      "Yeah. I used to joke with him that if I had medals like that, I'd have worn them in the bath. He never liked to talk about all that though; used to say that it wasn't what was on the outside of a man's chest that mattered but what was on the inside. He felt like I did about it."

      "How do you mean?"

      "That none of that was important. We'd did our bit, but hero or not it was all the same in the end. The only thing that mattered was coming back."

I found myself nodding.

"It's not so easy to fit back in though, Morgan, is it?

Times after that it's always been much lighter though. He stops by Dutch's sometimes or we go someplace else and talk about baseball or whatever."

"His wife told me about his drinking..."

"That's no secret, but he doesn't drink all the time. It's just that there's something wrong with his drinking gearbox, you know"?

Not being sure what he meant, I shook my head.

"Like a gearbox; his gets stuck and it's either set on neutral or ramming speed. Nothing in between. He doesn't drink every day, but sometimes when he gets going, he can't stop."

I nodded.

"Does he have any other bad habits? Gambling, or women, maybe?"

Marty bristled a bit at this, as I thought he might.

"Nothing that I know of. At least not that we ever talked about. He plays cards once in a while but that's not serious, just social.

He still loves his wife though. I am sure of that."

I signalled for refills, and we sat in silence. I guessed Marty was reflecting on their friendship.

The drinks arrived.

"When's the last time you saw him?"

Marty thought for a bit.

"Let me see. That'd be about a week ago last Monday. He stopped by the bar on his way home from work. That's his way sometimes."

I did a quick calculation. That would have been Monday, September twenty eighth.

"Was there anything bothering him? Something on his mind maybe?"

"No, the opposite. He was the happiest I've seen

him in ages.

He's had a rough time you know, the last eighteen months or so what with the separation and all. Jack's a family man at heart and he's crazy about those boys.

We ended up going on somewhere else and watching the game. We both love baseball and Jack's a Dodgers fan like me. Has been since he was a little boy."

"You go to the games?"

He shook his head.

"Funny thing is he never really wanted to go to the game, just liked watching it on TV. It was the play-offs. Not the second game at the Coliseum, when they won the pennant, but the first one, there in Milwaukee.

It was a great game; really close. We won with a home run in the sixth.

It was a nice evening, you know?"

He looked wistful, thinking about this time spent with his friend.

I don't really follow baseball and glazed over a bit when Marty was telling me about it, but something about what he said had registered on my subconscious for a fraction of a second. Whatever it was, it was gone before it landed properly.

Not being able to think of anything else for the time being, I planned on running him home and signalled for the check. Salvatore brought this over and I surprised and delighted him by pulling one of Kitty's pristine hundred dollar bills out of my wallet.

"That was excellent as usual, thank you. I know I'm a little behind with my tab, but this should take care of it and stand me in good credit for a while." "Indeed, Mr. Morgan. Thank you." Salvatore beamed, his faith in mankind, or at least in my corner of it and my ability to pay my bill, restored.

Suitably fortified and in much better spirits than when we'd arrived, we left Vincenzo's.

I asked Marty where he wanted to be dropped off and inevitably, this involved a journey back across the city to a rundown district out by the port on the Lower West Side.

As we criss-crossed the city, I probed some more.

"You still in touch with anyone in the business. Do you know how it's doing"?

"Ed from the warehouse lives in my neighbourhood and I bump into him sometimes. I don't know the guy they got in to replace me, though. He says they're going gangbusters over there; busier than ever.

That night I told you about, Jack was buying drinks for everybody. He told me he had money coming, so not to worry about it."

"Did he say where it was coming from?"

"No and I didn't ask. I guessed it was a bonus from the business of some kind."

The conversation waned and when I eventually dropped Marty off, he thanked me for dinner and told me to make sure I found Jack. I promised to do my best, bid him goodnight, and told him to be careful, which he brushed off.

Not surprisingly there was nothing else out there on Kitty's list, so I headed for home but planned on making one more stop on the way, this time in a slightly more upmarket neighbourhood.

5. Casa Laguna

The Casa Laguna was a drive across the city away from Marty's place but a whole world away in looks and class. Over on Franklin in East Hollywood, it was one of those old Spanish hacienda style buildings that had been the height of fashion at the end of the twenties, but still had panache to spare thirty years later.

It was where Jack lived, in a serviced apartment in one of a series of low-rise buildings set out around an open-air courtyard. It was a little after nine when I pulled into a guest bay out front.

Before trying my luck at the reception, I took the envelope Kitty had given me out of my jacket pocket and sealed it, then wrote Jack Conlon's name on the front, resting awkwardly on the dash.

I went in and approached the desk.

"I'm here to see Mr. Conlon in 12a."

The desk clerk was a bookish and officious looking man in his early thirties. There was nothing by way of a response other than a blank stare.

"I have an urgent message for him. Any chance you could buzz me up?"

I retrieved the prop envelope from my inside jacket pocket and held it up hopefully.

"I'm sorry sir. I'm not allowed to do that."

"Could you call him on the phone, please.? See if he's happy for me to go up or come down and get it himself?"

Laughing boy smiled at me neutrally, in a way that made it clear that what he really wanted was for me to go away. Nevertheless, he stepped across to the house phone and dialled.

After about thirty seconds with the handset to his ear, he

put it down and told me what I already knew.

"He's not answering sir. Perhaps you'd like to leave your message with me and I'll see he gets it."

I hesitated, playing hard to get.

"Well, I'm not sure, you see I'm meant to give it to him *personally*. Do you know if he was in earlier and just gone out? Maybe he'll be back soon, and I should wait."

"I'm sorry sir, I don't know if Mr. Conlon is in our out. We've just changed shifts and I haven't seen him."

He held out his hand for the envelope.

I tapped it against my other hand in a show of reluctance.

"Well, okay."

It was empty of course, but it didn't feel like it on account of the padding, and I handed it over figuring the worst that could happen was that Jack would get an empty envelope from what he might recognise as his wife's stationery set.

The desk clerk turned to the back wall, which held a bank of cubbyholes and posted the envelope into one. I couldn't make out the labelling but could see that there was quite a bit of mail in this one compared to the others. If it was for him, he hadn't picked any up in a while.

Like he had sixth sense, the clerk turned around abruptly and caught me leaning forwards over the counter, peering at what he was doing. I felt foolish.

"If that's everything, then."

It wasn't a question, more of an instruction, an identifiable edge of hostility in his voice now. He didn't like me, and the feeling was mutual.

Deciding to cut my losses, I about turned and left.

Outside, I decided on a tour of the perimeter, trying to appear nonchalant, but examining the layout of the place and looking for apartment 12a. Maybe I'd be able to catch a view or see if the lights were on or something: I wasn't sure what.

It was a two-storey building, with balconies and there were fire escapes every so often down to the street from the upper level. I guessed it was probably one set of apartments on top and another underneath and that they were smallish: one- and two-bedroom places.

It was dark, and my vague plan didn't yield much as the apartments weren't numbered on the outside and there was no other signage visible.

Working my way back to my car and just about to call it a day, I glanced up and noticed a sign for Franklin parking just along the road on the other side.

Since I hadn't seen a parking lot on my way around the building and there were only a few bays out front, I figured that this would be where the residents parked, which gave me an idea.

Parking attendants, valets and suchlike had been useful sources of information in the past, so I headed over there to see who I could find. Besides, it was a pleasant evening, and the night air was cool and refreshing. It felt good to be outside after spending much of the day cooped up in the office or in my car, crisscrossing the city.

The car park turned out to be a two-storey affair, with an entrance ramp leading back from the avenue and a barrier partway up, next to a cubicle for the attendant. A light was showing through the window, and I could hear a transistor set playing what sounded like 'Mack the Knife'.

I knocked and heard the radio dial being turned down before a fresh-faced and pleasant looking young man, who I judged to be aged around twenty-five, appeared and slid open the window divider.

"Excuse me, is this the car park for the Laguna?"

"Sure. Just bring her on up the ramp to the barrier here and I'll let you through."

"I should explain. My car's over outside the

Laguna. I'm not a guest there and I don't need to park it.

I'm looking for one of the residents, a Mr. Conlon from apartment 12a. Do you know if he would happen to park here?"

"I'm afraid I'm not meant to talk about the guests."

I opened my wallet and held out my licence for him to see. He was young enough that it might just impress him a little.

"I'm a PI. Name of Morgan. The thing is Mr. Conlon has gone missing, and his family is worried about him. I'm trying to help find him."

Evidently, the kid wasn't that impressed with my credentials. He stood his ground and shook his head.

"Sorry, Mr. Morgan."

At least he was polite.

I stood there and frowned, but the fact that he said he wasn't *meant* to talk about the guests gave me hope. Before returning the wallet to my pocket, I fished out a less than pristine five-dollar bill and set it on the counter in front of him.

As a rule, I'm not overly keen on this approach, but thought it might be worth a try on this occasion. Besides, I could afford it for once.

He looked at it, then back at me before picking up my crumpled offering.

"Well, okay then. I like Mr. Conlon and if you're trying to help, I guess it'd be alright."

"Is he parked here now?"

"Sure is. I'd know his car anywhere. It's on the first level, just up over there."

He pointed off to the right.

"So, when did you last see him?"

"I can't say for sure. I only work the evening shift here, so don't know everything that happens, but it must be over a week now. His car is in the same spot, so I don't think it's been moved since.

I can't say about the week before as I was off on account of my wife having a baby".

The way he said this last bit, with undisguised glee, I figured it must be their first.

"Congratulations. Mind if I take a look at Mr. Conlon's car?"

"I guess that'd be ok. She's a real beauty. A white Jaguar XK150 right in front of you at the top of the ramp – you can't miss her. Don't be too long though, Mr. Morgan."

"I won't, and it's just Morgan by the way. What do I call you?"

"Pete."

"Thanks, Pete. I'll see you in a bit".

This last delivered over my shoulder as I was climbing the ramp.

I didn't know what a Jaguar XK150 was exactly, but thought it was one of those little English sports cars they made. When I got to the top of the ramp, it turned out to be a thing of beauty and a joy forever.

With curves in all the right places and swept back lines, the graceful coupe looked as if it was travelling at a hundred miles an hour just sitting there. Up close, it was also bigger than it looked from a distance.

It had a sumptuous red leather and wood interior set off against white paintwork, finished with gleaming chrome work and wire wheels. I couldn't help but smile walking around it.

Of course Jack Conlon would drive a car like this. Who wouldn't, given the opportunity?

I tried the doors and the trunk out of a sense of duty, as much as anything else, but they weren't budging. The roof was up, so I couldn't make out a great deal inside, other than a beautiful dash with all the dials.

Acting like a proper sleuth, I looked for any and all tell-tale signs. Dents and scrapes, mud splashes, bloodstains, bullet holes or anything else that might be useful. If the car had any such secrets though, it wasn't giving them up: there wasn't so much as a scratch on it.

Finally, I took down the licence plate in my notebook, as much out of habit as anything else. The familiar act felt like something a real detective might do and restored my sense of professional pride slightly after not finding anything else noteworthy.

Eventually I gave up, walked back down the ramp to the office and knocked on the door, in time to hear the radio announcer giving out the station's handle 'KBCA 105.1'. The volume dropped off again and Pete appeared at the counter.

"I don't suppose you've got the keys for that beauty, have you Pete?"

I gestured with my thumb back up the ramp.

He laughed.

"Not a chance, Morgan. Only Mr. Conlon gets to drive her. He's got them."

Which figured.

I fished out another one of my cards, which made for two in one day – a near record for me.

"Will you do me a favour, Pete. If Mr. Conlon comes back for his car or you hear anything about him, will you let me know? If I'm not around, there's a number for my messaging service.

By the way, what time do you finish?"

"Will do. Not too long now, I'm off at eleven thirty, after that the guests have to fend for themselves until we open again at six tomorrow."

"So long then and thanks."

He seemed like a nice kid. If nothing else, at least I'd contributed to junior's college fund,

It wasn't late, but it wasn't early either and had been a long enough day already. I wasn't in the mood or in any way prepared for a stakeout on the off chance that Jack might show up, so headed back over to the Plymouth and for home.

On the drive, I imagined what it would feel like to be Jack, behind the wheel of the Jaguar at night, cutting through the soft air and throwing it fast into tight curves, maybe up into the Hollywood Hills somewhere.

It would feel fantastic, of course.

Stepping through the front door of my apartment, I felt dog tired from the day's exertions and found myself awkwardly trying to massage the back of my neck and in between my shoulders. A dull ache had developed there from when the big ape had caught me in Dutch's bar.

I showered, washing away the grime of the city and playing hot water on the sore spot, which helped some. Then I fixed a nightcap, a stiff brandy, and climbed into bed in my bathrobe with a book, as is my way.

Before long I nodded off and slept the undisturbed and dreamless sleep of the innocent, which must have been as much of a surprise to them as it was to me.

6. Subterfuge

I woke early, as is my habit, stumbled out of bed and on through to the living room of my small apartment, where I was greeted by glorious autumn sun streaming around the edges of the blinds. I went across into the kitchenette and put coffee on, then wandered back to the bathroom to observe my morning routine.

Instinctively I timed my shave just so that the coffee would be ready and have had enough time futzing on the hot plate to be piping hot when I was through. I can't function adequately in the morning without at least two cups of the stuff - strong and black.

Breakfast consisted of two slices of toast, hot and thickly buttered, freshly squeezed orange juice and the black coffee, steaming and bitter. One of the unadulterated pleasures of living alone is to be able to indulge oneself like this, unmolested. Of course, there were downsides, but not too many that came to mind that morning.

During breakfast, I tried to recap what I had learned so far, which was seemingly not a great deal, other than that Jack Conlon was a popular guy all round, with a lifestyle most people would envy and had gone missing. There were the two heavies in the bar who also seemed to be looking for him, but it wasn't a lot to go on and was circumstantial at best.

I went through my mail, which I'd been too tired to bother with the night before and as usual, it was mostly bills, some of which I could now pay thanks to the money from Kitty. I made a mental note to take a trip to the bank on Monday morning and deposit some of it in my checking account.

Then I checked in with the messaging service, to see what they had for me. Kitty had left a note to call her as soon as I found out anything, but it was slim pickings so far, so reckoned that could wait until later. There was also a message from Tom Delaney at the LAPD, one of the few friends I'd kept up with from my days on the force, who was just checking in with me.

Again, this was nothing that couldn't wait, so it was time to get going and undeterred by my lack of progress, I made a plan for the day.

First would be a trip out to the docks, to see what I might be able to pick up at the warehouse, since Marty had told me they worked Saturdays. Although lacking any special insight, I had a vague impression that any activity at the docks would take place either early in the morning or late at night. I don't know why I thought that to be the case, but it seemed about right.

Then a journey to the Laguna, to see if Jack had showed up or, if not, to try and gain access to his flat. Failing that, maybe there would be something I could find out from his neighbours.

All of which should take up much of the morning. Depending on what this turned up, I'd go back to working my way through the other contacts on Kitty's list in the afternoon.

Full of resolve, I dressed quickly for the California sunshine in casual slacks, a neutral shirt, and a fleck sports jacket. After the feedback from Agnes yesterday about my noisy size nines, I picked out a pair of loafers with a softer sole, then checked my look in the mirror.

I could have been anybody from a football dad going to his son's game to a middle-aged lothario conducting an affair, which was just the type of anonymity that I was aiming for.

Before leaving, I rooted around in the cupboard in my hallway and gathered a couple of props I thought might come in useful.

Sometimes, the act of just getting going is enough to

simulate progress and make one feel like one is doing something worthwhile. It felt good to be driving down to the ocean on this sunny day, even if it was down to San Pedro Bay and the sprawling Port of Los Angeles.

Marty said that the place was close to the office, but in my haste I had forgotten to take the address, so started over on that side of the docks, over by Wilmington. I pulled over at the main gate to ask directions, where the guy told me that the bonded warehouses were over in a secure area by the customs building, which was not far away, but fenced off from the rest of the facility and with its own entrance.

I drove alongside the security fence, which was double layered, about twelve feet high and topped with barbed wire, it dawned on me that as well as the usual sort of imports and exports, with duties to be levied, there would be high value goods like alcohol and tobacco in here, which would need to be protected.

My mood became less buoyant as I realised I didn't have a plan about how to get in and there wasn't much time to formulate one on the short ride over from the main gate, either.

I came to a gate which had an entrance barrier and a stop sign, with a guard post next to it, manned by a guy in uniform. I drove on past the sentry box and swung the nose of the Plymouth round, up to the fence.

As I stepped out of the car and up to the guard post, the uniform came outside carrying a clipboard and I reached back into my pocket for my wallet and licence. Not being able to come up with an alternative, I chose the direct approach and opted to tell the truth, or at least a version of it.

When I got closer, I could make out the guard's uniform and badge, which identified him being with the Los Angeles Port Police. The port had its own small force to secure and patrol the facility, but I'd never had any dealings with them, so wasn't sure what to expect.

"Morning. My name's Morgan. I'm a PI and I need to get to the Elegance warehouse, to speak with the guys there."

"You have an appointment?"

The guard consulted his roster, flicking through a couple of sheets of paper on the clipboard.

"No, I'm afraid not. I'm working a case and I'm trying to locate some property that's gone missing."

"Missing. You mean stolen?"

We all look at the world through the lens of our own experience. Larceny of one sort or another must have been pretty much the stock in trade of the LAPP and something they were always looking out for.

"I don't know yet. Maybe.

That's why I need to get in and speak to them."

"Okay, but you're not allowed on site without an appointment or the right clearance. Let me go make a couple of calls."

He took my licence, stepped inside, and wrote the details down methodically in some sort of log. He then placed the calls, which I couldn't make out, before coming back outside.

"The office here says it's ok for you to be here Morgan, but you can't take your car in. It's strictly no unauthorised vehicles on site.

I need to check with the warehouse that they're happy to have you up there, but the guys there aren't picking up. Probably loading up or outside somewhere.

If you hang on here, I'll try them again later."

This was not what I'd hoped for. I didn't want him to telephone ahead and tell them I was coming. There were some pretty tough characters down here on the docks, and instinct told me they might not talk to a detective, private or otherwise. I would need another approach to get anything out of them.

Marty had been forthcoming, because he was Jack's friend and the unusual way in which we got acquainted quickly established an element of trust, but it would be a different story with these guys.

I thought I'd try and appeal to the guard's humanity, always a bit of a gamble.

"I'd really like to get this wrapped up. It should be just a formality – it's an insurance matter and I just need to be able to say that I've spoken with them.

You've got my licence details and your office is happy, couldn't I just go on up?"

"Relax. What's your hurry Morgan? Like I said, I'll call them back in a bit."

I made a show of looking at my watch.

"The thing is I've made a date to see a certain somebody for coffee later on and it's not the kind of appointment I'd like to break, if you know what I mean."

I'm too embarrassed to say for sure but might even have winked as I said this last bit.

Luckily, he may have missed it, as just then a truck coming out of the port pulled up to the barrier on the other side. He went across to talk to the driver and check the paperwork.

They greeted each other by name and obviously got on, as I could make out banter and laughter. The officer came round to the back of the truck with the driver to check the contents against the manifest he was holding.

Figuring they would be more interested in checking what was coming out than going in and seeing my opportunity, I looked at him hopefully, lifted my wrist and made a pantomime of indicating my watch as they made their way back along the near side of the truck.

He called over to me.

"OK - you might as well go on up. I'm going to be a while here. Turn left through the gates and Elegance is the third building along on the right."

"That's great - thanks. I appreciate it. I'll just get the paperwork from my car."

I was genuinely grateful and had an idea.

Fake IDs, or aliases, as I prefer to think of them, can come in handy in my profession and when I started out on my own, I'd had some made up for me by a forger I know. What can I say? I have friends in low places.

No police or federal authorities you understand, so nothing strictly illegal, but morally a bit of a grey area, admittedly.

I keep these in the glove box of my car and selected one I thought might be useful, together with a clipboard and ballpoint pen. Then I chose a particularly dowdy tie from the three that I'd brought with me and put it on.

Removing my sports jacket and laying it on the passenger seat, I took a pair of round, horn-rimmed glasses out of the top pocket and put them on. I don't need spectacles, but these had plain glass lenses and were purely for appearance's sake.

Once through the barrier, I headed over towards the warehouse, rolling my sleeves up to add a final touch to my new look; that of an officious, busy-body type.

Pausing briefly, I jotted a few things down on the clipboard, so that it wouldn't look like blank paper if anybody happened to catch sight of it. I wrote down the date and the time, the title of the business and the names of some of the employees I already knew.

The building was a large brick affair, pretty much identical to those on either side. There was a sign on the top corner facing me, with the name Elegance and an arrow directing me down to the back of the building, towards the quayside.

I did as instructed and eventually rounded the corner onto a broad quay, stretching off into the distance. Light was reflecting off the water onto the warehouse entrances on my left, which were dappled in morning sunshine.

The Elegance entrance was a huge sliding wood and glass door on rollers, open most of the way across and letting the fine day into the hangar-like space. The interior was scattered with pallets and large packing cases, piled on top of each other and organised in rows, with aisles running down them towards the back of the building.

Instinctively, I wanted to look around before bumping into anybody and started working my way down the row furthest away, keeping an eye out and walking softly.

Some of the crates were very large, presumably containing pieces of the sort of statement furniture I'd seen in the showroom and whatever the stuff came packed in. These would be hard to steal and noisy to move, which probably explained why there was nobody around at the front of the warehouse.

There were stencils on the sides the crates and I worked quickly jotting down information a couple of pages further back on the clipboard, figuring that I could take a closer look later on.

The stuff seemed to be organised in rough piles and there were all sorts of numbers and codes, as well as writing in French, Italian and German. There were words I didn't recognise but took to be the names of ports of origin and ships and such like, as well as the Elegance address and more familiar names like San Pedro and Los Angeles.

Working my way back down the aisle, I could hear voices, but couldn't make out what they were saying, or where they were, for all the piled-up crates in the way. I put the clipboard under my arm in and headed on.

I passed a particularly tall pile of furniture on my left and came across a sort of alcove hidden in the boxes, where two men sat on upturned chests with cards in their hands, engaged in what looked to be a game of crib.

One was older than the other and I thought this might be Marty's friend Ed who he told me about. The younger one was stocky, with a couple of days' worth of dark stubble around his fleshy face and had been in the act of chewing something but was now stock-still.

As I was taking this in, he took his right hand away from his cards and sitting back, rested it casually on his thigh. It was a natural enough looking move, but it didn't escape my attention that it brought within reach a viciously sharp looking dockers hook, sitting off to his right-hand side.

"No need to get up, gentlemen. I can see you're on your break. Excellent: we're all in favour of that at the NLU."

Neither had any intention of standing and both looked at me blankly.

"I'll need to see your union cards, please. We can't have any non-union labour working here in the port."

Getting into character, I had modified my usual way of speaking to a more clipped, precise sort of delivery and had taken out the fake ID, which I was holding up for them to see.

It identified me as one Stanley Karnowski, an official from the National Labor Union. This was a real enough, but long since defunct organisation, sufficiently generic to be applicable to most situations. It was laminated, with a younger photograph of me, an impressive looking crest and some phony address details, registration number and other such gobbledygook.

As far as I knew, impersonating an official from a non-existent union was not a crime in the State of California, but it was not without its own risks in a highly unionised environment.

"Who are you? You're not the usual guy. What's his name, Ed, the one who comes around?"

"You mean Tony."

"Yeah, him."

The one I now knew to be Ed took over.

"We're covered by the longshoremen, here. How come we didn't know you were coming?"

"Well, you see I'm from the *National* Labor Union. This is a spot check. We have to make sure that the union officials down here are doing their jobs."

"Checking up on them as well, huh? That figures."

This from the one who wasn't Ed and who then spat tobacco juice just past my right foot with a practiced aim.

I acted my part and stepped back, pulling the clipboard up against my chest fussily and pulling a face.

"Take it easy, Mike, the guy's just doing his job."

Mike grumbled something about me being a pencil pusher, but in due course they both produced union cards and handed them over.

I made a show of examining these fastidiously, writing down names, dates of birth and union membership details.

"Is there anybody else? I have Jack Conlon and an Agnes Moreno on my list."

Ed did the talking again.

"You've got duff information.

They work at Elegance but not here. They're at the showroom over on North Avalon."

"Do they ever come here to the warehouse? They still need to be members or at least affiliated to a union if that's the case."

"Mr. Conlon comes occasionally, but you'd have to ask him yourself. I haven't seen him in a couple of weeks though."

"And what about a Martin Donaldson?"

Mike snorted and Ed said:

"You're way off. You're wasting your time and ours. Marty hasn't worked here for three years at least."

"This is most unsatisfactory." I tut-tutted.

"The last name I have is a Mr. Jenner? I hope he's here at least.

"Yeah. He's the boss but he's not around right

now. He's off back East, taking care of some family business."

Mike chipped in:

"He's from Brooklyn. New York City – it's a big place, you may have heard of it. The greatest place in all the world."

"Yeah, yeah. If it's so great, how come you're out here now then?" This from Ed.

It had the air of a familiar and long-running dispute, about to reignite.

I held my hand up politely to interrupt.

"I'll have to come back in that case. When will he be here next, Mr. Jenner?"

"I think he said the thirteenth, that'd be next Tuesday."

I smiled broadly and clicking the biro shut, attached it to my clipboard fussily, then set them back up under my arm.

"Thank you, gentlemen, you've been most helpful. I'll be running along now, and somebody will be out here again next week. Good day to you both."

I turned smartly on my heel and left, feeling eyes on my back all the way up the aisle until I rounded the corner to the warehouse entrance. I headed back to the barrier, saluted the guard with a wave and climbed back into the Plymouth.

Taking off the tie and spectacles, I was glad to get back to being myself again and replayed the conversation on the drive over to the Laguna, trying to work out if I had learned anything or what any of it might mean.

It was a beautiful Saturday morning in October, one of those bonus days when autumn felt like a continuation of summer. It was a day for spending out at the beach, or up in the hills, but instead I was driving around the city in my car, telling lies to people I'd barely met.

7. Distraction

To catch a break in the case I was going to have to make the running myself.

When I reached the Laguna a little after ten, the parking slots out front were taken, so I swung on over to the garage where I'd met Peter the night before and drove up to the barrier.

An older guy, around sixty and bald as a coot, who I figured for the day guy, came to the window of the booth. He had a cigar stub wedged in the corner of his mouth.

"I'm visiting Jack Conlon at the Laguna in 12a."

"Popular guy. Head on up. Anywhere on the first level. It's free until eight, but there's a charge after that."

He handed me a ticket.

"Thanks, I'm not planning on staying that long."

I took the ticket and drove on up to the first floor, which was fairly empty and parked nose out about half a dozen spaces along from the Jaguar, which hadn't moved.

Something about what he said was playing on my mind and on my way back down the ramp, I stopped and rapped on the window. The guy pushed his bulky frame up with some effort and wandered over.

"I see Jack's Jaguar is still up there."

I hoped this would help to establish my credentials as his friend.

"When you said that he was a popular guy just now, did you mean something specific? Has somebody been asking for him, maybe?"

He narrowed his eyes at me.

"You a cop?"

So much for the credentials.

"No."

Extracting another few dollars from my wallet, I

deposited them in front of him, this time having no illusions they might be going towards a college fund.

He scooped the money up without looking at it.

"Not somebody but *bodies*. Two of them. A mean looking guy was asking after Mr. Conlon. I didn't like the look of him, so didn't tell him anything.
His partner stayed down there on the avenue by his car, so I didn't get a good look at him, but he was big."

He pointed off down to the bottom of the ramp.

Al and Louis.

Everything went still as I focused in on what he was saying.

"When was this?"

"Yesterday afternoon. Not long before I got off at three."

Which would have been a few hours before I ran into the pair at Dutch's bar. It wasn't just coincidence: they were looking for Jack.

"You said you didn't see the other guy, but did you get a look at the car maybe?"

"Sure did. A green Hudson Hornet sedan. Fast car."

"Thanks."

I nodded, and walked on down the ramp, then crossed over to the Laguna, where I carried on past the entrance and did the same tour of the building as the previous night, only this time in reverse.

About halfway round, there was a gap between the blocks, with a view through a gate into the inner courtyard, containing the obligatory pool and a few empty easy chairs. It was probably where the pool guy came in and out with his cleaning gear and I tried the gate surreptitiously, but it was locked, as I knew it must be.

In daylight, I could make out some of the apartment numbers and although I couldn't see 12a, the ones on the top level on the opposite side from me were all numbered

a. From these, I worked out that Jack's place would be one or other of two apartments in the right-hand corner relative to the entrance. Having established the geography, I circled via the back of the building to this spot and crossed the street.

There are only so many times a man can tie or untie his shoelaces without attracting attention and a man standing around twiddling his thumbs looking awkward stands out. A man smoking a cigarette in the morning sunshine on the other hand is exactly that; the sort of presence you wouldn't register.

I'm not what would generally be considered a smoker, only being partial to the occasional small cigar, but carry smoking materials as they can be useful. I took up position just down from a mailbox on the corner, lit and puffed on a Pall Mall, enjoying the pleasing aroma of the tobacco smoke.

I checked my watch every now and then for good measure, acting the part of waiting for another party, just in case anybody was watching. All of which bought me about ten minutes to observe the building.

Pretty much nothing happened. Neither of the corner apartments had windows open or lights on, but it being not long after ten on Saturday morning, this was not unusual. I couldn't see movement or activity in the neighbouring apartments on either floor.

A curtain twitched up in the far-right hand corner apartment and I turned away, casting my look downwards, so as not to be observed and to get a better view out of the corner of my eye. It happened again and I felt a surge of adrenalin, until I realised it was just the material catching in the draft from an air conditioning unit which was mounted underneath the window and whirring faintly.

All of which was getting me nowhere.

I had to get inside the building and needed some sort of a

distraction. Focused on the task in hand and thinking hard, I looked around muttering to myself until I spotted something.

There was a smoking stand at the bottom of the short flight of steps just outside the entrance to the apartment building, with an ashtray on top and a trash can underneath. It would be for guests to use coming and going from the building, waiting for cabs or whatever, and it gave me an idea.

I wandered over to it and taking some paper from out of my notebook, wadded it up into a ball. Checking that the coast was clear, I set fire to it with my lighter and dropped it into the trash which had built up underneath in the can.

It is not without good reason that arson, is considered a felony offence in the State of California, but I figured it would only be a small fire which would burn itself out quickly. Besides, it was a particularly ugly smoking stand, I told myself as I strode purposefully into the Laguna, hoping nobody had seen me.

I nodded pleasantly to the desk clerk, relieved it wasn't the guy from the evening before but an older man and hurried over to the payphone booth in the left-hand corner of the lobby, playing the part of a man needing to place an urgent call.

Inside the booth, I turned my back to the desk, to obscure my true purpose and to watch the main entrance. Then I settled down to one side of an imaginary conversation, neither too loud or too quiet, waiting for my moment which should take no more than a minute or two to come.

A guest came into the lobby, through the inner door to the courtyard on the far side of the desk over my shoulder and carried on out through the main exit. I counted down in my head: three, two, one...

He came bursting back through the entrance door gesticulating at the clerk.

"Fire! Come quickly!"

The two of them rushed out to tackle the fire, the desk clerk grabbing an extinguisher from behind the desk. I calculated that it would give me a maximum of about a minute and a half before he put the fire out and returned to his post.

Sliding out from the booth and over behind the desk, I made directly for the cubbyholes on the back wall. Mail theft is also a crime in the State of California, although if my memory serves, it is only a misdemeanour. Nonetheless, I quickly grabbed the letters from pigeonhole 12a, addressed to Jack Conlon.

Having picked out my own envelope from the night before, I put some of the more obvious advertising circulars and uninteresting looking stuff back in the cubbyhole, hoping to make the theft less obvious. The rest I took with me, jamming it quickly into my inside jacket pocket.

Time to move on to phase two of my hastily conceived plan.

Moving to the end of the desk nearest the connecting inner door, I leant down over the counter, trying to locate the buzzer, which I knew must be there to let guests through. I had one eye on the scene outside where the fire was being extinguished way too efficiently for my liking.

I located the buzzer and was about to press it, when a youngish couple, who had been talking, came through the door and were distracted by the unusual scene being played out in front of the entrance. They paused in the doorway and interrupted their conversation.

"Thank you."

They barely noticed as I slipped past, making out they had held the door open for me.

I crossed a short hallway with some potted plants, occasional chairs and a side table with a coffee urn and cups, newspapers on the side, and a magazine rack. The whole space had a colonial chic air and would have been a very inviting place to relax if I'd had the time.

Not hanging around, I carried straight on through another set of open double doors into the courtyard around the pool, which I'd caught a glimpse of earlier.

This was another elegant space, combining richly worn terracotta tiles underfoot with the faded pink adobe walls of the surrounding buildings. The overall effect was that you were in a large villa or private house, as opposed to an apartment building. It was a delightfully cool space and would offer sanctuary from the heat on even the most brutal of summer days.

I made my way along one side of the courtyard towards the corner where I knew Jack's apartment was and came to a tiled staircase leading to the upper balcony level. Coming out at the top, the door to 12a was directly ahead in the corner of the building, at a right angle to the one for the other apartment I had been observing from across the street, which I now knew to be 11a.

I had hoped for some sort of internal corridor or that the doorway might at least be set back somehow, affording me some protection from prying eyes. Instead, I felt very exposed on the balcony, since the doors were all arranged around the courtyard, looking inwards, and facing each other.

I pressed the buzzer and waited a few minutes without getting an answer, then hit it again with the same result. I pushed against the door, which held firm and then knocked as loudly as I dared without attracting unwanted attention. Nothing.

Next, I put my ear to the door and listened, but the only sound coming from inside the apartment was the air conditioner, clattering away faintly in what would be either the living room or the bedroom.

The activities I was about to engage in were covered by laws relating to burglary, trespass, and unlawful entry or possibly a combination of all three. In my time on the force, it had been pretty routine to break in to gain access when required; although I wasn't with the LAPD anymore, of course.

There was a cylinder lock at the top of the door, which wouldn't give too much trouble, as I had lock picks with me, but I knelt to look at the keyhole lower down, which was for a mortise lock. One which might take a whole month of Sundays to get anywhere with.

Squinting, at the keyhole, I encountered something odd. I should have been able to see clear through to the inside, but couldn't, as there was something in the way. Most likely the key, which must have still been in the lock on the other side.

Meaning that the apartment was locked from the inside. I didn't like where this was going, and the hairs stood up on the back of my neck, telling me I had to get in there.

Taking a step back from the door, I noticed a small gap running along the bottom edge, probably not much more than a quarter of an inch. It may have been there intentionally to allow for a draft, but whatever the reason it gave me an idea.

I knelt down and re-folded two sheets of the beautiful, thick writing paper with Kitty's lists on and pushed these carefully under the door alongside each other and slightly overlapping, directly underneath the lock. I slid them in as far as I dared but kept an inch or so protruding from outside.

Next, I selected one of the lock picks from my set but turning it round so that the slim handle was pointing away from me, offered this up to the keyhole and slid it in gently. If I was right and the lock was fully locked from the inside, then the key should be in the down position and I might be able to locate the end of the shaft and tap it gently right back through the lock.

The theory was sound enough, and I'd made the target

area as big as possible, but it would all come down to luck as to where the key might land or bounce on the other side.

Applying gentle pressure back and forth, I played the shaft of the key with the pick handle until I heard it drop out on the other side of the door with a tinkle. I bent down further, ever so slowly pulled the sheets of paper towards me and felt pleased with myself to see the key was nestling on top of the little pillow I had made to cushion it's fall.

The key clicked the mortise lock open with a clunk and I tried the door again, in case the latch was off, which it wasn't, so turned my attention to the cylinder lock.

I was carrying some frames of old film stock that can be slid in between the lock and the doorjamb, but this is fiddly and doesn't always work, so opted for picks instead. I stepped in close to the door to cover my actions, but figured if anybody asked, I'd flash my badge and come clean about my concerns.

Getting a tensioner in, I drove a pick into the back of the barrel and worked it forward along the pin tumblers, eventually managing to line them all up, so that the barrel would rotate to open the door. Once inside, I got my picks out and put the lock on the latch before closing the door softly behind me.

Stepping over the threshold I was hit with a wall of frigid air, which got me wondering why anybody would want to crank the air conditioner up so high on a sunny, but not overly hot October morning in the cool apartment block.

The thought troubled me, and I had a sense of foreboding as I went further in.

8. Meeting Eric

Inside, Jack Conlon's place was elegantly simple, but the thing that got my immediate attention was the place had been ransacked.

I turned right into a short hallway with oak parquet flooring under a stylish, modernist rug and saw an attractive sideboard which should have been standing against the wall, lying with its drawers and contents spilled out. A walnut bureau facing me at the end of the passageway had received the same treatment.

Catching movement at the end of the hallway, my hand came up instinctively to my hip before I realised that it was just my reflection in a mirror above the bureau. The place was eerily still, and I sensed that whatever had happened here was long since over.

Venturing further inside the apartment, I rounded a corner to the left at the end of the hall where it opened out into a living room. At which point, the fact that the place had been tossed was no longer the main thing occupying my attention.

What took its place was the man sitting on a persimmon-coloured couch just inside, with his head turned in my direction at an unnatural angle and eyes staring straight ahead. A man who was dead. Unmistakably, very dead.

I checked his neck for a pulse in any case, but there was none, and he was cold to the touch. Rocking his head back slightly so that it rested on the back of the couch, I could see a fine trickle of dried blood at the corner of his mouth.

I recognised him from the photograph. Not the one which Kitty had given me of Jack, but one on the wall of his office. It wasn't the man I'd been expecting to find here: not Jack Conlon, but his business partner Eric

Jenner.

"What are you doing here?"

I wondered out loud.

He said nothing. The dead know all the answers, but they're not telling. They can be most disobliging in that regard.

Eric Jenner was dressed for a night out in a white tuxedo with black tie, but there was no indication if he'd been on his way out or coming back in. Bending down to look at the body more closely I could see two neat little holes very close together in his white shirt just under his ribcage, where his jacket fell open.

It looked like he had been shot through the heart and at close range with something small calibre, most likely a pistol. Either that, or the killer was some sort of an expert marksman to get the shots so tight together, as those little things lack accuracy over any kind of range.

Looking at the set up, I favoured the first theory.

There were no shell casings, so they'd either rolled off somewhere or maybe the killer had picked them up or used a revolver. Assuming he'd been killed here, which seemed likely but might not have been the case.

I'd have to call it in and sooner rather than later, but before the boys from the PD trampled all over the scene, I decided to look around myself. Besides, I wasn't looking forward to making the call and had some thinking to do with regard to my own situation, which was none too peachy.

Having worked homicide at LAPD for a couple of years, I knew how they operated and thought. There were some detectives over who thought the first person to see the victim dead was a solid suspect, before troubling themselves too much about finding the last person to see them alive.

In any case, I wasn't what you'd call popular over there, for reasons we don't need to go into right now.

Once I got myself off the hook, Jack Conlon would be in the frame as the next best suspect. The two men were known to each other as friends and business partners; the victim was in his apartment, and he'd disappeared.

My mind was racing ahead, and I would have to let all of this play itself out later. I needed to focus and work fast.

Much like my own place, the layout was compact, comprised of the short entrance hallway opening out on to the living room I was standing in. Off this on the right-hand side were two doors, both ajar and leading to what looked to be bedrooms. Past the couch there was an archway off on the other side to the left, where I could see a kitchenette and a short passage, which I presumed would lead to the bathroom.

Firstly, I crossed over to the air conditioning unit at the far end against the window and switched it off, using a handkerchief and being careful not to touch the controls directly. It was freezing and the noise was getting on my nerves: I could turn it back on later.

Then carefully picking my way around the wreckage, I did a tour of the apartment, which confirmed it had been thoroughly searched. Not professionally, more in a desperate scramble.

The kitchen drawers and cupboards were open, with the contents spilled out on the surfaces. It was the same story in the bathroom.

The mattress in the main bedroom was off to one side and the chest of drawers had been turned out onto the bed. Similarly, the nightstand had been rifled and the contents spilled out on to the floor.

At the bedroom window, I could see that it was actually French doors leading to a Juliet balcony. Gingerly I tried the handle, which was unlocked and looked outside. It was a short drop down onto a lawn bordering the sidewalk below, and although not connected, a short step across to the fire escape running back along to the living room window.

It was easily achievable for even a reasonably athletic person. My guess was the killer had locked the apartment door from the inside and left this way through the bedroom. They'd probably cranked the air conditioning up before going, in the hope that the body wouldn't be discovered any earlier than needs be in the spell of warm weather we'd been enjoying.

There was a second much smaller bedroom facing back into the courtyard, which Conlon used as a dressing room. The contents of a built-in wardrobe were piled up on a chaise, with the suit jacket and pants pockets turned inside out. There was also a pile of shoes all jumbled up in the corner.

I reasoned that whatever the killer had been looking for had to be small, if it could be hidden inside a shoe or in a pocket.

It seemed unlikely that Conlon would toss his own apartment, so what had happened here? Had Jenner done this and been disturbed, or had it been someone else either before or after his murder? Maybe the two guys from the bar were behind it: I knew they'd been to the Laguna, looking for Jack.

Another possibility was that it had been done to cover something else up.

I went back into the living room area and looked at the scene again, checked behind the pictures and the mirror looking for a safe, but found none.

There was a bookcase over on the wall behind the sofa and the books had been gone through and dropped down the gap between it and the couch with the body. Again, the act of flicking through books implied something small or thin, like you might use for a bookmark. Maybe money or a letter or a photograph; something like that?

Looking down behind the couch, I couldn't see exit holes to correspond with the ones on Jenner's front, so maybe the slugs were still in him, or somewhere in the back of the sofa, in which case the homicide boys would have something to go on. If he had been shot here.

The front of his trousers were clean and there were no scuffs or drag marks on the tips of his shoes or anything to suggest he had been moved here.

Looking back into the hallway, from where the body was positioned, I could see a brutal looking .45 automatic poking out from under the overturned drawer of the sideboard, not ten feet away from where Eric Jenner sat, waiting for eternity.

If Jenner had been shot with that, there would have been huge holes in him, the back of the couch and on through the bookcase into the wall behind. I left it well alone, figuring it didn't have anything to do with this set up and was probably Conlon's service piece, kept in the drawer.

Jenner might not have known it was there of course, or not had time to get to it or thought he didn't need it. Maybe he knew his killer, had a gun trained on him or was incapacitated in some other way.

I patted the dead man down and fished around in his pockets with my handkerchief, I didn't find the things you might normally expect, no keys, wallet, cigarettes, or lighter and so on. Nothing like that.

Looking more closely at the body, I tried to determine how long he had been dead. His workplace had told me that he'd been away for about a week, but it didn't seem that long. More like a couple of days, although there was no real way for me to tell.

Remembering my own situation and the hastily grabbed letters in my pocket, I sat down at a small table and chair next to the hatch into the kitchen area and had a look through them. There was a corner bar straight ahead of me and I eyed the bottles thirstily but decided against taking a belt from one.

Focusing back on the task in hand, I could see that Jack

Conlon used a messaging service like my own, where telephone messages were transcribed and delivered to the front desk of his apartment building.

Working quickly, I established that a number were from Kitty, naturally enough, a couple from his friend Marty and the rest seemed to be work related; either from the office or from clients who were following up orders. There was even a message from his country club asking him to renew his membership. It was all pretty routine stuff which wasn't telling me anything.

A handwritten letter in the pile of mail stood out from the rest. It was stamped and had come as a regular delivery, seemed almost empty and was from a distinctive cream stationery set. I set it off to one side and thought again about my own predicament.

I could demonstrate a legitimate reason for being at the apartment in the first place, although I'd have to fudge how I got in.

I didn't think I'd left any tool marks on the cylinder lock, but it wouldn't do to be caught in the apartment with my lock picking set, which would be enough to lose my licence. If I had gained access with the key though, that would be a different matter, as technically I wouldn't have broken in. It might still constitute trespass, but Conlon wasn't around, so who was going to bring charges? So far so good.

Not being able to put the post back or to leave it in the apartment, I'd have to admit to taking the messages, which the police would want as evidence. These might earn me a rap on the knuckles, but other than that one letter, they weren't strictly speaking mail - just internal memos – so I didn't think that was even a crime.

Remembering the mailbox on the corner across the street where I'd waited before, I had an idea. Say what you like about the US Postal Service, it does a pretty good job of providing high security safe deposit facilities, for short periods. You put the goods in one end, and they usually turn up at the other end a few days later.

Mailing items to myself that I didn't want to get found with was a technique I'd used before, and I routinely carry postage stamps, but was lacking an envelope.

Looking around, I saw the bureau back at the entrance to the hallway and went over to look in the top section. Sure enough, there was some stationery in there and I fished out a decent sized envelope, which stopped me in my tracks when I pulled it out.

The envelope was identical to the letter I'd left over on the table. I crossed back over and compared the two side by side. No doubt about it, they were like peas in a pod, definitely from the same stock of high-end stationery. Although I couldn't swear to it, the handwriting looked like the entries in the desk diary at the office, in Jack's own hand.

I was willing to bet that he'd used the same trick and mailed this letter to himself. It was a possible lead to Jack, and I wanted a look at the thing but was running out of time. I'd been there long enough already and could hear sirens approaching, probably in response to my little spot of arson outside earlier.

It was one thing to call the police in myself, but another thing entirely to be discovered there in the apartment with a dead man.

Quickly addressing the blank envelope to myself, I placed the little lock picking set and celluloid film inside, then folded Jack's letter so that it would fit into the new envelope and sealed the whole lot down. I attached postage stamps and probably put more than was strictly necessary to make sure and tucked it inside my jacket pocket.

It may have been a rash move, but I didn't want to get caught with the letter and told myself it probably had nothing to do with Jenner's murder. Besides, it was his property, and the police didn't know about it. It was my only lead so far to Jack and I needed to stay one step ahead if I was going to get to him before they did. Pretty soon they'd be looking for him as a matter of priority.

Taking the bundle of messages with me, I walked back through to the hallway. On the way, I noticed keys on the floor in the corner by the sideboard that I hadn't seen on my way in.

There were two car keys on a fob with a Jaguar emblem, along with a Yale key. It was sorely tempting to go over and take a look in the Jaguar, but I'd better leave something for the boys in blue to do. Out of curiosity, I picked them up with my handkerchief and tried the Yale key in the apartment door. It fitted.

Like many people, Jack Conlon was probably in the habit of pulling the door to behind him and not using the mortise lock, which is why he only had the Yale key on the fob and the other one had been on the inside of the door.

I left the door on the latch and went back outside to lock up with the mortise key. I'd tell the boys downtown I'd found it like that and managed to finagle the mortise key out of the lock, which was nearly true. They'd know I'd picked the other lock but wouldn't be able to prove it and I guessed it wouldn't matter.

Retracing my steps back down the staircase and along the side of the courtyard, I paused briefly in the hallway to help myself to a cup of the coffee on offer. It wasn't piping hot, but it was good and strong, so I had another, in the certain knowledge that it would be better than anything I might get down at headquarters in the long hours to come.

I walked confidently across the lobby and out through the main doors, past the scene of my earlier crimes and trying not to look guilty as I passed a fire truck parked along the street. I went around the corner to the mailbox, enjoying the autumn sunshine and ruing the fact that I wasn't going to be seeing much more of it that day.

The guys at the PD wouldn't want me to talk to anybody at the Laguna, so I went back inside, and this time placed a real call from the phone booth in the lobby to Tom Delaney on homicide. I told him briefly what I'd found and that I'd meet him outside the building.

I said that I was happy to cooperate and come in for questioning but didn't see the need for them to arrest me, even though I knew I would be considered a suspect initially. I went outside to wait for him and to have a think.

The homicide guys would want to know how I came to be there and there was only so much they'd swallow about client privilege before they lost patience. They'd interview Kitty in any case, so I'd sweat it out for a bit before telling them sooner or later that I was trying to find Jack for her.

They'd be mad there wasn't a lot else I could tell them and probably think I was holding out on them, even though I wasn't really. I knew they'd warn me off from trying to find him myself but wasn't convinced they were looking for the right guy in any case.

If I was right, Jack Conlon wasn't the murderer, but he was in a whole lot more trouble than he realised.

9. Sunset

The boys at headquarters hadn't been too hard on me but hadn't exactly given me an easy ride either. Tom Delaney was good to his word and let me come in without being arrested, which meant I wasn't an out and out suspect.

They knew I wasn't the real killer, although a couple of them might have enjoyed seeing me on the hook for a while. It didn't make sense for anybody to ransack an apartment, commit a murder, then call the police and wait calmly for them to show up.

As a single man and one with antisocial tendencies, it wasn't always easy to demonstrate my whereabouts at a given point in time, but eventually they worked out that the timings were also all wrong.

It turned out Jenner had been dead for at least couple of days and there was no connection between me and either him or Jack until after the event, when Kitty had come to my office. Which got me wondering again about a question that had been occupying me all day.

In the end, they lost interest in me as a suspect and wanted to know everything I could tell them about Jack Conlon and his whereabouts instead, which wasn't a great deal.

I did my best to co-operate and shared most my observations, even if there were a few sins of omission, by way of details left out. They knew I'd broken into the apartment but couldn't prove it and it wasn't that much in the grand scheme of things.

They'd find out anyhow, so I gave them descriptions of the guys who'd been looking for Jack at his apartment block and told them about the green Hudson Hornet, although I left out the bit about the gunplay and the rumpus when we'd met at Dutch's bar.

Which earned me the glittering prize of having to look through endless books of mugshots, which was entirely fruitless. Probably because they were from out of town, maybe somewhere back East, like I suspected.

Eventually, they had to let me go and Tom was decent enough to run me back to the Laguna to pick up my car as he was coming off his shift. He took the opportunity of the drive over there to lecture me about the wisdom (or lack thereof) in me carrying on my own investigation.

Not wanting to lie to him any more than I had to, I listened in silence, rather than agree not to look for Jack. Tom knew I would keep searching and I knew that he knew it, which made for an awkward journey.

He dropped me at the car park, and I went up the ramp to retrieve the Plymouth and saw the young man, Peter, back on duty. When I handed him my ticket, although it was past eight, he said that under the circumstances I wouldn't have to pay, which was good of him.

I asked if the police had looked at the Jaguar yet and whether they had found anything. He told me they had been up there earlier but didn't think they'd taken anything away.

Good kid that he was, Peter said that he didn't believe Mr. Conlon was responsible, even if there was a dead body in his apartment and I told him that I was inclined to agree, even if the police weren't. I bid him a good evening and saluted as I came back down through the barrier and headed for home.

Back at my apartment, I showered and made proper coffee, which gave me time to take stock of my situation, which was a delicate one. I wasn't investigating Eric Jenner's death, but looking for Jack Conlon, which amounted to pretty much the same thing.

I'd kept the existence of Kitty's list from the police, but they'd compile their own version soon enough, with names of Jack's known associates and regular haunts.

They would be knocking on all the same doors in the days to come and there were a lot more of them than of me.

I was dog tired but to get any kind of a head start on the boys in homicide, I'd have to jump to it. First, I telephoned Kitty at home and brought her up to speed.

When I told her about Jenner, her reaction was neutral, but I couldn't tell whether this meant anything. It can be very difficult to gauge somebody's reaction over the telephone, even if you know the person well, which I didn't. The police had been in touch and would be out to interview her, so it was possible she already knew about the body at Jack's place.

She'd heard nothing from Jack and was insistent that I keep looking for him. I explained the perils of having to tread carefully around the police investigation, but promised I'd give it my best shot. I asked her about the two hoods from the bar, just in case, but she had no idea who they were or what it was about.

We hung up and I thought about the dead body in the apartment.

Eric Jenner had been dressed in a tuxedo and black tie when I found him, so the odds were that he was either going to or coming from some kind of a function or night out. There were plenty of bars and dinner venues on Kitty's list, but one stood out as being a good place to start.

Sunset Boulevard had faded from its glory days, as most of the big action had moved out to Las Vegas. Famous clubs like Ciro's and the Macambo had not long closed down, but there was still a market for those who wanted a more local night out, and the Strip was the place to go for it.

Club Havana was a relatively new place, but I chose it because it would likely have a dress code. The Cuban connection didn't really make a lot of sense geographically, but I guessed it was trying to evoke the glamour of places like the Tropicana in Havana, now that the island was off-limits.

Nightclubs, with their fake ambience and overpriced drinks have never appealed to me. Naturally, I'd never been to the Havana, but from the little I'd heard, it would be no exception. Like it or not, I was heading there and to add insult to injury, would have to dress for the occasion.

Most people think that they look good in tuxedo. I don't and I know it. I hate the things. The truth of the matter is that with one on I look exactly like a boxing referee, which more than one person has told me to my face. This is particularly the case if I happen to remove my jacket.

Apart from the whole referee bit, I had a good reason not to take my jacket off. In light of recent developments, namely gunplay and murder, I planned on giving an old acquaintance an outing.

Although I don't like guns, it sometimes pays to have one to hand in my line of work and consequently own a couple: I'd rather have one and not need it than need one and not have it.

I crossed over to the safe behind the mirror over the mantelpiece in the living room, dialled in the numbers and retrieved my hammerless Colt .32 automatic from its resting place, together with the shoulder rig it lived in.

After taking out the magazine and checking the action, I re-inserted the clip and put the holster on so that the unobtrusive little gun fit snugly under my left armpit. Then I put on my tuxedo jacket and went across to check the overall look in the mirror. You'd never know it was there and even a light patting down wouldn't give it away, although a thorough one would.

Suitably attired, I hailed a cab outside my apartment building, figuring that arriving by taxi was a safe bet; a neutral option, that wouldn't say anything about who I was, or wasn't, should anyone happen to be watching.

I took the short ride down to the Strip, looking and feeling like a prize idiot in my monkey suit. We pulled up at the Havana and I paid the cab and went in. My heart sank as I took in the décor and the atmosphere.

There were excessive numbers of potted hothouse plants; mambo music; the sickly-sweet smell of rum cocktails; incessant chatter and the forced laughter of other monkey suited habitués and their glamorous partners, all having the most amazing time. Except for me, who wanted nothing more at that moment than to go home.

The only thing missing was a parrot in a gilded cage and I wasn't convinced that there might not be one somewhere in the place.

The whole set up was trying to evoke the recent past when America's rich and famous citizens used to go to Cuba to party. Them and the kingpins of organised crime, of course. Let's not forget about those.

That was under the excessively corrupt Batista regime, before Castro and Guevara won their unlikely victory, ushering in a new era of communism on the island. All of which was deemed to be distinctly un-American activity, particularly when they kicked out the mobsters and shut down their gambling operations.

Personally, I couldn't see what all the fuss was about. If a bunch of people on an island in the middle of nowhere wanted to organise themselves differently to the rest of us, then good luck to them I say.

The problem being that this island wasn't in the middle of nowhere, of course, but just off the coast of Florida.

Fighting the instinct to leave, I pressed on.

The bar was about a mile and a half long and deciding to start there, I took up a position about three quarters of a mile along it and signalled to the bartender in the time-honoured tradition.

It had been a long day and I could use a drink in any case. The barman, a jovial looking thirty-something wandered over.

"What'll it be?"

"Can you set me up a whiskey sour: straight up and strong?"

"Coming right up."

He sidled off to make my drink.

While he was away, I had the sensation I recognised him from somewhere and was trying to recall the details. Granted he was a bartender, but I thought it might be something else. I've always been good with faces, but less so with names.

A few minutes later, he set the drink in front of me and waited for my verdict.

It was in a coupe glass, which I eyed with some suspicion, but when I had a sip, it tasted surprisingly okay. I nodded my appreciation.

When I had finished busying myself with the drink, he looked sideways at me.

"Aren't you Morgan, who works homicide?"

This was said with a big smile, which can make all the difference.

"I was. That is: same Morgan, but no longer on the PD, although I'm still in that line of work. I'm freelance now.

I know your face, but you'll have to help me with the name. Forgive me."

He reached across the bar, and we shook.

"That's okay. It's Mikey Russo. You must meet a lot of people in that kind of job."

"Too many and not all of them good.

I remember now. That guy Newman: strangled his wife and tried to make out she hung herself. Nasty business.

You lived in the apartment across the hallway. We interviewed you as a witness."

"That's right. You put him in San Quentin, didn't you."

"Yup."

We both pondered this.

"You still live there, Mikey, out in Lincoln Heights?"

"Nah. I couldn't stay at that place after that. It was too creepy.
I'm out in Montebello now. Got myself a fiancé over there too."

"That's great. I'm happy for you."

"I've not seen you here before, Morgan: it's not one of your regular spots, is it?"

I laughed at the thought.

"Not exactly. Actually, I'm working."

A waitress approached the bar and Mikey excused himself to take her order. He came back five minutes later, with another drink for me.

"This one's on me, Morgan.
She was a nice lady, his wife, Mary. I liked her. I'm glad you put that no good bastard where he belongs."

"Thanks, Mikey. May everybody be where he belongs."

I tipped my glass to him.

"Is it another case you're working?"

"Sort of. Actually, I'm looking for somebody: a man named Jack Conlon. He's disappeared and I'm told this is one of his watering holes.

You wouldn't happen to know him? Know if he's been in lately?"

Mikey looked at me a little more cautiously now.

"Sure. Everybody knows Mr. Conlon. He's a really good guy.

He's not in any trouble, is he?"

I looked at him levelly and spoke with what I hoped was sincerity.

"Up until this morning, I thought I was the only one looking for him, but the guys from LAPD will show up here soon. They think he did something bad, but I'm not so sure.

Do you know a guy called Eric Jenner? He's one of Jack's pals and I think he might come here too?"

He looked at me blankly.

"He'd be about my age and height, a little heavier set, with salt and pepper hair. Has a scar on his cheek here."

I held up my hand to my left cheek.

He nodded now, remembering.

"I've seen that guy alright with Mr. Conlon like you said, but I didn't know his name. He's quiet; you know. Is he in trouble too, this Jenner?"

I felt the thin ice I'd been on start to give way.

"Eric Jenner is in as much trouble as a man can be, Mikey. He's dead.

I found him this morning at Conlon's place. The police think Jack might have something to do with it.

If they knew I was here talking to you about it, I'd be in a lot of hot water, but I might just be able to help Jack if I can get to him before they do. I don't want to get you in any trouble, but do you know if either of them has been in recently?"

He thought it over.

"Okay Morgan. If you think it might help Mr. Conlon.

I won't say anything about you being here if the police come around.

I've not seen him in here for some time, maybe a fortnight, but I'm pretty sure that guy Jenner was in here a couple of nights back."

I nodded my encouragement.

"That's good, Mikey. Now think what night was it exactly and did he have company? What sort of time would it have been?"

"I couldn't swear to it, but I think it was Wednesday. About nine pm, just after the early show.

We're pretty quiet then, mid-week.

There was another guy. I didn't get a good look at him, but he was shorter and kind of heavy. That's about all I can remember."

"That's really good, Mikey. Be sure and tell the police what you told me about this other guy. It might help Jack.

By the way, has anyone else been here asking about either of them?"

He shook his head.

"Nobody's spoken to me.

You might want to talk to Janet though; Mr. Conlon's friendly with her. She's a singer here. She was the act that night too. She might know Jenner or that guy he was with."

"What's her surname? How do I find her?"

"Stick around, Morgan. You're in luck – she's on tonight. She'll be back in a bit and should finish just after ten. It's Janet Paris, but that might not be her real name, the Paris bit, I mean.

She's pretty good, blond, and easy to look at. Make your way into the lounge back there and you'll catch her act."

He indicated an archway with a door and a sign marked 'Lounge' at the far end of the bar.

"Could you get a message to her, Mikey? Tell her that I need to talk to her about Jack after she comes off? I can meet her here at the bar and maybe you could point me out."

"Sure thing."

"Oh, and leave out the part about Jenner, will you?"

He nodded.

"Thanks Mikey, I owe you."

I dropped some money on the counter for the drink and made my way over to the Lounge entrance, to take a table for the show.

The flunky there asked whether I had a reservation and made a show of consulting his table plan, humming and hawing before telling me what I already knew: that they would indeed be able to fit me in somewhere in the cavernous room, which was about the size of an aircraft hangar.

At the table, I ordered another drink, but declined the dinner menu, since I was feeling slightly nauseous, which I put down to all that bad coffee downtown.

The act began.

Janet Paris was indeed blonde and good looking, and the figure-hugging red cocktail dress she had on wasn't hurting the overall impression. She sang well, if not exceptionally, and it was pleasant to sit there and listen, so much so that my nausea gradually left me, or at least I stopped noticing it.

With her husky voice and classic chanteuse delivery, she went through a retinue of mostly swing and blues numbers. She flirted with Jazz in the odd Blue Note number, but thankfully avoided the abominations of bebop and scat.

You had to listen hard for it, but her accent was off somehow. Not the singing voice, which was silky and natural, but when she spoke between numbers. I figured she was maybe from somewhere further East, but it had mellowed a bit out here on the West Coast.

In any case, there were so many imports; waifs and strays chasing the dream, it was getting so that there weren't many natives around anymore. I wondered what her story might be and guessed it was probably some version of this attempt at reinvention. I didn't know whether I'd get the chance to find out, or whether it really mattered, come to that.

Her set ended, and it was time for me to head back to the bar for my own turn in the spotlight. Knowing roughly her act would end at ten, I'd already taken care of the drinks bill and had tipped the waitress generously, on account of the money from Kitty still being in my pocket.

I was feeling mellow and melancholy, which might have been down to Janet's singing or the four (or was it five?) whiskey sours I had on board. Heading back to the bar and being a creature of habit, I resumed my earlier position on the same stool and signalled to Mikey.

He nodded his acknowledgement and came over after serving a young couple an unwise looking tropical rum concoction.

"How was that Morgan?"

"She's really quite something isn't she? I'm glad I caught her act: thanks for the tip."

"Another whiskey sour?"

"Just a beer. I'm in danger of getting a little ahead of myself here.

Can you set one up for Miss Paris, too? Whatever she normally drinks."

"Coming right up."

He came back a few minutes later with my beer and what looked like a large bourbon, straight up in a shot glass for Janet. I was glad that she wasn't having one of those fake-looking cocktails, for both sentimental and financial reasons.

Mikey must have pointed me out to her at some point since she appeared behind my shoulder and quickly took the stool next to mine.

There are worse ways to make a living.

I stood up, all chivalry and for some reason bowed very slightly. I held out my paw, surprised to find it was not adorned with a knightly gauntlet after all.

"That was some set. You sing beautifully, Miss Paris."

She looked at my extended hand doubtfully, before giving it a quick, perfunctory sort of a shake.

"Let's get something straight. I'm only here

because Mikey said that you're okay and that you're trying to help Jack out of some sort of a hole. So, hurry up and get on with it, Morgan."

All business. She took an impressive belt on the bourbon, but I was pleased that she still had the good manners to raise her glass to me first.

I tried to throw her off balance.

"What's your relationship with Jack Conlon?"

"Three strikes and you're out, Morgan. That was strike one."

I regrouped.

"Ok then. How do you know him?"

"Assuming that I even wanted to, I wouldn't know how to begin to answer that question. Strike two."

Her words were issuing an ultimatum, but there was something troubled and sad about the way she said them, which got my attention.

My last shot.

"Is Jack Conlon capable of murder? I found a man called Eric Jenner dead in Jack's apartment this morning and the police are looking for him. They think he may have killed Jenner. I happen to think otherwise.

They'll get around to this place pretty soon, so if you know anything that might help me find him before they do, now's the time to tell me. If not, then I guess its strike three and I'll be going home, which I have half a mind to do in any case."

When I dropped the news about Jenner, I watched closely for any kind of a reaction. If she did know anything, then she was as good at acting as she was at singing. The shock that flickered on her face looked genuine, but then again, who knew? After all, this city was full of actors of one sort or another.

I had succeeded in getting her attention though, and she looked directly at me.

"Okay Morgan, but not here. Let me go backstage

and collect my things and then meet me outside in five minutes.

What are you driving?"

"A cab. I'll get one and meet you outside."

"Make it a couple of blocks down at the traffic light, not right outside the front here."

"Good thinking. I'll see you shortly, Miss Paris."

"Call me Janet."

I nodded and headed out to hail a cab.

She knew something alright and for the first time since Kitty had walked into my office, it felt like I might have caught a break on the case.

It didn't take long to find a taxi; the hour wasn't late, and the ridiculous tuxedo business helped. The driver probably though he was onto a good thing when he saw me standing there like a prize chump.

He must have thought I was on to an even better thing when Janet climbed in next to me. When she did, he tried to catch my eye in the rear-view mirror, no doubt to wink at me conspiratorially, but I wasn't playing ball.

I couldn't tell him where we were headed until then, which made me feel foolish and a bit seedy. Being cautious, neither of us said much on the ride over to her place, which made for an awkward journey and added to the overall impression of two people who barely knew each other.

Ever the gentleman, I paid the cab as she went to open up. The driver didn't wink at me after all, but he might as well have done: the grin on his face was as wide as a Cheshire cat's. I wanted to wipe it off for him, which would have been uncharitable, as he wasn't really imagining anything that hadn't already crossed my own mind.

Her apartment was like a small, drab version of Jack's place and I guessed it had only the one bedroom. We crossed to a couple of easy chairs set at right angles to each other next to a small coffee table and she gestured for me to sit.

"Like a drink, Morgan?"

"Doesn't everybody?"

She smiled.

"Sometimes I think drinking alcohol is almost the entire point of being a grown up. I've got both types: bourbon and rye. What'll it be?"

"In that case, I'd like a bourbon, straight up."

"Excellent choice."

She disappeared into the kitchen area, came back with two highball glasses with a more than generous slug of bourbon in each and set them on the table. She sat and offered me a cigarette, which I declined, then lit one for herself.

I sat back saying nothing.

"Back at the Havana when you asked me about how I knew Jack Conlon, I wasn't being funny, Morgan. You see, there's more than one answer to that question.

You should know too that I'm in love with him, but he doesn't love me back. Not really."

I listened to her confession like a priest. Who knows? I might have actually been one in a different life, which would have been just my luck.

"My own story's not that interesting and easy enough to tell.

I'm from Hartford, Connecticut but left when I was about twenty-one and went to New York for about six years. It was after the war, and I found work there singing in the theatres and shows. It was exciting at first, but after a while I didn't really enjoy living there anymore.

Then I moved to the Midwest, lived out in Chicago for another five years, again working theatres and clubs, but I was lonely, and the winters got too cold for me."

Involuntarily, I raised my eyebrows at the thought of the woman in front of me being lonesome.

"A friend of mine got a job in Las Vegas at a place called El Rancho and wrote me. After a while I joined her working there and later, on the Strip. It was fun for a bit, but I got tired of Vegas: the fakery of it all out there in the desert gets to you in the end.

I headed west again and pitched up here in Los Angeles; last stop, on the edge of the ocean. It's taken me fifteen years to work my way from one side of this country across to the other. Now there's nowhere left to go."

She paused for a hit on her drink, before carrying on.

"I started singing at the Havana when it opened about nine months ago. A couple of months after that, the man you're looking for, Jack Conlon, started stopping in there. His friends, like Eric Jenner, would come by too.

You told me he's dead, but I'm not a hypocrite: I never liked him and couldn't understand why Jack stayed friends with him.

For what it's worth, I'm sure Jack didn't kill him, though."

Another pause.

"So how did it start, with you and Conlon?"

"The first time I met him, I was intrigued. I felt drawn to him and wanted to find out his story.

You see, I'd grown up with a different Jack Conlon back in Connecticut before the war. I mean a different boy, but with the same name. We went to the same high school and were sweethearts at an early age, teenage stuff.

He broke it off when he joined the army and went off to the war. I wrote to him a few times, but never heard back and didn't know then whether he ever got the letters or just didn't want to know any more.

After that it just sort of fizzled out."

She took a long pull on her bourbon and on the cigarette, before resuming.

"So, when I met him, the Jack here, I was stunned. Here was a guy with the same name as my childhood sweetheart. I couldn't get over the coincidence.

I didn't let on, but every time I met him or his friends, I tried to find out a bit more of his background. Some of it came out in conversation – he's a drinker and a natural talker with a lust for life, but it took a while to piece together.

All the time I was getting to know this Jack, I liked him more and more until eventually I fell in love with him, and we fooled around some. He was separated from his wife by then."

She gave me a quick upward glance, but I was in no place to judge her and was keen to hear the rest.

"That's not the whole story, though."

She gathered herself again and then told me one of the saddest stories I've ever heard.

"No. The Jack I knew back then was an only child, brought up by his mother, after his father skipped town when he was little. She died of a heart attack when he was fighting in Italy.

The local paper ran a story about him being some sort of hero, saying that he'd had been injured and ended up in a POW camp, I couldn't get any more details from them and there was nothing after that.

He never came back to Hartford, just disappeared and I didn't know whether he'd stayed in Europe or gone somewhere else. I thought maybe there wasn't enough for him to come back to."

She looked infinitely sad and tired then.

"It took me a while to work it out, but there had been pointers from the beginning, little things.

The LA Jack was always reluctant to talk about his background and I thought he might be from New York, but Jenner told me that he came from Connecticut. Whenever I asked Jack about it, he'd change the subject, or make excuses somehow.

He'd fought in Italy too, been injured and taken

prisoner. Jenner and Jack were tight, and they'd been in the same unit. Then I remembered from the story in the paper that it was the same unit my Jack from Connecticut had served with.

That's when I finally put it together. Their stories weren't just similar, they were identical.

You hear about men who go to war and come back different people, because of what they've seen or what they've done, but in this case, the Jack Conlon I knew back then and the one I know now are just that. They're two different men."

It was my turn to take a long pull on my drink. I didn't know what to say or ask, so let her carry on.

"I needed to know what had happened to the real Jack, the one I knew from Hartford; why he was impersonating him and who he really was. So, I confronted him one day when we were alone, and it all came out.

His real name is Jackie Meyer. The switch happened more or less by accident when most of their unit was wiped out. They'd been taken prisoner and the real Jack was killed escaping with Meyer, who switched uniforms and dog tags with him before being injured and recaptured himself.

He woke up in the hospital in a POW camp with a different identity and just carried on being Jack instead of Jackie."

She paused then to extinguish her cigarette and we both sipped our drinks. Then she carried on.

"I wasn't sure how I felt about him for a while after that, but the more I thought about it, the more I could understand why he'd done what he'd done. Who doesn't want to wake up one day as somebody else? Have another go at life?

I'd fallen in love with him by then in any case."

I sat perfectly still and thought about the wild story she

had just told me.

"So, who else knows his real identity?"

"As far as I know, only Eric Jenner. They were both in his unit, so he would have known the real Jack Conlon.

Jackie and Eric grew up together, poor boys from Brooklyn; went to the same orphanage there."

A penny dropped with me. Marty had said that Jack had been a Dodger's fan since he was little, but the Dodgers had only moved to LA from New York a couple of years before.

"Why'd he disappear?"

"I don't know the ins and outs of it, but there's something going on down at the docks there, not just the usual furniture business. Something else.

Whatever it is, it went wrong somehow, and Jack took off.

Jenner showed up at the Havana the other day with another guy I don't like.
I think he's got something to do with it all."

"Short, fat guy?"
She nodded.

"His name's Mazza."

"Where is he now – Jackie or Jack?"

"I think of him as Jack. I don't know where he is, but I ran him down to Del Mar and know how to reach him.

It's not where he's staying, but if you leave a message at the front desk of the Fairmont hotel there in the name of Meyer, he told me it'll get to him."

It was late and I'd had a bit to drink, but if I made coffee for the drive, I could be down there in a couple of hours. It might wait until the next day, but I couldn't be sure.

"That's quite a story, Janet. What will you tell the police?"

"Nothing. They'll hear the rumours about Jack

and me, but I'm not telling them any of it. I told you because I want you to find him and help him before they do. You'll do that, won't you?"

I wasn't sure how I was meant to help exactly but was willing. Keen to get going, I stood up.

"I'll try. By the way, would you happen to have a gun, Janet, and know how to use it?"

"There's one around somewhere. Jack gave it to me. Why do you ask?"

"I ran into a couple of tough guys from out of town looking for Jack: a big guy called Louis and a smaller one called Al. They drive a green Hudson Hornet. Keep an eye out for them and that gun close by."

My head reeling from the story, I bid her goodnight and leaving the apartment block, headed out into the autumn night, towards the streetlights to hail yet another cab. Only I never made it that far.

Her block was set back and as I stepped out from the shadows into a pool of light under a streetlamp on the sidewalk, a flash of green appeared at speed from my right and the Hudson Hornet pulled up fast at the kerb.

The rear window was wound down and I was looking down the barrel of a large automatic, with a calibre about the same as a small Howitzer. Subtlety wasn't their strong point.

Whether I had been distracted thinking about the story, or my senses had been dulled by the booze, it was too late. I had hesitated and missed any opportunity I might have had.

"Get in."

With little choice, I edged towards the door as the mean looking one slipped over to the other side of the back seat of the Hudson with the gun trained on me.

"Seeing as you ask so nicely."

Cursing myself for not being vigilant enough and for the last bourbon, I slid in next to him and closed the door.

"Put the window up and no funny stuff, Shamus. Where's the heater?"

I considered my options as I wound up the window and either going for the gun or lying to him about it didn't seem like good ideas. He was going to find it in any case.

"Left armpit."

He transferred the hand cannon to his right paw, then dug around awkwardly with his left, unclipped my little .32 from the shoulder rig and pocketed it. I felt suddenly very alone without it.

"Anything else?"

"No."

He patted me down thoroughly for good measure, then transferred his gun back over to his left hand, close in to my ribs.

"Hit it, Louis."

Louis threw the car into gear and the Hudson peeled off from the kerb, gaining speed impressively.

I remember thinking that a bad situation only gets worse. This was just before the one called Al raised his arm and slammed me hard, just above my right temple with the butt of the large automatic, proving the point most emphatically.

There was an explosion of light and blinding pain before I lost consciousness and dropped into a dark ocean of deep-sea dreams. I dreamt I was back at sea, pitching and rolling in my bunk in a storm at night, lurching one way and then another having nightmares, feeling the shapes of monsters and drowning men closing in on me.

10. Louis and Al

I came to lying on a floor somewhere, still wearing the tuxedo, with a searing pain in my right temple and a question burning deep inside what was left of my shattered consciousness. I had been drifting in and out, so couldn't remember all the blows, but there were some peaches in there for sure, even for someone like me with a long history of violence to his person.

Punches and kicks had rained down on me across what might have been half an hour or more before I finally blacked out again and they'd had to stop. The big guy, Louis, did most of the damage, but when he got tired of using me as a punchbag, Al would take over for a bit. One had used a sap and the other a knuckleduster, so as not to hurt themselves unnecessarily. Thoughtful.

They knew their work and were a lot more thorough in their interrogation than the boys at homicide, although their bedside manner left a lot to be desired. They hadn't had the chance to start in on the torture before I passed out, although the big guy broke a couple of my fingers and the recollection of the pain nearly made me sick.

The questioning centred around a box I knew nothing about; did I have it, know where it was, or what it was. This was the theme they came back to over and over. When, naturally enough, I couldn't answer any of these questions, they turned to the subject of Jack Conlon. Did I know where he was, did he have the box and so on.

They never asked about Jenner being dead in Jack's apartment. Maybe they didn't know, or perhaps knew everything there was to know about what happened to him.

I couldn't tell them what I didn't know but managed to hold out on what little information I had about Jack's whereabouts, reasoning that it might keep me alive a little longer.

The questions eating away at me (apart from about that damned box) were whether they had been following me, or Janet, or whether I had been set up. Back there at the Havana before we left, she'd had the chance to make a phone call backstage.

What about Kitty? It was on account of her I'd been looking for Jack in the first place and came to be in his apartment with a dead man. Could she have a part in all this?

I wasn't going to find out the answers to these questions or anything else unless I did something about my situation. Time to focus and think things through very carefully.

I had underestimated these two. They were taking their time, had done this before and would kill me for sure when they finished. It hadn't been a prolonged beating, but the problem was I wasn't going to be able to hold out much longer. My willpower and natural stubbornness could only last so long, and my body wasn't going to take another session.

In a funny way, I was lucky that Al had hit me too hard in the car in the first place to subdue me, and I'd passed out again quickly. It meant they hadn't tied me up, which was good, although I was in a sorry enough state.

The damage included pain in my head and my face, mouth and eyes which were all swollen; broken fingers, (luckily the little finger and the ring finger on my left hand); a dull, persistent ache across my back and kidneys and a sharp pain in my chest, which only hurt when I breathed. I had a mouth full of blood and exploring gingerly with my tongue, discovered that a couple of teeth had been loosened.

I seemed to be in a room with no windows, like a large cupboard, or storeroom. It was dark, with the only light coming from a crack under the door. Sitting up painfully, I edged my way over, reached up with my right hand and tried the handle gently, desperate not to alert my captors to the fact that I was conscious again. It was locked from the outside, naturally.

Paying the door close attention, I could make out that it opened inwards, meaning that the stops would be on the outside, so I'd never be able to kick it out from inside. Assuming I had the strength or the opportunity, both of which seemed unlikely.

Tired and confused, I definitely wasn't thinking straight and part of me wanted to keep sitting there on the floor and not have to think about anything ever again.
That would be giving up though, which would leave me as good as dead.

Adjusting to the light, I closed my eyes for a bit and then reopened them, trying to ignore the stars and flashes in my vision courtesy of the beating I'd taken. After a while, I could see a little in the gloom, and worked my way around the walls of the small room mainly by touch, peering into the darkness, trying to find anything to help me out of my predicament.

There was very little in the way of furniture or shelves with anything on them, or items attached to the walls, either high up or low down. If this had once been a storeroom, there was no sign of what it had contained and nothing I could find to use as any kind of weapon. There wasn't even a light switch and only one electrical outlet low down, about a quarter of the way along the side wall, back towards the door.

The tour hadn't taken long, and it was only in the last corner that I found the only object of any kind; a standard lamp, which must have provided the illumination in this windowless space. I fell into despondency, trying to figure whether it would be better to spend the last however long alone here with my thoughts, in darkness or in light, before they came for me.

Feeling around the lamp with my good hand, I reached up inside the shade and pushed the switch across, but nothing happened. Sticking my hand up slightly further, I could make out that there was no bulb in the holder, which settled the matter.

It was a shame; a shard of glass might have been useful, even if I didn't know what I would do with it, and it wasn't going to even up the odds against two armed men. To lift my spirits, I set about discovering whether the lamp could be used as a weapon of some kind.

Largely by feel, I could determine that it was an all-in-one metal construction of some type, maybe brass, with a heavy base and would have a hollow shaft where the flex came up to the top. I examined this and couldn't find a join anywhere along its length.

I unscrewed the brass retaining ring and placed the shade with the wire cage holder carefully down on the floor so as not to make any noise. Which left me with a long thin metal tube, with a heavy weight at one end. It would be practically impossible to wield it as any kind of a weapon in the narrow room, with no way to swing it, even if I'd had the upper body strength to do so.

Using the base to smash the lock might have been worth a try, although it would make a racket and alert them, removing any element of surprise. Even if I did manage to shear the handle off, the door would still be locked from the outside.

The door opening inwards made it harder to rush whoever came through it, but I might be able to jump them and for a long while this was my plan. Considered objectively, it was pretty hopeless, but I might be able to inflict damage on one of them, which seemed better than nothing.

The fact that I didn't know when they might be coming for me made the tension and the waiting worse, but they would be eager to resume, and I knew it would be soon. Then I had another idea. One you might legitimately describe as a lightbulb moment.

Partly to occupy my mind, I went through elements of the lamp at my disposal, from top to the bottom. There was the lightshade with a thin wire cage that attached it, but this didn't seem to offer much; then the bulb holder and switch unit, which was of little consequence; the stand underneath, which I'd already considered.

Finally, there was the length of flex with the plug, protruding out of the bottom.
Of course: the flex! If I could get it loose, I might have something. I reached down and gathered it up, realising that it hadn't even been plugged in when I tried the lamp earlier.

Working quickly, I reached up with my good hand and unscrewed a second brass ring securing the switch assembly to the top of the shaft. Then I yanked hard, pulling the holder up sharply and stripping the ends of the wires away from their terminals in the process. As I did so, the sharp pain in my ribcage intensified alarmingly and I had to stop myself from crying out.

I lay the lamp down gently on its side, slumped to the floor and wedged my feet against the bottom of the lamp stand. Then I wrapped some of the cord and the plug around my right wrist and tried to pull the flex out of the bottom and back down through the hollow column.

On the third heave, it gave out against decades of grime and shifted, throwing me back flat to the floor. As I lay there panting and in pain, even though I had stopped believing some years before, I prayed that I hadn't made too much noise.

The flex could be used as some sort of noose or garrotte, but my chances were slim against a fit and healthy body coming head on through the door and I had a different idea in mind. A potentially lethal application of electrical theory, owing much to the thinking of Franklin or Faraday.

I stripped the ends of the two copper wires down with my bloodied teeth, which hurt like hell, and shuffled over to the door. Then I carefully wound the end of one wire to the spindle end of the handle and wrapped the other a few inches further along the grip.

The wooden door wouldn't conduct electricity, but the metal handle might. My plan was to plug the cable in and electrify the handle, sending a jolt through the shaft into the hand of whoever was on the other side, which might prove lethal to them but be nearly as dangerous to me.

I would only get one shot and had no way of testing whether the combination of outlet, plug and flex were in working order. The lamp had been dumped in the storage cupboard at some point and may have not been working for years.

Timing would be everything, as I'd have to wait for the person on the other side to unlock the door and then start to move the handle. Hopefully, it wouldn't be the cleaner, although by the looks of the place, it hadn't been touched in years.

The end with the plug just about reached the wall outlet and I sat there poised with it in my good hand and rehearsed the motion of jamming it into the outlet and throwing myself to one side, away from the cable.

After that, I'd still have to get out of the room and the house, but I'd have the element of surprise and would have to take my chances. If I was lucky and it worked and didn't kill me, it might maim or incapacitate one of them and even up the odds a bit.

If.

After a while, there was the sound of footsteps and muffled voices. People were moving around some distance from the door. My watch had stopped, so I had no way of knowing how long I had been out for or what time it was, but my best guess was that it was morning, and they were stirring into life for another day of killing. Me.

Then a snatch of conversation, closer by, responding to a muffled voice I couldn't make out, further away.

"Sure....... do that...... wake up laughing boy."

Then the distinctive noise of a screen door further off banging shut followed about thirty seconds later by the sound of an engine starting outside. Not the low growl of the Hudson, but something rougher and less tuned; more like a truck.

There may have been more than two of them, but however many, one had now left, or was at least outside somewhere. This was my opportunity: I would have to attract the other one to the door.

I was just about to call out when I heard footsteps close by, followed by an unexpected, polite knock at the door.

"You awake in there, Morgan?"

It was the big guy, Louis. He obviously thought he would have no problem handling me on his own. I waited, playing dumb.

"I'm coming in and no funny stuff. If you try anything I'll plug you right through the door."

From outside came the unmistakable sound of the slide being racked back on an automatic.

The key scraped all the way around in the dry lock unbearably slowly until there was a click as the door unlocked. I carefully lined up the pins to within a quarter of an inch of their corresponding sockets in the wall outlet, watching the door handle with absolute focus.

It seemed to take an age with my hand hovering there, but eventually there was the faint scraping of metal and the end of the door handle dipped cautiously down, at which point I jammed the plug into the outlet.

At the same time, I threw down on my side and across the tiny space, needing to get away from the electrical death trap and avoid catching a bullet, if he managed to get a round off.

Looking down past my feet, I saw the door handle sparking satisfyingly for a fraction of a second before there was a loud bang, not from his gun, but probably from the fuse box blowing out somewhere. Then nothing.

Not wanting to electrocute myself, I yanked the plug from the wall socket, forced myself up and leaning against the wall for support, went over and opened the door fully inwards. The big guy was slouched on the floor across the other side of a narrow passageway with sunlight filtering in from the left.

Squinting into this I could make out a short corridor leading back towards the kitchen, and guessed I'd been locked up on the ground floor in what was probably a pantry. The corridor was in semi-darkness and there was a sickening electrical burning smell. A fuse box, mounted on the wall opposite me further along the passage was smouldering and making an arcing sound.

His .45 automatic was on the floor where he must have dropped it and I stepped over his legs to pick it up, then popped out the clip and cleared the action carefully with my undamaged left thumb and index finger, before readying it for use again.

Louis groaned, behind me, evidently still alive. If I met these two again somebody was going to die. I didn't want that somebody to be me and thought about finishing him off, but it would have been murder, which I draw the line at.

In the end I settled for kicking him as hard as I could muster on the right side of his head, making sure he was out cold. His left hand was burned where he'd been holding the door handle, meaning that the gun must have been in his right. To even things up a bit, I stamped down hard with my heel on his gun hand, breaking the index and middle fingers.

It wasn't quite a tooth for a tooth but might stop him

shooting anybody for a while and I figured he'd get the message. What with the burns on his other hand he'd probably need help going to the bathroom for a while, which might test his close relationships.

It was a vicious and vindictive thing to do, but I didn't feel bad about it.

Going through his pockets, I retrieved my wallet, licence and the billfold with Kitty's money. In addition, I relieved him of his own wallet and driver's licence and the thing I'd been hoping to find most: a set of car keys.

I stood and listened for a full two minutes, counting the seconds, but heard nothing, so crept gun first along the corridor, as quietly as I could. I'd heard Al, if it was him, go out and an engine of some sort starting up earlier, but couldn't be sure he hadn't come back or that there wasn't somebody else around.

The passageway opened into a large kitchen area where the windows were shuttered, but light was coming in through cracks in the blinds. I guessed that the lights must have been on before I'd blown the fuse box.

There was left over food on the table, burger wrappings and a bottle of bourbon with two glasses. I picked up the bottle, uncorked it painfully with my bloodied mouth and took a long hard belt. The pain made me wince and it was rough stuff, but agreeable enough under the circumstances.

My little .32 was over on the countertop by the sink and I retrieved it with the good fingers of my right hand, nestling it back under my arm in the empty shoulder holster I was still wearing. The keys to my apartment were next to the gun and I pocketed these too.

I was two-gun Morgan then, which made me feel braver, but it was still nowhere near enough to risk another encounter in my current state.

Time to make good my escape.

Cautiously, I made my way to the screen door at the

back of the kitchen, passing another doorway on the right-hand side on the way over. This opened onto a second hallway and framed on the other side of this was a further opening, through which I could make out a chair in another room.

It was where they had worked me over the night before and in the half-light, I could make out sticky dark spots, little pools of liquid under the seat. It was blood: my blood. It made me shudder to think how it might have played out and I suddenly felt old and weak.

I needed to get home and lick my wounds. Also to get myself cleaned up and out of the evening wear. If anybody saw me like this, covered in blood, I might end up being interviewed down at The Glass House again.

Outside I could see that it was an old, derelict looking property and set back: a quiet place, chosen well. I guessed they must have broken in and were using it as a base of sorts.

They'd probably helped themselves to another vehicle somewhere along the way too. Something less conspicuous than the Hornet, maybe this is what I'd heard earlier on, when Al went out for supplies or whatever.

I found the green Hudson round at the back, mostly out of sight but with its nose poking out of an outbuilding. I was mightily relieved when the engine caught and threw the car into gear, pulling around the front and out onto the street at speed, making a mental note of the house number displayed on a post on the way out.

I had a vague recollection of the car climbing up into the hills the night before, when I'd been swaying in and out of consciousness, so headed downhill on instinct. It turned out that I was up in Laurel Canyon somewhere and the road was Laurel Terrace Drive, which wound its way down a small canyon to a junction with the boulevard, at which point I knew where I was.

Although there wasn't much traffic, I drove gingerly

back towards the city, paranoid that every car or truck I encountered might be driven by Al. Gradually this feeling passed, and I began to consider my options more clearly.

Going to the police wasn't on. It wouldn't get me anything other than another spell at the station and a stern telling off, neither of which I needed. Kidnap and assault were definitely on the naughty list, but electrocuting people wasn't on the list of approved activities either.

I needed to turn the tables on the two goons and keep them busy for a while, or off my tail for a day or two, at any rate.

Going home wasn't the safest of bets, since they'd seen my driver's licence, but Al hadn't taken my apartment keys when he left earlier, so I knew he hadn't gone there. Once he went back to the house and found Louis, he'd be too busy to pay me a visit for a while, so I went home. It took all my mental strength to negotiate the drive.

Safely inside, I took a long shower, as hot as I could stand it, then took stock of the damage in the bathroom mirror. It didn't look all that bad. For somebody who'd maybe been in an automobile wreck. I wouldn't be winning a beauty competition any time soon.

My movements in the shower told me that at least a couple of my ribs were cracked. I already knew about my fingers, which had hampered my driving and took a roll of tape from the bathroom cabinet after showering and bound them together.

My dentist wasn't going to be happy the next time I saw him. The lacerations in my mouth and the swelling in my gums felt huge when I explored these with the tip of my tongue. The top teeth on the left-hand side hurt and were somewhat looser than they should have been.

With trepidation, I got iodine and cotton wool from the bathroom cabinet and saw to the cuts and grazes around my eyes and mouth. It hurt like hell, but I cleaned myself up and took more painkillers than was strictly necessary.

The bruising was bad and would get worse, but a pair of dark glasses would cover up a fair bit and it was still sunny outside. That and a trilby, if I didn't mind looking a little old fashioned, which I didn't.

I shuffled into the kitchen and put coffee on, then made up an ice pack and held it to my temple. While the coffee was coming through, I helped myself to a stiff one from the bottle of Irish whisky I kept for special occasions and near-death experiences in general, which helped some. Needing to think clearly, I kept it to just the one.

Nowhere was safe. I had no real way of knowing what they knew but had to assume they'd studied the contents of my wallet. As well as my home address, they knew my name and would be able find the office easily, so I'd have to be careful there.

I would have to get down to Del Mar soon and didn't know if it could wait but it was going to have to. It was Sunday morning and every fibre in my being was telling me to hit the sack for a day of rest, but something needed taking care of first.

I dressed, painfully, including the .32, which wasn't going to be leaving my side for a while, then headed outside cautiously, doing my best to disguise the battering I'd taken.

Despite the fact we'd gotten off to a bad start, I liked the Hornet and took it for a farewell spin on the short ride to the nearest station house, where I parked right on top of a traffic light opposite, much to the annoyance of my fellow motorists.

I left Louis' wallet open at his driver's licence on the passenger seat and stashed the gun in the glove box after wiping both down with my handkerchief. The .45 might have been useful and certainly packed more punch than my own piece, but it would do me more good to have the police out looking for them.

Working quickly, I wiped down the other bits of the car

I'd touched like the steering wheel, gearshift, and door handles. The police probably wouldn't bother fingerprinting the car, but I figured it couldn't do any harm.

Wearily, I walked a couple of blocks further up to a bank of payphones, fished out change with some difficulty and placed an anonymous call to the LAPD. I gave them the address off Laurel Canyon, told them two suspects in the murder of Eric Jenner were holed up there and gave them names, descriptions, and details of the Hornet, before hanging up.

On my way back down the street, I saw that a patrol car had already stopped alongside the illegally abandoned Hudson and an officer had the driver's side door open, with his head inside it. He'd radio it in soon enough, which should buy me some time.

God bless parking restrictions in the State of California I chuckled to myself, for the first time, although even this was a source of some pain.

I thought about getting food, but was too tired to bother so walked home as steadily as I could manage, noting that the painkillers were starting to kick in. The low buzz I was getting from them and the booze was the best I'd felt that morning.

Slipping back into the apartment, I locked up thoroughly, then stopped to look in the refrigerator on my way to the bedroom. I don't know what I expected to find, since I hadn't been shopping or put anything new in there for some time. It was an act of mindless optimism; the kind I like best.

Opting for the bottle of whisky instead, I took that to bed with me, together with the painkillers, which I'd left on the table in the living room. The sun was shining brightly outside, so I drew the bedroom curtains tight and placed the Colt on my nightstand, close at hand. If anybody wanted me or was coming for me, they'd have to come right in and get me.

I thought about calling some people but didn't have the energy and disrobed instead, leaving my clothes on the floor where they fell. Somewhat unwisely, I took some more painkillers with a large slug of the whisky just to be sure, before climbing into bed. The liquor burned my mouth and throat on the way down and I shuddered as I drank it but knew it would have the desired effect eventually.

My sleep was almost immediate and deep, but interrupted by fitful tossing and turning. I woke up several times feeling feverish and covered in sweat. Such dreams as I can remember were violent and confusing.

Echoing my interrogation, I dreamt of a box, but this was one that I was lying in, somewhere in a sepulchre buried under a mountain of rock, deep underground. It didn't take Freud to work that one out.

11. The Box

The body knows what it needs, and it pays to listen sometimes. Although it was barely midday on Sunday when I took to my bed, I slept through fitfully until waking in the early hours of Monday morning.

I wasn't going to be able to get any more sleep and needed the bathroom in any case, so I got up, put coffee on, showered and shaved. My various wounds hurt more than the day before, but the sleep had done me some good and at least my head felt relatively clear.

My stomach was growling, which I took to be a good sign. I'd have to attend to that before long, but in the meantime made do with a diet of coffee and painkillers while planning my next move.

My priorities were: breakfast; the office; Del Mar. When I stopped by the office, I'd also put in calls to Kitty and Tom Delaney, to see if there had been any developments.

Still in my robe, I packed for a short stay down in Del Mar in case it took a while to make contact with Jack. I fished out some overnight things and a tan leather Gladstone bag of good quality that had served me well for some time.

It had been a while since I'd been anywhere and while I was packing, had a childish sense of excitement like that of going away on vacation. I had to pull up short and remind myself that it would be nothing of the sort.

My cover story was as a travelling salesman, and I dressed in lounge suit with open neck shirt and comfortable shoes. It was standard issue California casual attire, except for the shoulder holster and the Colt.

I selected a suitable fake ID for the journey from my small collection and regarded myself in the full-length mirror in the hallway before setting off, deciding to add some sunglasses and a hat to the outfit. I didn't look quite as rough as I felt and might get away with it if I kept these on.

Not taking any chances, I held the gun with my good hand inside the jacket pocket on my right side and carried the Gladstone awkwardly in my left until I reached the car and could put it in the trunk.

I made it to the Plymouth without incident and set off to eat with no specific destination in mind. All my usual eateries, either near the apartment or the office, would be off limits as I didn't want to pick up a tail.

Checking my rear-view mirror more often than usual and taking a seemingly randomly sequence of turns along the way to be sure I wasn't being followed, I headed in the general direction of the office, planning to stop somewhere anonymous in neutral territory.

Driving through Westchester, I spotted a coffee shop I'd not seen before called Pann's, which fit the bill, so parked a couple of blocks down and around the corner off La Tijera Boulevard. Before leaving the car, I had a good look around to reassure myself nobody had been following me and relaxed a little.

It's difficult to eat when you are tense and I was a little jumpy, so holstered the Colt which had been on the seat next to me and took it along for company, being careful to button my jacket up on the walk to the restaurant entrance. I have a carry permit but didn't see any reason to advertise.

The place was futuristic in design, with modern décor and I hoped it would have substance as well as style. The coffee smelled good, and I ordered some as soon as I sat down, having requested a booth at the back on account of how I looked. They had been happy to oblige.

Since I didn't know how the day ahead would pan out, my intention was to breakfast well, although I would have to order carefully, since my mouth was in a delicate way and not up to chewing anything that might resist.

My coffee came and I ordered the omelette with cheese and onions, which I figured I could get down, followed by a short stack with blueberry sauce and orange juice. Pancakes wouldn't normally feature on my list but would be easy on my teeth and fill me up.

I declined the offer of toast, which came free, as well as all manner of meat products and caught the waitress giving me a sideways look. I thought this might be because of the order, but then realised I was sitting inside with sunglasses on and had been reading the menu over the top of them. Taking these off to appear less creepy, I saw her shocked reaction and she asked what had happened to me.

I told her I was a stunt double, had been working on a car chase scene which went wrong, ended up in a wreck and was lucky to be alive. I had no idea why these words came out of my mouth, but the waitress seemed to believe it and was looking at me in wonder.

She was young and not unattractive, a description which seemed to fit most of the people one met in this town: I guessed she was here following her own dream. I don't think I had been deliberately lying to impress her: it just felt less complicated and somehow more authentic to be somebody else for a while.

Which got me round to thinking about Jack Conlon again.

Thankfully, the coffee was excellent, and I washed down a couple more painkillers with it before ordering more. When the food came, that was good too and I ate well, trying to empty my mind of distractions. Only the occasional stab of pain from my mouth reminded me who I really was and what I was meant to be doing.

After I'd finished and the waitress had brought my check, she asked who I had been stunt doubling for. I told her it was Cary Grant and she looked at me doubtfully, not least because he was at least several inches taller than me.

Unreasonably resenting his manifestly superior height and not being able to drop the performance, I told her he insisted I had to wear lifts in my shoes to play him and this was why I'd lost control of the car in the first place.

She asked me what he was really like.

To my shame, I slandered him, saying that he was a tyrant on set and an absolute heel of the highest order. Again, I had no idea why I said this and was sure it was not true at all and that he was probably one of the nicest men imaginable.

She broke into a broad smile, leaned in close to me conspiratorially and told me she'd always thought his nice guy act was too good to be true. Genuinely delighted, I gave her a large tip and she was still smiling broadly when I left the place.

I picked up the Plymouth and carried on to the office in much higher spirits, feeling better for eating well. Downtown, I parked a couple of blocks down from the office and was vigilant on the walk back, the cautious routine becoming second nature by now.

After collecting my mail from the locked box downstairs, I walked up and along the corridor, put my key in the outer office door but found it already unlocked. It was possible that the cleaner or the janitor had left it that way, but I doubted it and became suddenly very alert.

I stepped to one side of the frame, placed the mail down silently and readied myself, getting the Colt out and up out into my right hand. I listened carefully at the door, but there was no noise coming from inside and the odds were that if anybody had been inside, they were long gone, but I wasn't taking any chances and went through the door gun first.

The outside door had been picked professionally but

inside was a different story. Once out of sight, it had been quicker and simpler for them to smash the lock on the inner door, which was hanging loose.

Pushing this open with my foot, I found the office had been comprehensively ransacked. As it was Monday and I'd not been in since Friday afternoon, it could have happened at pretty much any time over the weekend.

Not having the time or energy to deal with it, I nipped back out to retrieve the mail and locked the outer door from inside, so as not to be disturbed. The drawers in my desk had been gone through but there was something I had come to collect, so I cleared a space and sat down.

Opening the top right-hand draw of the desk, I reached in and found my snub nosed .38 in the hip holster that I kept there. It was time for an upgrade, so I took off the shoulder holster and replaced the .32.

Still small and neat, this one had a lot more stopping power and was plenty of gun for any situation I might find myself in. I swung out the cylinder and checked the chambers, closed it back up and clipped the holster onto my belt just above my right hip.

Flipping through the mail, I came across the package I'd sent myself from the mailbox outside the Laguna and set this to one side. It seemed like a long time ago but had only been a couple of days and had probably only been delivered that morning.

The other items of mail were bills and such forth, nothing that couldn't wait, so I put these aside and set about opening the small parcel. First, I tipped out the little lock picking set and transferred this to my jacket pocket, figuring it might come in useful on my trip to Del Mar.

Next, I unfolded the letter addressed to Jack that I'd swiped hastily from his apartment building and studied it more closely. I tried to recall the handwriting from going through his desk diary back at his office with Agnes and still thought it matched. Although I couldn't make out the date, the envelope had a San Diego postmark, which fit: Del Mar was down there in San Diego County.

It looked like Jack had sent himself this letter sometime after he'd gone down there. But why? Might it contain what whoever had tossed his apartment had been looking for or the reason why Eric Jenner had been killed?

As I held the thin envelope in my hand, remembering how Jack's books had been gone through I looked up at my shelf of reference volumes on the back wall. They were mainly law books, furniture to reassure my clients really, but these had been systematically gone through and dumped on the floor too.

Whatever it was, they'd been looking for something small and thin enough to conceal in something like a book and the letter would certainly fit that description.

It occurred to me that if I'd had this on me when Louis and Al had picked me up, I might be dead too. Dismissing the thought with a violent shudder and needing to see what was inside, I opened the letter, committing what I knew to be a California penal code violation. With luck, I could let Jack have it back when I caught up with him.

I'm not sure what I'd been expecting but all it yielded was a disappointingly small and anonymous looking brown ticket with a series of numbers on one side and a perforated tear along the top. Squinting more closely through my puffed-up eyes, I could make out the letters LAUS in faded lettering, where the red ink used had been running out.

It took about twenty seconds for the answer to come to me, which seemed obvious when it did: Union Station. I was looking at one half of a ticket for the luggage store there. The type they attach to your bags, tear off and give you one half, so it can be matched to the other when you pick them up.

So, I had another stop to make before going down to Del Mar but needed to make those phone calls first. Retrieving the telephone up from its current resting place on the floor about two feet away from the desk, I replaced the handset in its cradle and checked the line before busying myself with the calls.

First, I spoke with Tom Delaney and asked whether there'd been any developments. He gave me the silent treatment for a full thirty seconds, to the extent I thought my handset might have been damaged, before telling me about the anonymous tip off concerning Al and Louis and the green Hudson.

He pressed me about whether I'd been responsible for the information and where in hell I'd been yesterday when he'd tried to get hold of me. I crossed my fingers while I told him I didn't know about any of it but uncrossed them when I said I'd felt unwell and been in bed catching up on my beauty sleep with the phone off the hook. At least that part was true.

He didn't believe me, but I know Tom well enough and could tell he was pleased they had some sort of a solid lead on Eric Jenner's murder. The two suspects were known villains, as I had suspected, had been seen at the apartment and fit the frame well enough.

It turned out they were both Canadian and were wanted in Chicago for murder and more besides. That explained not being able to place the accents. While on the phone to Tom, I had a flashback of them speaking French to each other in the car. Or had I just imagined that?

He was still keen to talk to Jack Conlon though and reminded me not to try to find him and to call them when I had any information.

I asked if there was any information about the murder weapon and he said that it was something small, probably a .25, but the bullets were a bit messed up from bouncing around inside Jenner's ribcage. It was an unusual weapon, not unheard of but lacking in power, which is probably why the bullets hadn't gone straight through.

I could tell Tom didn't think it fit very well with the profile of the two heavies and from what I knew of them, neither did I. After we'd hung up, this troubled me for a bit, but eventually I shrugged it off and put a call into Kitty. The phone rang for a while before she picked up and when she did, she sounded tired on the other end, like she'd been resting.

There wasn't a lot to report. The police had been out to see her about the business at Jack's apartment, but they were separated, so she hadn't really been there and didn't know much about the set up or the neighbours and so on.

She'd given them a list of friends and acquaintances and told them what little she knew about Jenner from what Jack had let slip down the years, but other than that, there wasn't much.

I warned her about the two heavies and told her to be extra vigilant, especially with her boys. The police had already gone through that with her though.

She asked about whether I'd had any developments and I told her I was following up on a lead which looked promising but wouldn't know more for a day or two. She seemed to come alive on the other end of the phone and wanted to know more, but I told her to sit tight for the time being.

It wasn't the time to open up to her about Janet's story and I didn't know how much of it was for real in any case. If her husband turned up, he was going to have to be the one to tell her about it all and I didn't envy him the task.

She told me to be careful and we hung up.

Janet was the other person I wanted to call. I'd been going back and forth over her story and had some questions to ask her about it and it wouldn't do any harm to warn her about Al and Louis again. There was another thing nagging away at me too.

I didn't have her home number and it was too early to reach her at the club. Short of going over to her apartment and taking potluck on her being at home, there wasn't much I could do. I didn't have the time or the energy for that. It would have to wait. I hadn't been to Union Station in a while but was headed there now.

Rummaging around in the desk draw on the left-hand side, I dug out a small box of shells for the .38 for the trip to Del Mar, just in case. Then opting to leave the office as it was, rather than tidy up, I locked the outer office door on the mess and retraced my steps to the Plymouth, with my hand close to the gun at my hip.

I drove carefully all the way to Alameda, changing direction and weaving around until I got tired of it and figured that anybody tailing me would have done too. I parked up the street outside the station on a meter and fed it some change.

The station building was an exotic mix of art deco and mission revival, but I wasn't there to admire the architecture. After hunting around for a few minutes, I found the sign for the luggage store, which was over to one side at the head of the platform.

On the way there, the thought struck me that I didn't know what I was picking up. My expectation was it would be something that like a parcel or a suitcase, containing the box I'd heard so much about, but what if it was several items or something that wouldn't fit in the trunk or on the back seat of my car?

No, wait: if it was more than one thing, I'd have more than one ticket. That's how these places worked. I only really had my right hand to work with, so hoped it didn't turn out to be too cumbersome. By the time I'd thought this through, I'd already reached the counter.

There being no queue, I fished the ticket out of my pants pocket and presented it to the middle-aged guy there.

"I'm here picking up."

He nodded, bored looking, the action habitual and non-committal.

Vigorously chewing gum, I could feel him looking at me sideways without seeming to, trying to figure out what sort of a customer I might turn out to be. He must have had a lot of experience dealing with all sorts.

After examining the ticket closely, he disappeared around the back, returning about five minutes later with nothing for me, but flicking through paperwork.

He was chewing furiously now, which I took to be a bad sign.

"Yeah, we got it, but there's a problem."

This delivered between chews.

"What sort of problem?"

"It's been here too long. This is short-term storage: nothing's meant to be here more than two weeks. It's gone over that. There's a fine to pay on top of the storage charge before you can get it back."

"How much is it?"

He ran his finger down the manifest.

"Let's see. Its seven dollars for the storage and a five dollar fine, so that'll be twelve dollars total. You're lucky it's only Monday. Another couple of days and it would have been shipped out altogether."

Weighing it up and deciding there was no real choice, I filled out the obligatory forms, or rather my alter ego, the sales rep Mr. Rogers, as it said on my phony driver's licence, did and paid in cash. After stamping the paperwork in triplicate and issuing me with a grand looking receipt, the attendant finally went around back to fetch my item.

I didn't know what I'd been expecting, but when he returned a few minutes later, I was at a complete loss. What he laid on the counter was an actual box, but much larger than I had anticipated. It was rectangular, about the size of an overly large suitcase, not much less than three feet long and two feet by two feet in cross section.

The construction was old and looked like rosewood,

with antique clasps and hinges and a carrying handle about halfway along on the top, at the balancing point. I'd watched him place it up on the counter and calculated with some relief that although it was an awkward shape, it didn't seem all that heavy.

I wondered what the hell could be inside it.

He was obviously thinking the same thing.

"Say: what have you got in that awkward old thing, anyway?"

"I'm a stage magician and these are my props."

He looked at me sceptically.

"Sure, if you say so. What happened to your face?"

"Somebody didn't like my act."

He snorted.

"Okay pal. It's your business. I get it."

Surreptitiously, I tried the box and thought it weighed in at around twenty pounds: heavy enough, but not so bad that I'd need a trolley. I desperately wanted to look inside but in privacy; somewhere secluded and away from the city, without all these people around making me paranoid.

Slowly, I made my way back across the station and out up the street to the Fury, where I stashed the box easily enough crossways in the large trunk, wedging it in place with my overnight bag.

Whatever the hell it was, the box was in my possession, at least for the time being. As far as I knew, nobody knew where I was so I could take my time examining it later.

I drove like a nun out of the Downtown area, taking a circuitous route to the east of the city, before heading south to pick up US 101 down to San Diego. It was a beautiful day for a coastal drive and heading out on the highway and leaving the city behind, I let the Plymouth off the leash, driving as fast as I dared without risking getting pulled over by the highway patrol.

The sunshine and sea air gave the illusion of freedom

and for a blissful couple of hours, it felt for all the world like I actually was going on vacation. I pictured myself escaping the city, fleeing my troubles, across the border and beyond into Mexico, carefree and with a sense of elation.

12. Del Mar

Although I didn't know the area well, I'd had occasion to go to Del Mar, the last time being a couple of years before on a case I'd been working, and I thought about it on the drive down.

I'd worked a few like it before; one of those thefts from big houses and grand old families that come up. Often, these turned out to be inside jobs; a servant or maybe one of the grandchildren knowing where grandma stashed her gems and faking a burglary.

Usually, people went wrong when they tried to get rid of the stuff, which they'd stolen on impulse. They weren't thinking straight about where to lay it off and either did so too quickly or didn't realise how small the market is for second-hand jewellery without any proof of ownership.

Sometimes it was a family member doing it for the insurance money; an injection of cash to help keep up appearances. All well and good provided they didn't get caught, or weren't tempted to keep hold of the stuff, sell, or pawn it somewhere else, in which case it was just the little matter of insurance fraud.

It was pretty routine, and I'd worked these sorts of jobs from both ends – on behalf of the insurance companies and for the families. In this particular case, the grandson had a dope habit, had gone on a week-long high and washed up in Del Mar with the family jewels, or so he'd thought. He'd planned on heading for Mexico when he hit the jackpot, only that never happened.

The twist was that the stuff turned out to be fake. Evidently, somebody in the family had got there before him, pawned, or sold the diamonds some years back and replaced them with paste. They were quality fakes with genuine mounts: good enough to fool most people even close-up and still worth something.

I'd found him when he ran out of money, which hadn't taken long, then retrieved the stuff from a jeweller's and took him home, which had been the messy part. It was all hushed up afterwards, of course.

My thoughts turned to what Jack Conlon was doing there and whether he was also making for the border, which couldn't have been more than thirty or forty miles away. On arrival, I went looking for the Fairmont and found it quickly enough, on the seafront, where I reasoned it would be.

Tired, with no way of knowing how long it would take to contact him and wanting a good look at that box, I decided to take a hotel room to use as a base.

The Fairmont looked a little above my pay grade, but I decided to take a room there: it was convenient, and I needed to leave a message at the desk in any case. Janet had told me Jack wasn't staying there, but who knew? I figured he'd have to be close by somewhere.

It was the easy solution and lazy thinking like that could prove dangerous, but it would give me a chance to scope the place out. The hotel was out of season quiet, which worked both ways; I might stand out, but so would anyone who might come looking for me.

I checked in using the phony driver's licence under the name of Mr. Rogers, my only luggage the box and the Gladstone bag, both of which I was insistent on taking up to the first-floor room myself.

I was pleasantly surprised to find that it was bigger than the double I'd booked, more of a small suite situated at the front of the hotel, with a sea view and a balcony. These were both options I'd declined when checking in, but guessed they'd given me a better room on account of the time of year.

Comfortable without being fussy, the place had a large coffee table with a couch and a couple of easy chairs, as well as a breakfast table and two dining chairs positioned over by the balcony to make the most of the view.

I crossed back to the door, hung out the do not disturb sign and locked it from the inside, putting the chain across for good measure. Going to the balcony door, I checked that was locked, then drew the curtains and switched on the lamp by the coffee table, before fetching the box from the foot of the bed.

After setting the rosewood container down lengthways on the low table, I went about opening it up, folding down one end, which was hinged at the bottom with a pair of latches at the top.

Squatting down to look inside, I could make out two sections running the length of the box, which were stacked on top of each other. As I slid the top one out, I discovered the two were joined together and a sheaf of paperwork resting on top of them fell out, which I put to one side.

I carried on pulling the two long sections all the way out of the box, stopping to move one of the chairs out of the way to make more room as they emerged onto the coffee table. When finally free of the box, they turned out to be hinged together, with the top bit folded up on top of the lower one. They were also of a different wood to the outer rosewood box, which I fancied might be cypress or some such.

Folding the top section down flat next to the first one revealed that this in turn was two pieces hinged together, so that the third piece swivelled around to sit parallel to the others. The hinged joint between these second and third parts was tapered, so that when fully expanded, the contraption I was looking at was roughly triangular.

Each of the sections was hollow and contained wires running along the long axis and secured at both ends, like the strings of a harp, with long ones on my left running all the way down to short ones on my right. There was a mechanism along the edge facing me, with little wooden pegs held upright, one for each corresponding string.

My initial impression was that it might indeed be a musical instrument of some sort. Either that or a device for the mass torture and beheading of rodents. What did I know?

Tilting the box up for another look, I discovered a shelf built into the interior at the bottom, containing a final long flat piece which had been underneath the others and I had overlooked. When pulled out, this turned out to be in two sections and held a series of white on black keys, which when offered up to the mechanism in turn slotted in neatly.

When the puzzle was finally pieced together, what was in front of me was some kind of portable keyboard, like a harpsichord, with reversed out keys. The whole thing was ingenious in design and when folded up and housed in the rosewood box could be carried around with relative ease.

Shaking my head, I sat there dumbfounded, with absolutely no idea what to make of the object or what it meant.

Absentmindedly, I depressed a couple of the keys and got a distinctly unmusical noise. Not surprising given the thing's obvious age and the sea voyage it had recently been on. Not to mention that the wooden frame meant it would have to be constantly retuned at the best of times.

It was undoubtedly old, at a rough estimate maybe two hundred years or more, and a rare thing (I'd never heard of one for starters) meaning it probably carried some value accordingly. It didn't seem to me the kind of thing people would get worked up enough to kill for though.

Was there something else about it; something that I was missing? Did it have some sort of a secret, or had something else altogether already been removed from the box? Remembering the paperwork, I picked the sheaf up, smoothed the sheets out to take a better look and started leafing through.

The top one was some sort of an importation licence, attached to a customs receipt, showing that the item had been imported and duties paid at the Port of Los Angeles on September eighteenth. It was made out to Elegance at the warehouse address and had Eric Jenner's name on it but had been signed for, with a signature which looked like the surname read Conlon.

The next sheets were in French, which I know a little, with markings for the grand port maritime de Marseilles dating from the middle of July, a couple of months before arriving in the U.S. I made them out to be some sort of inventory and was struck by one heading, which read '*objet*', next to which was what I took to be a description of the item. Here the words '*clavecin brise*' were written, although I didn't know what these meant.

The next sheets were similar in layout and design but written in Italian. They were stamped 'Porto Napoli' and dated a few days before the French ones, which I guessed might be about the shipping time from Naples to Marseilles, give or take.

Outside of a restaurant menu, my Italian isn't up to much, but I looked for a heading corresponding with the one on the previous sheets and found one that said '*articolo*' with the words '*cembalo piegatorio*' written next to it.

Whatever the item's significance was, it had gone from Italy and then on to France before arriving in the US, imported by Eric Jenner through the business he ran with Jack. Not long before there was some sort of trouble, Jack went missing and Jenner wound up dead.

I leafed through some more of the paperwork and there seemed to be other permits and licences, very ornate affairs with elaborate stamps and crests, mostly in Italian. Whatever it was, judging by the paperwork, it had spent longer in Italy than in France.

Then I found something that stopped me dead in my

tracks. A German document from the Nazi era, complete with eagle and swastika stamp and dated 1944. This one referred to a '*Reisecembal*' in several places, whatever the hell that meant.

None the wiser but more than a little spooked, I fetched the bottle of whisky I'd brought along for company from my overnight bag and took a long pull on it before sitting back down to think things through.

I looked the thing over and made a note of all the features, and when I eventually tired of the puzzle, dismantled and packed it all away again in the carrying case. At which point it became just an intriguing old box again, which I stashed at the foot of the bed.

I crossed to the table, wrote out and sealed a note for Jack on the hotel stationery, then made my way down to reception where I left it marked for the attention of Mr. J. Meyer, as per Janet's instructions. The note introduced me as Mr. Rodgers, a travelling harpsichord salesman from Connecticut, who'd just got in from Havana and wanted to meet up. It told him to come to my room that evening at seven, alone. I figured he'd understand what it meant.

Not feeling like taking the sea air and figuring it might not be wise in any case, I stopped by the hotel bar and picked up a couple of glasses with some ice. Although not usually in the habit of diluting my drinks with ice, the idea had appealed on this occasion, not least because the throbbing in my right temple had returned.

Back in the room, I locked the door and put on the chain, then unpacked my bag, which used up all of two minutes. I took a washcloth from the bathroom and packed it with some ice, then headed over to the couch to rest up and wait.

I set up bar on the coffee table with the two ice glasses, the rest of the whisky and the half-empty bottle of painkillers, then poured a glass for sipping, put my feet on the coffee table and self-medicated some. Holding the ice pack to my head I let out a deep sigh of satisfaction.

When the ice pack had melted, I put what was left of it in the bathroom sink and moved over to the bed with the bottle and glass, and made myself comfortable, unclipping the .38 and laying it on the nightstand. I took off my shoes and propped myself up with some pillows, not for the first time wondering why there were always so many.

Wanting a few stiff drinks, but needing to stay sharp, I set a strict two drink limit, sipping the whisky with the ice slowly. I stopped counting at three but felt considerably better and drifted off into a dreamless sleep, sitting there on the bed in my hotel room.

13. Jack Conlon

The knock at my door came a little after a quarter past seven that evening. After lying down to do some thinking, I'd drifted off into a light sleep, but came round quickly enough, reaching instinctively for the gun on the nightstand before getting up.

Although I didn't remember dreaming, a phrase from my subconscious with a nightmarish quality was going around in my head: *that which you seek also seeks you.*

It was from Rumi; some eastern wisdom I'd picked up along the way. I wasn't sure why it came to me, but recognised it for what it was: a warning, but what about? What was it that was seeking me? The box? I didn't see how that could be. Might it mean Jack maybe, or something else altogether darker and more sinister?

My earlier jitteriness gone and feeling calmer, I approached the door with some caution. Keeping the gun out of sight in my right hand but trained on an unknown target on the other side of it, I fiddled awkwardly with the chain with my left and opened it just enough to peer through the crack, from my position pressed up against the corner of the room.

Jack Conlon was on his own and I recognised him immediately from Kitty's picture since he made no attempt at disguise. He had the casual air of a man seemingly without a care in the world and looked relaxed and tanned.

Dressed elegantly for dinner, in a beige suit with brown loafers and a pale blue open necked shirt, his outfit wasn't unlike my own but looked far better on him than it did on me, notwithstanding the fact that I had been sleeping in mine. He obviously had a better tailor, and his good looks didn't harm the overall impression.

I opened the door fully and let the gun hand drop to my side, feeling a bit sheepish.

"How's the keyboard selling business?"

"A lot tougher than people realise. It nearly got me killed."

"So I see."

He seemed amused but was paying close attention to my gun hand.

"Why don't I come in and you can tell me all about it."

I moved aside and gestured for him to lead.

"*Mi casa es su casa.*"

He sauntered in like he did indeed own the place, crossed to the couch, and sat down. He must have seen the box at the foot of the bed, but his face didn't give anything away.

"You always answer the door with a gun in your hand, Mr. Rodgers?"

I grinned by way of a reply.

"Let's have a drink, but some house rules first. Did you bring a gun of your own to this party and are you thinking of pulling it on me? I've had rather a tiring day and if there's to be any business like that, I'd just as soon get it out of the way."

He thought, weighing up the situation.

"In answer to your questions: yes, I did, but no, I'm not.

I got your message and if you're here at the Fairmont, it can only mean Janet sent you and you already know who I am."

"Good. Then I'll fix us that drink. By the way, neither of us is who he seems: my name's Morgan, not Rodgers and I prefer it without the Mr.

I hope you like yours neat, I'm all out of ice."

After holstering my .38, I upended the two highball glasses, poured a decent slug of whisky into each, and handed him one.

"Cheers, Morgan."

"Cheers, Jack, or should I call you Jackie?"

"Janet told you. I go by Jack. Have done for quite a while."

He took a decent sip and nodded his approval.

"Yah. I want to ask you about that later, but first things first."

His eyes slid across to the foot of the bed and he gestured with his glass.

"I see you have the box."

"Yeah, how about that? Mind telling me what in the hell that thing is and what this is all about?"

He sat forward and thought for a bit, turning the glass around distractedly.

"An Italian friend once described it as the magical madrigal, but then his English wasn't that great. Turns out that it's neither of those things: it's not a madrigal and it's not magical. If anything, I'd say it's cursed."

"I was hoping for something a little more '*como se dice*' substantial."

He shook his head.

"It's a long story, but I have some house rules of my own.

I know how you found me, but I don't know whose interests you represent here, Morgan."

He began to reason things out, working his way through the situation.

"You've managed to get hold of that box and you've looked inside it, so you're not here for that.

You've been to see Janet and ended up here, which means that it can only be about me. What's your interest in me?"

As he'd been talking and playing with the drink with his right hand, the left had been moving slowly, almost imperceptibly across his lap and easing over towards the right-hand lapel of his jacket which was hanging open where he leant forward.

"It's a fair question, but I thought we agreed no guns. I didn't know you were a south paw, Jack. I'd like you to put both hands back where I can see them now. Slowly please."

My own had moved close to the gun at my side and he brought his left hand back out and turned both palms up to me apologetically. We sipped our drinks instead as I thought for a minute, deciding how best to lay it out.

"I'm here because your wife hired me to find you. She's worried about you and from what I can make out she's right to be.

The box is incidental. I picked it up along the way looking for you, although I'm interested in it now, of course, as it is at the middle of whatever's going on. On a personal level I'm interested too, because two tough guys beat the hell out of me trying to get to it. Or to you.

You breeze in here acting like you haven't a care in the world. You might not know it, but you're wanted for murder in LA, not more than a hundred miles away."

I paid close attention, studying his reactions.

"Who am I supposed to have killed?"

He was smiling. Still the easy charm. This was it: I had to go in hard and see how he reacted.

"Eric Jenner. I found him dead in your apartment a couple of days ago. At first the police thought I might have done it. Now they think you did."

There are probably as many reactions to news about the death of somebody close as there are people on the planet, and I was watching minutely for any trace that might betray what he knew about the death of his friend. I wasn't expecting what happened next.

Conlon froze; completely still. He didn't move a muscle in his face and his breathing stopped. Even his drink halted in mid-air between his mouth and putting it down on the table. It was like he had been turned into a marble statue.

With his service record, he must have seen a lot of death. Either he was registering genuine shock, or he had real acting talent. When he eventually came out of the trance, all the earlier breeziness had gone and when he spoke, it was as if from a long way off.

"Eric's dead? What happened?"

"He was shot. Twice. Somebody got up close to him with a little gun, something like a .25 and made a real neat job of it."

A distracted frown creased his forehead, like he had just remembered something.

"What can you tell me about it, Jack?"

He shook his head as he returned from whatever quiet place inside himself he had gone to.

"Whatever else he might have been, Eric was my friend. He didn't deserve that."

I waited, but nothing more came, so I changed tack.

"What do you know about a couple of Canadians? French speakers: Quebecois. One called Alain Thibault and the other's a Louis somebody or other. They nearly killed me and they're looking for you."

"Alain Thibault and Louis Ricard."

"You know them?"

"Not exactly. Eric met them in Italy in the war, but I wasn't there then. They were in some sort of a special forces unit with the Fifth Army."

"They were at your place. You think they might have killed him?"

He thought it over, then shook his head.

"No. Eric was friends with them, and they were working for him. He thought they might be useful to have around when things started getting heavy, so he went to Chicago to see them. They work freelance there."

It was my turn to shake my head.

"Freelance. You mean they're hired guns, right?"

"I didn't ask what they do. We all had to make a living after the war somehow. Guys like that who don't fit back in so well come from all walks of life."

I inclined my head towards the box.

"How do you think they knew about that thing?"

"Eric probably spun them a yarn; told them he had money coming because of it or something. I don't see how he could have hired them otherwise."

"Why would they come after me?"

"If they're still around, it's because of the box. Maybe they double-crossed him or found out he's dead and decided to go it alone. Either way, my guess is they're working for themselves now.

You can't really blame them: there's not much of a future to look forward to in their profession."

Which wasn't that different from my own line of work.

"How'd this all start anyway?"

"May I?"

He'd finished his drink and got up to help himself to another and top mine up. I got the feeling he was weighing up how much he could tell me.

"There are two sides to Elegance furniture: the quality reproduction stuff at the showroom and a line in luxury antiques we import for the very wealthy.

We were dealing in that side of things when we started out just after the war; the items we imported weren't always what you'd call strictly on the level. We couldn't always prove where they'd come from and some of them had to be sort of smuggled in."

"Smuggling, huh? The way you put it sounds almost romantic."

"Don't look at me like that, Morgan. Everybody's got to start somewhere and that's how that business is. It's all legit now and the repro stuff is the future in any case."

He looked very earnest, wanting me to believe in his

business like an investor he needed on board.

"Legitimate although far less profitable, I imagine. How did you get around the paperwork and licences, that sort of thing?"

He shrugged.

"Mostly fake. Good enough to pass muster, but they wouldn't stand up to scrutiny from somebody who knew what to look for.

Our man in Italy, Battaglia, sourced the pieces and looked after the export documents; greased the right palms at the ports. Eric did the same at this end."

"I might need to ask you more about that later but tell me what this has to do with the trouble now."

"I didn't know anything much about that box at first: as far as I knew, it was just another antique shipped in from Italy.

About three weeks back, Eric was out of town, and I got a call at work from some angry guy with an accent saying he was expecting delivery of an antique box and it hadn't turned up and demanding to speak with Eric.

He sounded really pissed. I told him to relax, that Eric wasn't around, and I'd look into it."

"Anything unusual about that?"

"Other than that, he wouldn't give me his name, just that Eric had organised everything. Sales were usually down to me, but once in a while, he would come up with a contact of his own and the order would come about that way. There are frequently delays in shipping and deliveries get re-arranged all the time: that part was routine.

Eventually I got hold of Eric back East, who told me that it was for some big shot producer, had been paid for already and was supposed to go to a big house up in the Hollywood Hills somewhere. He was unusually agitated and asked me to take care of it personally."

He paused to light a cigarette and offer me one, which I

declined.

"Go on."

"Anyhow, the next day, I got another call. The same guy, but more insistent this time, saying that the item belonged to some people who wanted it delivered. I was to bring it to a certain place at such and such time and that would be the end of it."

"No name?"

He shook his head.

"Just an address."

"What did you do?"

"Ignored it of course. I don't like being threatened and he'd got my back up. I went to the customs house though, to see if I could find the thing.

It turned out the box had been sent to the wrong warehouse. Eventually they located it and I signed for it, then borrowed one of the inspection rooms they have there have a quick look and see what all the fuss was about.

Which left me none the wiser. I took it home and stashed it at my place, which was right about when I got the feeling I was being watched. Nothing concrete, just an uneasy sensation."

"What then?"

"Eric told me he'd be back that evening and I went over to find him. I wanted to know what was so important about that damned box and why he was so touchy about it. We had a long talk at his place. He was very agitated and told me that he knew more than he had let on at first.

He was in trouble again, but it would all be fine if he could just get hold of the box. Did I have it, or know where it was?

For some reason, call it intuition, I told him I didn't have it, but it was safe and I could get it in a couple of days, which seemed to calm him down a bit."

"What kind of trouble was he in?"

"You might as well know all of it, Morgan; it can't do him any harm now."

He refilled our glasses.

"Eric always needed money. Whatever he had, it was never enough for him. He couldn't adjust when he came back from the war and was always looking for a buzz, or for something new. Me, I'm still experimenting with this stuff."

He gestured with the glass in his hand.

"The business was doing fine; at least I thought it was, and we were earning a good living out of it, but Eric got into gambling. Nothing serious at first but it seemed to provide him with the thrill he was looking for.

He got in deeper of course, and his debts had mounted up. I'd helped him out in the past, but this time he didn't come to me."

"So where did he go?"

"He borrowed money from a guy called Franco Mazza. Loan sharking is his business if you can call it that."

Eric Jenner had been seen with Mazza at the Havana, which seemed to fit.

"Like all gamblers, he thought he could win the money back; it was a sickness with him. Gambling was how he had got into a fix, but in his mind, it was how he would get out of it too.

Eventually when his debts mounted up, he helped himself to money from the business and altered the ledger to cover it up."

"How'd you feel about that?"

"I just never thought he'd go that far. I'll freely admit I wanted to kill him when he told me. I didn't though."

It would have been a powerful motive, but for whatever reason, I believed him.

"What did you do?"

"I decided to help him instead, of course.

He kept going on about that box being his way out and pleading for me to get it for him, but he wouldn't tell me any more. Whatever trouble he was in, I had the thing and planned to confront whoever was responsible.

The next day at work I was at my desk planning what to do next when I got another call. Different voice this time, telling me they wanted the box, or else and not to involve the police."

"Or else what?"

"My membership of the Country Club would be cancelled."

He was looking at me pointedly now, but I failed to see the point.

"What? I don't get it."

"I'm a *life* member of the Stanley Hills Country Club. It's good for business: contacts and the like. My father-in-law's the chairman there and when I married Kitty, he gave me lifetime membership as a gift.

The point is that the membership only expires when *I* do."

I nodded, remembering something.

"Wait. There was a message at your apartment from the club, something about renewing your membership."

"After that, things got serious. That night I was coming back from early evening dinks at the club when two guys ambushed me at the hairpin down the hill from the entrance. Stepped out from behind some bushes and one of them took a pot shot when I slowed down: opened up with a Thompson."

I thought about this.

"I looked your car over but didn't see any bullet holes. You get a look at them? How'd you know it was a Tommy gun?"

"Unmistakable sound. It was dusk so I couldn't

see them well, although I didn't hang around for a closer look.

The thing is that they missed, but it was deliberate, a warning. They could easily have taken care of me."

We both thought about this. His car was pretty distinctive and would have presented a large target moving slowly on a tight bend. He was probably right.

"Then what?"

"There was a hand-delivered envelope waiting for me back at the apartment. Something about it stood out; something menacing made me not want to open it."

"You did though. What was in it?"

"A photograph; Kitty and the boys outside the house on the driveway. It was grainy, like a surveillance shot, taken from bushes by the road."

"Was there a message?"

"No message. Just an address. It was clear what I was supposed to do."

"You didn't go to the police?"

"I couldn't, Morgan. Think about it. I called Kitty to warn her to keep the boys out of sight. She wasn't in, but I couldn't risk going there if I was being followed.

I spent an uneasy night thinking things though in the apartment, making it obvious to anyone watching that I was in. Lights on, smoking on the balcony, radio turned up, that sort of thing.

Early next morning, I packed some things. I needed the box for my plan to work, so took it and caught a cab outside the front of my apartment block, not minding about who was watching.

I needed to get out of the city to keep any danger away from Kitty and the boys, so went to Union Station and very publicly bought a ticket to Sacramento, got on the train but got off further up the platform just before it left and doubled back to the left luggage office. I stashed the box there while figuring out my next move and mailed the ticket back to myself."

I tipped my drink to him.

"Neat trick. One I've used myself."

He acknowledged my salute.

"Been wondering how you worked that one out.

I put in a call to a friend at one of the studios and went to see one of the few people I can really trust."

"Janet?"

He nodded.

"She drove me here and I figured I'd lie low until somebody showed up looking for me. Turns out that somebody is you."

I thought about it all for a while, trying to decide how much of it might be true. I couldn't, so asked a question instead.

"What about Eric Jenner? What was he doing while you were running around town stashing boxes and the like?"

"Probably out playing blackjack. That's his game."

He smiled sadly at this point. It was more of a grimace at his error in tense and we both looked into our drinks.

"What do you think he was doing in your apartment?"

"I can't say for sure, but my guess is he went looking for the box after I told him I had it hidden somewhere."

"Any idea how he got in?"

"That's no mystery. He had keys to my place, as I do to his."

I hadn't found any on his body, which might or might not have been important. Maybe the killer had taken them.

"Who do you think killed him?"

He looked thoughtful for a minute, swirling his drink in his glass.

"Mazza, or somebody working for him maybe."

Something about his manner seemed off and I was frowning, dubiously.

"Killed by a money lender, without getting his money back first?"

"The kind of interest he charges, he's had his money back many times over. One thing you can't have if you're a moneylender though is people not paying on time."

"So, you think Mazza killed him *'pour encourager les autres'*?"

"Say what, Morgan?"

"Nothing. Just some French I picked up somewhere."

"Might come in useful. By all accounts, that thing's French."

He gestured over to the box with his glass, looking long and hard at the elephant in the room.

"What say you we take a proper look at that thing: see if we can't figure it out? I never really got the chance earlier."

I'd been thinking the same thing myself and brought it from the foot of the bed to the coffee table.

"Why don't you tell me what you know about this thing, while I set it up?"

I took the sections out and assembled them on the coffee table, more quickly this time, knowing how it went together, and had it laid out in no time.

"What I know I got from Battaglia in Italy when I finally got hold of him about a week ago. It's a *'clavecin brise'*, a folding harpsichord from the eighteenth century, so it's a couple of hundred years old.

A beautiful and rare piece, but this one's supposed to have come from the court of Frederick the Great. Provenance is everything with antiques, Morgan. If you can trace a piece back to royalty, it's worth a whole lot more."

"Is that what all the paperwork is? What about that Nazi stuff?"

He frowned.

"What?"

I leafed through the documents and extracted the one that had fallen out before.

"Here."

He took the letter and scanned it.

"Eric told me we were finished with that."

I looked at him questioningly.

"Never mind. I'll tell you later.

You've had a look at the thing, Morgan. You see anything that might explain why anybody might want it so badly?"

I shook my head.

He put the letter down and handed me my drink. I took a sip, appreciating the good liquor, even if it was my own and settled in to the familiar, warm embrace.

We spent time going over the instrument and then the case inch by inch: Jack at one end and me at the other, then he suggested we swap around, in case the other had missed something. Short of X-raying it, there was little more we could do to get it to yield whatever secrets it might be holding.

While we looked, I tried to blank my mind out, not speaking and to get myself into an unthinking state. I knew from experience that this could sometimes help to recall some lost detail from the subconscious. All the while, something was eating away at me like I'd overlooked it earlier on.

We were just about to give it up as a bad lot, when a detail came back from when I'd been asleep earlier, before waking with that Rumi quote filling my thoughts. I had been dreaming after all, and the fragment I could remember had been of my mother speaking French, teaching me the words for things.

Then I spotted something I hadn't paid attention to earlier. There was a tiny hole towards the front on the left hand-side of the instrument, where the keyboard joined the body. There was a shelf sticking out slightly which held the keys in place.

The opening wasn't much bigger than a woodworm burrow, with tiny gold leaf lettering over the top of it, which read *'l'huil'*. I knew enough French to know that this meant oil, and that's exactly what the hole looked like, some kind of lubricating point.

Which set me to thinking.

I don't know a lot about old musical instruments in general, and even less about old harpsichords, but I could tell the action was all wood or ivory keys worked by wooden levers. Why would it need to be oiled there?

Jack noticed how suddenly still I had become.

"What is it, Morgan? You find something?"

I was looking at the hole, trying to judge its diameter.

"Maybe. I'm not sure yet."

After walking over to the stationery set on the table by the balcony, I hunted around until I found a paper clip, opening it out flat as I came back to the coffee table.

I showed him what I'd found.

"It's this hole here, Jack. It says it's for oil, but I wonder..."

I pushed the unfolded paper clip gently into the opening. After it had gone in further than I'd thought it would there was a dry metallic click and a shallow, spring-loaded drawer popped out about half an inch, just enough for me to get a purchase on it with the tips of my fingers and slide it out.

The hidden drawer had been to the right of the tiny hole, its edges ingeniously disguised to line up perfectly with the joins in the wooden sections. I carried the little tray over to the table by the balcony and emptied it out carefully onto the glass tabletop, where Jack and I examined the contents. Jammed in tightly together so that there was hardly any space between them all were the following:

A small, rusted pin with a brass sphere at one end and about the same diameter as the paperclip, which I took to have served as the original 'key' and had been locked in the drawer, perhaps inadvertently.

A lump of green glass, like that from the thick end of a bottle, like a child might pick up on a beach. It was smooth in parts as if by the action of the sea and pitted in other places.

A piece of the marquetry corresponding with a missing bit of veneer from the facia above the keyboard and which I guessed someone had sought to keep with the instrument.

A small silver ring of purely sentimental value that might fit a child and was probably a keepsake.

A few tiny, uncultured pearls of no great value that might have come loose from a bracelet or a small necklace.

"What do you make of this stuff, Morgan?"

I tried to figure out why anybody would go to so much trouble to hide these trinkets. I settled on the theory they were childish objects and might have been locked in by accident and forgotten about.

"Looks like kids' stuff to me. I'd say that these things were locked in here a long time ago. We might be the first people to have seen them since."

"How about that? It's hardly worth killing for any of this stuff though, is it?"

I shook my head.

"That's what I was thinking. Tell me again where it came from."

"The Prussian royal family. Frederick the Great is supposed to have got it from his mother."

I started to speculate, thinking out loud.

"Do you think a little boy or girl might have

locked these things in here way back when? A royal child maybe? Might explain the ring and the pearls."

"You mean like a prince or a princess? What are you getting at?"

A thought struck me. I got goosebumps down my arms and the hairs stood up on the back of my neck.

Picking up the lump of glass, I took it across to the balcony window and held it up to the light for a closer look, turning it this way, then that.

"What are you looking at, Morgan?"

"It's not what I'm looking at but what I'm looking for. Come here."

His head was next to mine now and he was looking at where I was pointing.

"If you look through the stone, you see these little black bits here and here?"

"Yeah. So?"

"I'm pretty sure those are inclusions."

"Inclusions?"

"Little imperfections. Glass doesn't have them, but gemstones do. sometimes you get tiny bubbles in glass, but I can't see any of those either."

"How do you know any of this?"

I shrugged.

"I've worked a fair few jewellery thefts and insurance jobs in my time, picked up some knowledge and seen plenty of paste. It's so big and rough looking that it never occurred to me it was anything other than an old piece of glass but looking at it now, I'm pretty sure it's real."

"What? Look at the size of it though: a great big green jewel, like an emerald maybe? Why is it so rough looking?"

Jack looked at me incredulously.

I shrugged my shoulders.

"My guess is its old and uncut. It might have been

in there for a couple of hundred years, who knows? The more I look at it, the more I'm convinced, although we'd have to get it looked at by someone to be *absolutely* sure."

"You know anybody?"

"Sure, but not my usual contacts back in LA. It'd be too dangerous to go flashing this thing around there. Besides, there's the little matter of you being wanted for murder."

I was thinking now.

"There's a guy I met down here on a case a few years back, a jeweller. He's on the road back outside Escondido."

"Let's go see him".

He was grinning, excited as a schoolboy.

I laughed.

"It'll have to wait until tomorrow. Check your watch: he'll be closed now."

"If that thing is an emerald, it'd be gigantic, wouldn't it? What kind of money might it be worth?"

I thought some more.

"I can't say for sure, but it would have to be *a lot*. It's all to do with quality and size, and this one is old as well, with a royal connection. Definitely the kind of money people might kill for."

Our excitement faded: every silver lining has a cloud.

My mind was spinning with questions. Why was the stone still in there, not taken out and kept elsewhere? Was it possible nobody else knew of its existence? Or that the people looking for the box knew it had great value, but no more than that?

Another connection had been made somewhere deep inside my thinking muscle and I didn't like it one little bit.

"Say, weren't the Nazis big on Frederick the Great? Didn't I read somewhere that Hitler was a fan?"

Jack was nodding.

"Idolised him. Saw himself as the same kind of

warrior king, saving his nation."

We were both suddenly a lot quieter.

"Morgan, if we're going to dwell on the past, why don't we make it worthwhile and raise a glass to that little prince or princess or whoever might have put it in there?"

"I guess that can't do any harm."

His breezy manner restored, we drank to the little boy or girl from the eighteenth or seventeenth century, or whenever the hell it was. Historians seem to use a deliberately confusing labelling system.

"You're all out of whisky. What say you we split and go to the place I'm staying, have a drink and a bite to eat there. Looks like I'm buying."

Grinning, he brandished the emerald, then wrapped it in a handkerchief and put it in his jacket pocket.

"Sounds good, but I took a room for the night here. I didn't know you had a place."

"Well, I don't exactly. I'll explain when we get there.

Don't worry about this place – it's owned by someone I know. No need to check out and no bill to pay; it'll be taken care of. Just get your stuff and follow me."

I looked at him doubtfully.

"Relax, it's all fine, Morgan – I swear.

I'll take this thing and meet you outside in ten minutes. Follow me in your car: look out for a tan Chrysler station wagon."

He hefted the box up and we dismantled the harpsichord and put it away. For some reason I couldn't explain I wanted to protest, but the thing was his to take, not mine.

After Jack left, I gathered my things together, remembering at the last minute to collect my painkillers from the nightstand. As I was packing, I wondered if he was really going to be there when I came out or whether I might never see him again.

If that happened, what would I tell Kitty? Worst case

scenario: at least I'd be able to say I'd found her husband and he was alive and well.

I had no idea what I might be able to tell her beyond that though.

14. Casa Blanca

To my surprise, there was indeed a light brown Chrysler station wagon positioned just along the street as I exited the Fairmont. I gave a discreet tip of my hat to Jack and went around to the lot at the back to pick up the Plymouth.

I slotted in behind him and we drove along the coast a little further south for three or four miles before making a right turn into a long drive lined with laurel and bougainvillea. We twisted right and then made a long sweeping left turn, looping back around a small headland projecting out into the ocean.

At the end of the drive was a substantial yet understated ranch style property, nestling in on the ocean side behind a low hill, topped with a mixture of pine and jacaranda trees.

In a beautiful setting and totally private, the house itself was a dazzling white but so completely hidden from the road you'd never suspect it was there. We pulled up out front and Jack took the box off the back seat of his car and ambled over to the door. As I got out of mine, he called out to me.

"Bring your things, Morgan. This place has plenty of rooms. No point you driving back to the city tonight."

He had keys, so hadn't broken into the place after all, which was something of a relief.

As I stood there, scrubbing my lungs clean with sea air and enjoying the background scent of flowers, I felt comfortable enough with Jack although had mixed feelings about staying. His story was an interesting one that I wanted to hear more of, but his wife was my client.

In the end, a combination of tiredness and inertia got the better of me, on top of which my headache was kicking back in, so I shrugged my metaphorical shoulders and fetched my bag from the trunk.

The door couldn't have been much more than about nine feet tall and four feet wide; an impressive affair, studded with iron nails and grillwork, with one of those peephole hatches.

Inside felt beautifully cool on the warm autumn evening, and we stepped into a broad corridor running along the length of the house, disappearing away to both sides. The floor was laid with rustic terracotta tiles and there were animal skin rugs scattered along its length.

There was a Spanish mission theme, with whitewashed walls hung with tastefully chosen Mexican art and large mirrors in driftwood frames. There were colourful Aztec style sculptures and ceramics dotted around in little alcoves, which might have been recent folk art worth a few dollars or antique pieces worth a few thousand; I couldn't tell which.

It reminded me just how close to the border we were down here.

The place was subtle and arranged with such seemingly casual elegance I realised it could only have been the opposite: meticulously designed and carefully executed.

"Help yourself to any of the bedrooms down that end, Morgan."

Jack gestured back over my shoulder down the corridor stretching out behind me to the left of the front door.

"Then come on through to the lounge and I'll fix us a drink and something to eat."

This last was delivered over his shoulder as he wandered off in the opposite direction and I watched him round the corner at the end of the hallway.

I did as invited, went to the other end of the house and opened one of the doors into what turned out to be not just a bedroom but a small suite of interconnected rooms, going through to the back of the house. There was a balcony door there opening onto the ocean side.

I went over and cracked this open to take the breeze and help with my headache. After a few minutes enjoying the rhythmic lull of the surf breaking against the shore below, I broke away from my reverie and went to find my bedroom, which was through a door on the left of the living area.

An oversized and comfortable looking brass bed, with crisp bed linen of the finest quality was calling out to me, and I was sorely tempted to lay on it for a bit. Instead, I went through to the bathroom to freshen up and wash down a couple of headache pills. The towels were thick and luxurious; I imagined they were Egyptian cotton or some such. The whole place felt like an exclusive hotel.

Wondering what Jack's deal was here, I left my rooms and went back along the passageway to join him. The end of the hallway doglegged left and then right, before opening out into a vast living area at the back of the house, set down a couple of broad but shallow steps.

Stepping down these, the lounge seemed even more gigantic in scale. Double height, like a hotel lobby, it was set over two floors where the back of the plot dropped down towards the ocean. There were several different seating areas, and a huge stone fireplace was set into the wall to my right.

The whole of the back wall was floor to ceiling glass interspersed with terracotta brick pillars and offered what would be spectacular, panoramic ocean views in the daytime. A stone bar matching the fireplace was set into the far right-hand corner, where Jack was busy mixing drinks. I walked across a sea of beautiful oak flooring to meet him.

"I give up. What's the story with this place?"

I didn't know what it was called then, but he handed me a gimlet, which he'd mixed for both of us without asking.

"The Casa Blanca? That's what they call it. It's a

movie industry inside joke. It's owned by one of the studios, not the one who made the film as it happens, but one of the others. I forget which."

The wry smile told me there were no problems with his memory.

He suddenly looked serious and raised his glass.

"Let's drink to absent friends."

I knew he meant Eric Jenner. I'd never met the man and never would, on top of which what I'd heard about him wasn't good, so couldn't oblige him on that score. I had plenty of candidates of my own though, so raised my glass.

"Absent friends."

I nodded my appreciation of the drink, which was excellent, and we were quiet with our own thoughts for a while.

"I'm curious. Why would a studio have a place down here?"

"It's a bolt hole, Morgan, a place people come to relax in private. Movie actors and the like and their special friends. Or industry executives."

A thought struck me from my conversation in the diner.

"Film stars: you mean like Cary Grant maybe?"

"Possibly. I don't know. Why do you ask?"

"No particular reason. You were saying?"

"This place doesn't officially exist; very few people even know about it. It's a stop off between here and Mexico. The rich and famous go there to party and take advantage of the more *relaxed* regime. They use this place as a steppingstone, going there or coming back. It's just a short hop across the border, but a world away from the publicity of Hollywood."

Somewhere like this for rich and famous people to conduct their affairs in private would be useful and Jack made it seem like harmless fun, but I knew there would be a darker side. I'd seen at first-hand how the industry chewed up and spat out people without a second thought. One way or another, I'd dealt with enough of the casualties through the years and it didn't sit well with me.

"Handy for seducing young starlets, I imagine. Or wide-eyed waitresses with a headful of the movies. I can see how they'd be impressed with this kind of a set up."

"Get off your high horse, Morgan. I wouldn't know about any of that. I was in a fix and needed a place to stay."

I swept my arm around the room.

"Who pays for all this anyway?"

He looked bemused, as if the thought had never occurred to him; his laissez faire attitude clearly extended to not caring who was paying for his board and lodgings.

"I have no idea. It's off the books; that much I do know.

They keep it like a sort of hotel. There are no staff here overnight, but they come during the daytime and prepare meals; leave fresh flowers; make up the bedroom, that kind of thing.

I make sure I'm out or down at the boathouse, but they're paid to look the other way in any case. There are gardeners who come too, of course."

"Oh, of course."

He let that one go by.

"That station wagon comes with the place, too. It's anonymous and understated like everything here but with a much more powerful engine than you'd imagine to look at it."

I thought for a minute.

"So where do you fit in? You really mix in those kinds of circles?"

He refilled our glasses from a jug behind the bar.

"Of course. They're just people like you and me, Morgan.

I've had clients all over Beverly Hills and West

Hollywood for years: there are mansions up there full of our stuff. Not just the reproduction pieces; that's pretty good business, but also high-end antiques brought over from Europe. There's always money in that too.

One thing I've learned is that rich people are paranoid about getting ripped off. They've got too much money and don't know what they're doing, so like to feel they're dealing with friends."

"Which is where you come in."

He was nodding.

"Exactly. I fit in and I'm good at it. I look and dress the part and married well – Kitty's connections didn't do me any harm.

Friends become clients and clients become friends after a while. You start getting repeat business and referrals; you know how it goes."

I snorted.

"There's not a lot of repeat business in my line of work and not much by way of referrals. Leastways, not the kind anybody wants."

He laughed.

"I promised you dinner. Come on through."

Jack picked up his drink and I followed him past the end of the bar through a doorway and across a cavernous kitchen, then through an archway into a small dining area at the end of the house, which I guessed was not the main one but probably meant for the staff. It was comfortable, nonetheless and offered a view of the moon just starting to rise far out over the sea.

"I tend to eat here or in the living room in my quarters. The other rooms are all too big."

However humble his origins, Jack had acquired a taste for the finer things in life somewhere along the way. Somebody, who I guessed was not him, had gone to a lot of trouble providing a most agreeable selection of cold dishes laid out for us to dine on.

There was a beautifully poached side of salmon with hollandaise sauce, accompanied by a green salad and a potato one with delightfully subtle chives and just the right amount of bite on the potatoes, which is to say none at all.

It was simple but delicious and we washed it down with a sensational and elegantly chilled French white wine, a Pouilly-Fume, which went down very nicely. I could see how a man might get used to this sort of thing.

When we had eaten and exchanged pleasantries about the food, he asked me something I hadn't been expecting:

"What do you know about women, Morgan?"

I laughed.

"Women? You're asking the wrong guy.

Let me see. They say you should tell beautiful women they're intelligent and intelligent women they're beautiful. The idea being everybody wants to be seen as the thing they're not, or rather, to be seen differently by others to how they see themselves."

"Ah, but what about women who are beautiful *and* intelligent?"

"Those are the ones you stay away from. Even I know that. They're nothing but trouble."

"That might be where I've been going wrong. You've met my wife. What did you think of her?"

"Yes, I've met Kitty. Janet too. From what I can see, that's exactly where you've been going wrong. You've got trouble on both fronts."

He said nothing but suddenly looked sad.

Jack Conlon had his faults as we all do, but I liked him well enough, and in a different life we might have become friends. The way things were going in this one though, I wasn't sure either of us would live long enough for that.

I took his change in mood as my cue.

"Tell me about how you became him. How Jackie from Brooklyn became Jack from Connecticut. I know a little from what Janet told me, but I'd like to hear it from you."

He thought for a minute.

"It's really not as complicated as you might think, Morgan. It happened more or less by accident at first."

I raised my eyebrows but said nothing, waiting for him to carry on.

"It was in Italy in January of 1944. Jack was a Lieutenant, and I was a corporal. We'd fought our way up from Salerno and were captured one morning after an action south of Monte Cassino. We'd been surrounded and had to surrender, and I'd been wounded slightly in the arm, a graze really.

That afternoon, we were being taken to a POW camp somewhere behind their lines by open-top truck, under guard and feeling pretty low. I can't say for sure what happened: either a mortar round or an artillery shell fell in front of us and exploded, but the next thing I knew, we were on our side in a ditch at the side of the road.

Jack was already outside, taking a rifle from one of guards who was lying there unconscious. He was fearless like that: one of the bravest men I've ever met.

From the amount of blood on the ground, I'd say that the driver and the other guy in the front both bought it. Jack and I took off, instinctively making for higher ground up the mountainside on the other side of the road and headed for a promising looking treeline further up.

The other guard appeared on the road below us and was taking shots at us from down in the ditch behind the truck. There were rocky outcrops and shrubs on the lower part of the slope; not much by way of cover but better than nothing. Jack returned fire and kept the guy occupied while we made for the trees.

When we got there, it turned out to be the edge of a had plantation of pines, which gradually got denser and darker and offered better cover. It was carpeted with pine needles and soft underfoot.

It was only when we'd gone further in, and Jack caught up with me that I realised he'd been hit. I don't know if it was from the explosion, or if he'd been shot by the guard down below, but he was panting hard and looking sort of grey.

I helped him further into the woods and we circled around for a bit, trying to throw anybody who might have come after us, but nobody did. We could hear fighting down below and more artillery, so my guess is we got forgotten about or something more important came up.

Less edgy by then, I examined him in the light of a little clearing, where a tree had come down. He had a puncture wound halfway up his back below his left shoulder blade, which may have been from a bullet but more likely a piece of shrapnel, as I couldn't find an exit wound anywhere.

I had no medical kit of any kind or morphine to help him, and the wound wasn't in a place where I could apply any kind of a tourniquet. I knew it wasn't good, but the wound wasn't bleeding much, and he seemed in good spirits, happy to have escaped.

Night came and we made camp as best we could, hunkered down out of sight in a little hollow where I covered us both up with pine needles and branches. I realised his best chance of getting proper attention would be for us to go back down the hill and surrender at first light, as soon as the fighting stopped.

That night on the mountain was the coldest I can ever remember. I'd lost my jacket in the action that morning, was dog tired and my arm was hurting like hell. We lay there shivering, and I only drifted off for a bit sometime just before dawn. When I woke up maybe half an hour later, I knew instinctively that Jack had died in the night.

I forced myself up to check him over and sure enough he was cold to the touch, not breathing and unresponsive. I can't say what happened for sure, but my guess is he must have been bleeding internally from his wound and just bled out and never woke up.

When the sun came up and things started to warm up a bit, I used the butt of the rifle to scoop out a shallow grave for him under the trees and buried him there on that mountainside. Then I used one of his bootlaces to lash together a rough cross out of bits of branch and marked the grave that way. I don't know if he was really religious, but it seemed like the right thing to do."

He shrugged.

"I took his dog tags, which I wore with my own, and his jacket to keep warm: he didn't need it anymore and wouldn't have minded. There were some letters in one of the pockets from his girl and I took one for the return address, figuring I'd write her and tell her what happened when I got the chance.

There was a pause as he remembered his fallen comrade and I refilled our glasses, not wanting to break the spell.

"What next?"

"I tried to figure out where the fighting had been the day before and which way would be the best bet to make it to our lines. I took the rifle along for company with the few bullets left; if I ran into the Germans again, I had no choice but to surrender.

Avoiding the road, I wandered back down the mountainside for half the day without seeing anybody except a few goats. Eventually I came to a low ridge with a settlement nestled in the bottom of the valley beyond it where there was a broken-down bridge, where I figured the fighting had been.

I'd cleared the ridge and was making across a field for the first farmhouse I saw to get a drink of water, when there was shooting, and somebody was shouting at me in German. I made the cover of a wall at the edge of a field, threw the rifle over it and was putting my hands up to surrender when a grenade went off just the other side of the wall.

That's all I can remember. After that, nothing."

"Until?"

"I woke up a week later with my head bandaged in a transit camp hospital near Bologna, much further north.

Naturally enough, they thought I was Jack Conlon: I had his jacket with a lieutenant's insignia, as well as his dog tags. The thing that clinched it was the letter from his sweetheart, Janet, in my pocket. Like I said, it happened by accident at first.

The Nazis were running the north of the country and we all knew how they had it in for the Jewish prisoners. It seemed prudent not to be Jackie Meyer for a bit.

They wanted to know about the dog tags for Corporal Meyer and questioned me about this and other matters when I was well enough. By that time, I'd decided to carry on being him and told them that Meyer had died, and I'd buried him back on the mountainside.

It was simple. I was friendly with the Lieutenant and knew about his background, like that he came from Connecticut and his mother had died. I had plenty of time to think there in the hospital and the more I did, the more it made sense to carry on being him.

Eventually, my shrapnel wound healed and I was discharged from the hospital into the camp proper, where I kept to myself. There were perks to being an officer, and I got better treatment than the ordinary Joes in there.

I felt bad when the letters caught up with me from Jack's sweetheart, but I never read them and knew he never wrote to her anyway, so I just did the same. He'd told me he wanted to make it easier for her to move on if anything happened to him.

The only other fly in the ointment was at the very end of the war when the camp was liberated, and we were to be debriefed by US military intelligence".

"Military intelligence: now there's an oxymoron."

"Say, an oxy what?"

"Never mind, I'm interrupting. I'll fill you in later."

"So, I knew they'd have a file on me – on Jack – and a photograph. We looked a little alike, but not enough to fool them."

"What did you do?"

"I arranged an accident just before my interview. Tripped and fell so I ended up with a nosebleed and two black eyes. There was an orderly in the infirmary I was friendly with who made sure my head was bandaged up good and proper, although I might as well not have bothered.

They were only really interested in the Germans and as I'd been in there a while, there was nothing up to date I could give them. It was a rubber-stamping exercise: they never even bothered fingerprinting me, which was lucky.

I told them about the grave on the hillside where Corporal Meyer was buried, but I could only give them an approximate location and they weren't that interested. I don't know if it was even followed up on.

Next thing I knew I was being shipped back for demobilisation, issued with new identity papers, and sent on my way. I even had a decent amount of money set aside from a Lieutenant's back pay while I was a POW – can you believe it? They even threw in another medal on account of my wounds."

"What then?"

"I'd made a pact with Eric that if we made it through, we'd both come to sunny California and try our luck: there was nothing waiting for me back in Brooklyn in any case, except more poverty and petty crime. No family and no sweetheart.

So I came straight out here, then set about finding out what had happened to him. It turned out our unit was pretty much wiped out at Monte Cassino and never regrouped, so I guess I was lucky to have missed that show.

He spent the rest of the war fighting through Italy and made sergeant, assigned to a different part of the Fifth Army. He'd survived and gone back to Brooklyn although he thought I'd been killed, which I felt bad about.

I took a risk and wrote to Eric, explained about the switch with Conlon but telling him to keep it secret, then spent a nervous couple of days waiting for him to call me on the number I'd given him. I didn't know what to say to him and worried about how things might go.

In the end, I explained things to him pretty much as I've done to you, and we smoothed things out. He couldn't believe I'd made it out. It didn't take much convincing for him to join me out here, and we set about starting new lives."

"What was it like: becoming somebody else? Taking over another man's identity like that?"

He thought it over for a bit, while I refilled our glasses.

"The truth was it felt easy at first.

Everything started working out, like my luck had changed overnight and it felt like my destiny unfolding. I had a new ID, new status and new opportunities being presented to me. It was like I was leading a better life: his life.

LA was exactly the right place for me.

Living under a different name is perfectly normal there: people do it all the time. Think of all the actors and those other folk in Hollywood changing their identities to follow their dreams. It's no big deal. Nobody much cares where you come from: it's where you are going to that matters.

So, I set about reinventing myself. I had the money to dress better, and worked on losing my accent, even had voice lessons to help with that. If I hadn't wanted to attract attention, I might have even had a shot at the movies."

"Congratulations on that accent, by the way, I'm a native and hardly picked you up: just the odd vowel sound here and there."

"The Dodgers even ended up moving out here a couple of years ago. How about that? It was like an omen or something."

"Yeah, how about that? We're getting ahead though. What did you do for money when you were starting out? Your army severance pay can't have lasted forever."

"Right. That's where the furniture came into it: when Eric and I first started bringing stuff over from Europe."

"What gave you the idea?"

He looked at me, like he was weighing up whether or not to tell me something.

"You remember that Italian orderly I told you about in the transit hospital?"

"Sure. What of him?"

"He was called Alessandro and was working there against his will. By that point, the Germans were running things, but he wasn't a fascist like some of the others and realised once we'd invaded the mainland that the war in Italy was coming to an end.

He was from Naples and desperate to get back but stayed on to the end to help in the hospital. Just before I was due to leave, he came to me and said he had something he wanted to talk to me about: a proposal, but that it was risky.

I thought he wanted my help with the authorities or to get him to the US, but it wasn't that. After beating about the bush, he told me a cousin in Naples had discovered a stash of furniture in a warehouse down there; high-quality stuff from all over Europe.

The story was some German general had shipped it

there with a view to getting it away through the port before the end of the war. It was his own personal loot, meant to be headed for South America somewhere on a boat with him on board, only his plan got overtaken by events.

The cousin and some associates had liberated it under the cover of the chaos, but the stuff was way too hot to get rid of over there, without paperwork or proof of ownership. He thought if I could establish a market here, we might be able to sell it to some wealthy Americans. We arranged to stay in touch."

For the second time that evening, the hairs stood up on the back of my neck as the awful truth dawned on me.

"Wait a minute. You're saying you and Eric went into business importing and selling antiques *looted by the Nazis?* You knew where the stuff came from: didn't that bother you?"

He bristled at this, his guilt turning to anger.

"Look Morgan, whoever those people were, they were long dead. How would we ever even trace who had owned what? I'm not proud, but it was too good an opportunity to pass up. Think about it."

"But it was stolen from Jewish people, like you, who were murdered."

He shook his head.

"Whoever those people were, they were nothing like me. They had to have been rich and I was poor: there's a world of difference.

Have you ever been poor, Morgan, I mean really poor; had nothing?"

I thought about it.

"Well, there have been times I've had money and times I've had none. Don't get me wrong, I know which I prefer, but I can't truly say that there was a time I had absolutely nada."

"Well, I have and it's true what they say: when a

man has nothing, he has nothing to lose. I'd had a lifetime of being poor up until then.

Let me tell you what I'd learned about the rich: they have their own morality. Haven't you noticed how they never go to prison, but just get off with a slap on the wrist? The super-rich have politicians and the justice system in their pockets, and failing that, there are people on the payroll to do the dirty work. All at arm's length, so their money stays nice and clean.

They say about the cream that floats to the top of the milk, but if you look carefully, there's always a layer of scum on top."

"What about fighting Fascism and all that?"

"Don't make me laugh, Morgan. Politics is nothing but rich people telling poor people what to do. Power and wealth: it's all the same thing. They go hand in glove."

"What are you then, a Communist? Like those guys over in Cuba?"

"I'm not interested in changing the world, Morgan: that's the kind of thinking that starts wars. I just want to take care of my little corner of it. Anyhow, good luck to them, I say. Haven't they got the right to organise themselves as they see fit?

Human happiness is a rare commodity and I'm all in favour of a man making his own. Isn't that what this country is meant to be all about anyway: the pursuit of happiness?"

He'd given me something to think about, but much as I tried to imagine how a poor orphan from Brooklyn might see the world, it was all a bit too convenient for my liking.

I changed tack.

"So how did it work, the business?"

"I'd been thinking about Alessandro's idea and got in touch with him, via the number in Naples he'd given me, which was for a bar. I thought it was a shot to nothing, but he was there and excited to hear from me. He handled things at that end, and we set up a small shipment, as a trial run."

"What about this end?"

"Eric had been in with the Teamsters in New York, so he knew how to approach the union guys down at the port. My job was to develop the sales network; in fact, my first Hollywood contact came from that voice coach I told you about.

The first shipment went well, and after that Alessandro would send a monthly inventory of what would be coming in: an unbelievable pipeline of stuff to sell. We couldn't miss. Demand was high and after a while he started buying more antiques all over Europe for us and we only moved the occasional bit of the old stock.

One of Eric's fifth army buddies from after my time, Gabriel Battaglia, joined us and went over to work alongside Alessandro. He'd loved Italy, was keen to get back there and it gave the export business an American face, which we thought might attract less attention."

We talked until late about a range of subjects, and drank a fair amount, although it was nothing we weren't both used to, as neither of us were giddy teenagers. At one point in the evening, he shook a couple of anonymous looking tablets from a roll in his pocket and swallowed them, without hiding the fact. I guessed what they were.

"Bennies?"

"You've had them before? You want a couple? I was feeling drowsy."

"Sure, we had them in the navy to keep going on watch. Some of the guys on the PD use them for working nights. No thanks."

"We used them in the army too. They can be useful if you don't get too fond of them. Suit yourself, anyhow."

He didn't strike me as being tired, and Kitty hadn't

mentioned anything about drugs, when I'd asked. Maybe it was another bad habit he had acquired that she didn't know about.

We circled around to Kitty and Janet again.

"The day I married Kitty was the happiest in my life. Then we had the boys. I'd do anything for them, you know. You got kids, Morgan?"

"No. Leastways none I'll own up to."

He laughed.

"Shame. You should try it sometime.

Seriously though, it felt like the wheel had turned and I was at the high point of the ride. All my dreams come true. At the same time, I knew that it couldn't last, though. I had this terrible feeling, like it was all going to come crashing down.

Like my success contained the seeds of its own destruction."

I wanted to probe him about the money.

"So, what happened? Business was good, and you were going legit. Wasn't that enough?"

He thought about it for a while.

"The reproduction business took us in a new direction and was very successful and the aim was to drop the other stuff. Eric always needed more money though; it was never enough for him.

I can't blame him entirely. If somebody says, 'how'd you like to make some more thousands to add to the pile', easy money like that, it's hard to ignore. The lifestyle's got to be maintained, of course."

"Of course. I've seen the Jaguar."

I couldn't keep the edge out of my voice, and he looked at me hard, waving his hand dismissively as he spoke.

"That's just part of the act.

It's not just for me, Morgan: it's all for Kitty and the boys. I wanted to get her away from that bastard Earl and make a new life. He's a piece of work, pure poison, but she's been pampered all her life; had the best of everything. It's not easy to compete with that.

I couldn't hold it all together in the end."

"Why not?"

"I don't want to make excuses, but the war had something to do with it. With Eric, it came out differently; earlier. Eventually he settled on the gambling, like I said, that was his way of dealing with things.

It was easy being him to start with, but the pressure of trying to be a different person, a better person, got to me and I started to drink more than was good for me and things started to spiral at home until they fell apart.

Then the business with his girl Janet coming into my life, *his* life, like that freaked me out. It seemed too much of a coincidence, more like some sort of cosmic justice: kismet, or whatever.

I'd taken her life away once and then, when she fell in love with me, it was like I was taking it away from her all over again."

Maybe he did have a conscience in there somewhere, after all.

"Yeah, that's one hell of a story, Jack, but why are you hiding down here? Why the need to take off in the first place? You don't strike me as the type for dramatic gestures."

He smiled.

"Don't be so sure, Morgan, but as it happens, you're right.

Whatever plays out, I need it well away from Kitty and the boys. Here seems like as good a place as any."

"I found you, which means others will too. Maybe the police."

"It's not them I'm worried about."

A sensation started to grow on me; one I didn't like.

"Just what am I doing here anyway?"

"Let's just say I left a trail of breadcrumbs of sorts:

not just Janet. She's the only one I can really trust now that Eric's gone. I knew anybody who came to the Fairmont through her would be okay.

I left clues in other places pointing in this direction, to bring whoever is behind this down here, where I can deal with them. Then there's you."

I didn't like where this was going but let him carry on, needing to be confronted with the full extent of my foolishness.

"Me?"

"Anybody looking for me just has to follow you."

I was thinking furiously. I had been played and was none too happy about it.

"I was set up. I'm the bait in your trap down here, aren't I?"

"Not by me, Morgan. When you told me back at the Fairmont that Kitty hired you, I had a good idea, but not before. I swear."

"I was nearly killed trying to get to you."

"What you should be asking is who's calling the shots? Kitty might be looking for me, but I doubt it. For what it's worth, my money's on Earl. Either way, once you came on board, they had another lead to follow. You've no idea what that family is capable of. Their crest should be a nest of vipers."

I thought about it. My office had been tossed and I assumed it had been Louis and Al, but maybe I'd been hasty, and it hadn't been them.

"I wasn't tailed here from LA, I'm sure of that."

"Think about it Morgan: they wouldn't have to. If they knew I was somewhere nearby, all they'd have to do is wait for you to show up, then follow you. They'd just have to pick you up outside town somewhere: your Plymouth would be easy enough to spot."

What a prize chump I had been.

"That's what our little procession out here from

the Fairmont was all about. You with that box; showing the rabbit to the dog."

"You catch on quickly."

"Evidently not quickly enough. Here was I thinking we were getting along, but you've been keeping me here talking half the night on purpose. Now, why might that be, I wonder?"

"I like you, Morgan, but thought you might be useful too. Help to even up the odds".

He gestured to the box.

"Men are coming here to get that thing or to kill me. I don't know how many there might be, but you got away from those two heavies, so can obviously handle yourself in a tight spot."

I went to get up but realised I was already on my feet. Somewhere during the last few minutes I'd stood up, shamed by my own stupidity, and enraged by what I was hearing.

If only I'd listened to the voice inside my head earlier that evening: 'that which you seek also seeks you.'

I'd had enough of Jack Conlon and his easy-going morality, or lack thereof. It was too selective for my liking, too unquestioning about the consequences of his actions.

"I'm leaving."

"Don't be angry, Morgan. Like I told you before: these people play by their own rules."

"Whatever is coming for you, you'll have to deal with it yourself."

He was nodding silently as I turned on my heel and went to the other end of the Casa Blanca to collect my things. Still fuming at my own stupidity, I stepped through the front door and into the humid night air.

15. The Boathouse

I didn't hear a shot or pick up a muzzle flash, but as I came out of the front door and was crossing round the side of the house to get my car, a large chunk exploded out of a terracotta pot containing night jasmine on a low wall not far in front of me.

Knowing immediately what it was, I dropped my bag there on the drive, vaulted said wall and threw myself down on the other side, putting it between me and whoever was doing the shooting. I crawled along the lawn there until I was in shadow, then risked a peak, instinctively looking up to the small copse on the hill at the front of the house.

It was a good candidate for where the shot had come from, offering good visibility of the door and most of the frontage of the property. It was where I would have been.

I had trouble adjusting my eyes and couldn't be sure but thought I made out movement up there. It might have been my imagination, or the gunman making his way down the hill to get closer. The plan was probably to bump me off quietly at a distance and then move down to the house, but I had other ideas.

Time to move.

The .38 was in my hand and good for close-up work, but no match for somebody at distance with a hunting rifle or whatever. The chances were he wouldn't be alone, and I made for cover at the back of the house, unsure of whether to expect company.

It was a shaky plan, but I couldn't risk getting pinned down and my car was around towards the back, so that's where I was headed, even if I didn't fancy my chances on the winding driveway. My system was so flushed with adrenaline that I couldn't feel the various parts of my broken body complaining as I did an undignified belly crawl along the length of the wall to its end.

There was a gap there where the drive looped around the house. How I hated that expanse of ground between me and the cover of the wall on the far side, and the gravel surface, which would advertise my every movement. The gunman had probably already worked out where I was making for, but I would be a sitting duck otherwise.

Still in the shadows, I got into a low crouch and readied my gun. Counting down from three in my head and surprising myself by going on two, I sprinted hell for leather across the space, firing twice on the way over. My aim was shaky; a wild guess at where the gunman might be, my chances of hitting anything made all the more unlikely by being on the move.

There was a lean-to with roof and brick columns attached to a wall to the right-hand side of the property which served as the car porch, and another shot slammed into the brickwork over there as I ran, followed by the sounds of a ricochet and roof tiles shattering.

I made it to the other side and jammed myself up against the wall of the house, breathing hard. Again, there was no sound of the actual shot or accompanying muzzle flash, so the odds were the gun was fitted with a suppressor, which could only mean a professional shooter. Feeling my way along the wall, I pressed up tight against it, desperate to make it to the other end and around the corner before he or they caught up with me.

Just then, somebody killed all the lights in the house and around the perimeter, and I guessed Jack had heard my shots and hit the master switch, which was smart thinking. It was darker and I felt a bit safer.

Just as I got to it, a door cracked open about three quarters of the way along the wall and a rifle barrel poked out low down as a familiar voice hissed:

"Morgan: in here!"

I scuttled through and around behind him as he gently closed the door. Moonlight filtered in through a high window somewhere to the otherwise darkened interior and I could make out that we were in kind of short service corridor running out to this side of the house from the kitchen area.

Jack had an M1 carbine, a semi-automatic rifle which had been standard army issue during the war. I had no idea where he'd produced it from, but knew it was illegal and had no doubt he knew how to use it. He was a highly trained soldier and the combination of him, and this lethal weapon made for a formidable pairing, and it was one I was pleased to see under the circumstances.

"That come with the place too? I won't ask if you have a licence for it."

Even in the dark, I could sense him grinning by way of response and marvelled that he was actually enjoying this.

"You'd be amazed what you can bring back from a trip down Mexico way these days. I told you I've been waiting for them."

I was getting to meet a different Jack now: the soldier, his senses sharpened, relishing the fight to come.

"How many?"

"I can't say for sure. My guess is at least two.

One taking pot shots at me with a silencer from up on the hill but moving down here now. I didn't see anyone else, but he'll be sure to have company."

"You figure the other one is down here, around the back maybe or making his way around the far side?"

I nodded.

On cue, there was the sound of glass breaking somewhere over on the other side of the house: a balcony door or a window to one of the bedrooms down where I had been staying.

One of them was inside now.

"Seems like a good time to leave Dodge. You have

a plan, Jack?"?

He nodded in the semi-darkness and whispered.

"The boathouse: they keep a cabin cruiser down at the shore. They won't have got round to it yet and there's only one way down there. Follow me. I have to collect something first."

It was sound thinking; if there were only two of them, then it made sense they would both be occupied up here at the house for now.

If.

He led the way through to the kitchen, where he picked up a small rucksack out by the back door. It was pregnant with ugly, angular bulges. I didn't ask what they were.

"You've thought of everything, huh?"

He ignored this, intent now only on communicating his plan.

"One of them is back there in the house now and the other one will have worked his way around the side to the back soon. We're headed straight out the back about twenty yards directly across to a low line of shrubs back there.

I'll go first and you follow. That way I'll be able to give you cover to the back and the side of the house."

"Okay."

Not twenty minutes before, I'd been sick of Jack Conlon and his world and now I was trusting this man who I hardly knew with my life. It was better than any of the alternatives I could think of.

Jack opened the back door silently. The moon was up far out to sea, casting a watery light back over the landscape, which was both a blessing and a curse: it would aid our progress but make it easier for us to be seen.

He counted down from three with his fingers then sprinted across, putting on a real burst of speed, surprising me with his athleticism. Once in the line of bushes, he squatted and raised the rifle to his shoulder.

There were no shots this time.

He gestured across for me to join the party, and not waiting for a written invitation, I belted for all I was worth across the patio running around the back and tumbled clumsily into the bushes beside him, gun at the ready.

He signalled, two quick gestures with his hand towards the shore, turned and headed into the foliage as I fell in behind him. It was hard work having to keep hunkered down and going forwards at the same time, and he was much better at it than I was.

We picked up the path but kept off it to one side, moving through the shrubbery as quietly as we could. Our progress seemed painfully slow and although I couldn't hear anybody behind us, my imagination was working overtime. I kept looking back over my shoulder, expecting a bullet in the back at any moment.

Eventually the bushes became more spread out as the path wound its way through low sand dunes. I could hear the waves breaking down on the shoreline more clearly and see the outline of a squat building ahead.

As we approached, I could make out a double door at the front of the boathouse, which from above looked to be more of a low shed or wooden shack, nestled into a small bluff where the land gave way to the sea. I wasn't sure what I had been expecting, but the building itself didn't look promising, although the positioning would offer natural shelter and cover, which is probably why Jack had picked this spot for whatever he had in mind.

He must have reconnoitred the spot beforehand and knew to stay away from the front of the building so led the way to the top of some steps set off to the left which wound their way down to the shore at the back.

At the bottom of these we turned right and along a short stretch of quayside next to a small inlet. Built of stone and reassuringly solid, it led to a little jetty projecting out from the back of the boathouse. One of the doors at the back had been left open, presumably by Jack.

Once inside and with the door pulled to again, he produced a flashlight from the rucksack and swept its narrow beam around the interior until he found what he was looking for. There was a kerosene lamp and some matches sitting on a bench with some tools on it at the back, next to the winching gear.

From down here at the back, the structure was taller than at the front; two stories, with the whole thing raised up on thick beams, allowing for the drop where it nestled into the hillside.

The old wooden building would leak light like a colander, so we couldn't risk electric lighting, assuming that there was even any out here. The soft light from a hurricane lamp down at the bottom of the building would probably be safe enough though, as we were tucked under the bluff, away from the house and the path.

Although grateful to be able to see better, I was still nervous when Jack got the lamp lit. The space was U-shaped, with the tall doors we had come through facing out to sea and a gallery up on stilts running around the top on the other three sides. A staircase went up to the gallery, where the door I'd seen from the front was.

The whole thing was built around a narrow basin at the bottom, with a short stretch of slipway opposite the sea doors. Berthed in the space in the middle was a wooden cabin cruiser which we were alongside and which I guessed at slightly over thirty feet. It was already in the water; its dark bulk being slapped rhythmically back and forth by soft waves.

"You're a sailor, Morgan: why don't you look that thing over, check it for fuel and whatnot in case we need it to get away later?"

"Why don't we just go now?"

He shook his head firmly.

"This ends here, tonight. Besides, I don't much care for boats."

"What will you be doing while I'm looking her over?"

"Springing this trap and catching us a rat or two. I'm going back up there to prepare a reception committee. You go if you want to Morgan; I won't hold it against you. This is my fight and I'm taking my chances here."

My turn to shake my head. Whatever this thing was, I was very much a part of it now.

He hefted the rucksack back onto his shoulder. It made a metallic clanking sound as he did so, and I had a pretty good idea what was in it.

"When I'm done, I'll come back round to the door at the back here, so don't get trigger happy. Speaking of which – there's a .45 in here if you want a bigger pea shooter?"

"No. I'll take a couple of those bennies now though if you've still got them."

Since being shot at, I had been running on pure adrenalin, but knew it wouldn't last. This was no time to start feeling drowsy.

"Sure."

He handed me the little roll of pills.

"Give me about twenty minutes. Any longer than that, you take off in the boat and save your own skin."

I nodded and checked my watch as he set off.

After he'd left, I stepped aboard and busied myself with the little boat. I couldn't really claim to be much of a sailor, and it had been some time since I'd last messed about in the things, but it was familiar territory and the knowledge I might be doing something practical to improve our chances steadied me.

It might have been part of Jack's plan: giving me something to do to take my mind off things. Whatever the case, the boat regarded me indifferently, as if it might just

be about to set off on a pleasure cruise or a fishing trip, which is what I guessed it was used for.
Up close I could see that she was a hard top cruiser, about thirty-six feet long and powerful looking, with sleek lines.

Stepping across from the dock into the cockpit, I found the key in the ignition and although couldn't risk turning her over, carefully rotated it one notch around. The ignition light came on, followed by the gauges flickering into life, which was a good sign.

The fuel indicator settled at three quarters full, and the voltage looked good, but I wouldn't know about the oil pressure or the temperature until we were under way. Still, she seemed to be well maintained, and I had a pretty good idea she would start when asked to, which made me feel better.

The wheel and the rudder were moving freely and the settings for the throttle and the forward and reverse gears were as I expected them to be. Dialling back the ignition, I stepped off to arrange the mooring lines so that we could cast off in a hurry if necessary.

This was essentially a pleasure cruiser, primed and ready to go, and it occurred to me that there might be the odd bottle around, so I stepped back on board and into the covered cabin area, flicked open my lighter - 'all the better to see you with Grandma' – and jackpot! There was a fully stocked bar in miniature towards the bow over on the starboard side. It even had a couple of bar stools in front.

Aside from needing something to wash down the pills, I was going to need all the courage I could summon and wasn't fussy about whether some of it might come from a bottle. I liberated what looked like a good brandy, squeezed out the cork, and downed a couple of the bennies.

Suitably fortified, I stepped off and across to the other side of the boathouse, where I folded back and secured the door as quietly as I could. When all this was finished, I dimmed the hurricane lamp right down and waited at the back door by the quayside, where we had come in. Keeping the .38 in my hand and the brandy close by, I felt fraudulent and vaguely foolish sitting there and playing the soldier, or the sailor, come to that.

Jack came back after fifteen long minutes which dialled my anxiety levels right up. I heard movement on the quay outside before he hissed at me in a stage whisper.

"Morgan, it's me, don't shoot."

In spite of everything, I was pleased to see him. The rucksack he'd been carrying looked lighter and less bulky than before, without the metallic looking bulges.

"Okay, we're all set.

You take shore watch: keep an eye on the back here in case they work their way around from further along. I doubt they will, but it's possible."

"Right."

"I'm going to wait for them up by the path but can be down here in no time if you need me."

He checked his rifle and busied himself taking a couple of spare magazines out of the rucksack.

"Say; you sure you don't want that bigger piece?"

"No thanks."

While I'd been waiting for him, I'd cleared and reloaded my .38, which gave me six shots. I figured that if it took any more than that I was done for in any case.

I offered him the bottle and he took a big hit from it.

"Okay then. Be ready."

"What's the signal if they come?"

"You'll know when you hear it.

Oh, and Morgan, one more thing: keep clear of the path back to the house."

"And why might that be?"

He grinned, and I knew for sure then what had been in the rucksack and had a strong sense this was going to end badly. He spoke over his shoulder to me as he was going.

"Stay lucky."

"I intend to. You too."

I settled down to my night watch at the back door of the boathouse, with half an eye on the stairs up to the gallery off to my right. I wondered whether I might be better off on the upper level, but figured it made more sense to stay close to the boat.

Turning the lamp out fully, I let my eyes adjust to the moonlight filtering in through the back doors. It wasn't long before I had a slight buzz from the bennies and felt alert enough to risk another hit from the brandy.

They came about a half hour later, as I knew they must at some point.

There was a loud noise from somewhere up on the path outside: something like a flat crack and a crump together. At the same time, the front of the boathouse above me was peppered with shrapnel, punching tiny, spherical holes clean through it. A mine or a grenade of some sort had gone off up there.

The trap had been sprung and this was the signal for sure.

Immediately after this came the sound of rifle shots, a staccato of ones and twos, which I took to be Jack opening up with the M1, followed by a longer burst from an automatic weapon returning fire. I kept my head down low to the ground, waiting for the outcome.

A tense couple of minutes stretched by, and unable to take the waiting any longer, I steeled myself and ventured out to the quayside to meet my fate. Sometimes it comes down to a moment of action, weighed in the balance against a lifetime of regret. That or oblivion, and no lifetime at all.

I made the corner at the bottom of the steps and Jack called down to me urgently from above.

"Morgan, up here! Quick!"

I stumbled up the uneven steps and joined him not far from the path at the top where he was crouched next to a body.

"He's dead. I hit the other one, but he's only wounded.
Get rid of this one: use the boat."

Jack was breathing hard, and his speech was unnatural; strained.

"Thing is...he clipped me too. In the leg."

He indicated his left thigh, where there was a dark patch of blood. He popped a couple of little white pills which I guessed were painkillers, probably oral morphine of some sort.

"This is serious, Jack. This wound needs seeing to. We'll have to..."

He interrupted me sharply:

"No time. He'll be making for his vehicle. I'm going after him. Take this. You'll know what to do with what's inside."

He swung the little rucksack round to me, then took the emerald, still wrapped in a handkerchief, out of his pocket and handed it to me.

"This too."

When Jack told me what he wanted done with the emerald if he didn't make it back, I was surprised, but when I thought about it later there may have been a sort of logic, or at least symmetry to it.

"I'm trusting you to do the right thing, Morgan. Stay lucky."

Without waiting for a reply, he set off up the path, grunting with pain and using his rifle as a sort of crutch, leaving me with the dead man, frantically wondering what my next move should be.

I rolled him over, away from the path to get a better look in the moonlight. It wasn't a pretty sight. He must have been very close to the explosion, which had taken half of his face off: his own mother wouldn't have recognised him.

Going through his pockets, I found the thing I least wanted to. Even as I opened the wallet, I could feel the weight and make out the outline of the shield it contained. Flipping it out and tilting it to the moonlight with a sinking feeling I read the name on his credentials, which identified him as a police officer. Whatever I was involved in had just got a whole lot worse.

I knew him. It was Rudy Baker, LAPD, a dirty cop. Our paths had crossed before when he had worked vice at the same time I was over on homicide. Violent and to my certain knowledge corrupt, he was known to control his patch using what were euphemistically known as 'old fashioned' policing methods. We hated each other, and I wasn't sorry to see him dead.

Whatever else he may have been though, Baker was a serving police officer, and I was none too happy to have played a part in that death, even if it wasn't me who killed him.

Making a conscious effort to calm myself, I sat there trying to think the situation through, whilst listening closely to try and work out what might be playing out up above.

The way I saw it, my options were limited.

I couldn't call it in. There had been gunplay and getting caught down here with a dead LAPD officer - one I was known to have some personal history with – would mean a spell in San Quentin followed by a visit to the gas chamber for sure. I didn't need to consult the California penal code to work that one out.

Baker was out of his territory down here, which was unusual but could be explained by him looking for Jack. What with the silencer and the clear intent to kill, I was sure this wasn't an official operation, which got me around to thinking about who his partner might be.

Hand in glove with his day job, which afforded the perfect cover, Baker was rumoured to have been moonlighting as an underworld enforcer. I suspected he had a hand in at least one of the homicides I had investigated, where some evidence had conveniently gone missing.

The victim in that case was a convicted pimp and probable dope dealer, who nobody had shed any tears over, and had been beaten to death. There were rumours at the time that it was on account of his debts and allegations were made, although none of the witnesses went on record about it, for the sake of their health.

It was an even money bet that Baker's partner would be one Kurt Taylor, another nasty piece of work and a drinking buddy. Older and less well known to me, Taylor was also of this parish, so to speak and worked on the department, but before my time.

He transferred over to the LA County Sheriff's department after some unpleasantness involving the death in custody of an armed robbery suspect. It wasn't uncommon back in the day for interrogations to get a little too enthusiastic and for suspects to confess to multiple crimes, which helped with the clean-up rate.

Again, nothing was ever proven, but there was a cloud attached to both their names amongst decent officers, even if some of the senior ranks seemed to care more about their results than their methods. The corrupt actions of men like these and others doing nothing to prevent them, were why I had quit the force.

Whoever Baker's partner was, I couldn't be sure either of them had been trying to kill me or I just got in the way when they were looking for the box, or for Jack. On the other hand, they may have known I was here; followed me down from the city or waited for me to show up, like Jack said.

The more I thought about it, I realised it might have been these two who ransacked my office. It was chilling to think they might have been after me. I needed to find out who they were working for but would have to get myself out of my immediate predicament first.

A long ten minutes had gone by since the explosion and the gunplay, but there were no sirens up above, meaning this probably hadn't been officially sanctioned police business. Out here on this isolated headland, the small explosion from an anti-personnel device or the gunfire might not have registered with anybody else either.

Listening very carefully, I made out an engine gunning into life somewhere further away and another one closer by shortly afterwards, then the faint sound of gravel churning up by the house as a car peeled off. Their ride must have been out at the top of the drive as I hadn't spotted it earlier, so even money this was the other guy going, followed by Jack in the station wagon.

That left the Plymouth up above. I still had the keys in my pocket, and it was an undeniable link between me and what had happened here; one that would give me away for sure if anybody came looking.

Then there was Baker's body. If that was found here, the police would be all over the house and grounds and were bound to turn up other physical evidence, like my fingerprints, which would be everywhere.

I cursed myself and my situation.

If there were others who knew where Baker was, the game might be up, though he was a maverick operator and this was off the books, so maybe not. His partner might be able to get a message back before Jack caught up with him, but I couldn't worry about that right now.

Thinking with a cool head, I realised Jack was right: if I got rid of the body, there would be no reason for the police or whoever to come looking here or to connect Baker's disappearance back to either of us.

I picked up his gun and even with gravity on my side, had difficulty manhandling the body off the path and back down the steps to the shore; stopping more often than I would have liked to get my breath. Dragging the dead weight along the quayside and into the boathouse was hard work.

Inside, I got the lamp relit and busied myself finding something to wrap the body in. There was a pile of old gunny sacks upstairs on the gallery and some tarpaulins next to these. I picked out the oldest looking oil stained one and took it down to the boat.

On the way back down, I spied a fuse box mounted on the wall by the front door and a light switch below and to one side, which I guessed would be linked to a gantry switch somewhere at the bottom of the stairs. Needing to work quickly, and reasoning it was the lesser of two evils, I threw the switch, and the boathouse was illuminated by a couple of bare bulbs hanging high up, one at either end of the building.

It was risky, but I reasoned that the immediate danger outside had passed. There was little chance of me guiding the boat back in without light and hanging around until after daybreak wasn't an option.

Spreading the tarpaulin out on the aft deck next to the cockpit, I set about the difficult business of hauling the body on board, nearly dropping him into the basin at the last minute, which would have been a disaster.

I made sure that the doors on the oceanside were fully open and tied back, and that the winching gear at the back was disengaged, then went up to the bow to let go of the line there, returning to untie her at the stern.

Moving her forwards along the dock with a boathook and away from the short slipway at the back was tricky, but I needed to make sure the propellers were in deeper water before starting her up.

When I was sure this was the case, I turned her over and the engine sprang into life, sounding impossibly harsh and loud to my jittery ears in the still night. With the throttle at idling speed and engaging a forward gear, we were underway out into the darkness, and I was thankful that it was calm, with little wind.

We might have been putting out to sea for a spot of gentle night fishing or a cruise, but instead, I was setting off with my grisly cargo, wondering what I was doing. As I guided the small craft out along the jetty, I was grateful to see a light further along it on a short lamp post which would serve as a navigation light for the journey back.

I couldn't risk getting lost along the coastline and went as far out as I dared without losing sight of the lights in the boathouse, shrinking behind me. Once we had gone far enough, I pushed Baker's body over the side and threw his gun and wallet with the badge in after him. I fished around in the rucksack for the other .45 and threw that in too.

It had been them or us and I didn't suffer from sentimentality or say any last words or prayers: just heaved his remains overboard, then washed down the tarpaulin and the aft deck with a couple of buckets of seawater to get rid of the blood. I've wondered since about that moment and how strange it was he should share this final act with me of all people.

I had no idea what would become of his body, whether the currents and the tide would bring him back in somewhere or whether the sharks might get to him before that. It was by no means foolproof, but I couldn't afford to worry about it at the time. The wind had started to pick up and it took all my concentration to get back to the boathouse and manoeuvre the cruiser back into the berth.

Relieved there was no reception committee waiting, I checked my watch to find that a couple of hours had passed since Jack had gone after the other gunman. I didn't bother to reverse her in and probably couldn't have managed the winching gear on my own in any case, so just cut the engines and tied her up as best I could there at the mooring. Whoever looked after her would know that she'd been out, but I figured that would be the case anyway.

After securing the back doors to the boathouse, I folded and took the tarpaulin back to the upper level, where I stacked it under the others. Then bringing the rucksack and the bottle along for company, I killed the lights and went out through the front door.

The wind had picked up and the weather was changing fast, with cloud rolling in obscuring the moon and throwing the landscape into deeper shadow. I had to use the flashlight from the rucksack to pick my way back to the house.

Remembering what Jack said about the path, I stayed to one side of it, watching my footing carefully and checking for trip wires. Somebody had come this way as there were little pools of his blood dotted along; maybe his or the other guy's, who knew?

There wouldn't have been much point in him setting more than one booby trap, but I looked diligently as it wouldn't do to have the gardener getting blown up the next day. It just wouldn't be fair on the poor sap. There was remarkably little physical evidence of what had taken place, probably because it played out in the open, down by the shore and away from the house.

There were a few extra holes in the rickety boathouse, some broken tiles and whatnot and some shell casings, but I couldn't afford to worry about that and none of them could be tied back to me. Then there was a small crater and some blood in the sand amongst the dunes and along the path, but that would barely be noticeable after the next rain.

The urge to get straight in my car and head off was strong, but I wasn't feeling too good. Holding my nerve, I reminded myself that nobody had come yet and another ten minutes getting into better shape would be time well spent.

The door to the kitchen was open and I went through various cupboards until I found coffee and set a pot to boil on the stove. Then I went into the nearest bathroom and washed my face and hands and set about generally cleaning up my appearance, superficially at least.

There were a few new minor cuts and scrapes on top of the old ones, although I was careful not to examine my reflection too closely, in case I didn't like who I saw.

Back in the kitchen, I drank strong black coffee, scolding hot, as quickly as I dared without burning myself and weighed up the idea of trying to wipe down my fingerprints in the house. In the end I figured it would be hopeless and too time consuming, even if I could remember where I'd been, so simply didn't bother.

I'd pushed my luck far enough and needing to get going, picked up the rucksack and headed for the back door. Having an idea, I doubled back to the living room, and collected the box from where Jack had left it earlier, figuring it might prove useful.

This time I made it out to my car without incident and retrieved my overnight bag from where I'd dropped it earlier, scooped it up and set it in the trunk alongside the box. Sliding in behind the wheel, I fished the .38 out of my jacket pocket and tossed it on the passenger seat next to the rucksack.

As I did so, I felt the emerald wrapped up in the handkerchief and realised I had forgotten all about the thing since Jack had given it to me. I'm not usually given to irrational nonsense, but had a sudden and powerful insight, a moment of absolute clarity: I knew beyond doubt that it was cursed and resolved to get rid of it at the earliest opportunity.

It was a quarter past four in the morning as I pulled out of the driveway of the Casa Blanca back onto the main road and into the rain which had been threatening. It would make my drive back harder but would wash away the evidence of my sins, if not the deeds themselves.

   Unsure of what I was engaged in, other than saving my own hide, I was grateful nonetheless that my luck was holding, although I'd been gambling with it since the day Kitty walked into my office. If I had known then what I knew now, I would have thrown her out on her beautiful ear.

16. A Bend in the Road

The crash site was just to the south of Encinitas, at a sweeping right-hand bend on the road high above a ravine. I had a pretty good idea what had happened the moment I saw the highway patrol car with a recovery truck at the side of the road and the broken barrier on the ocean side.

It was raining harder as I headed north back towards the city, but there were tyre marks just visible on the verge, meaning it must have happened an hour or two back when it was dry; about when Jack would have been coming through.

There was no other traffic at this early hour and not wanting to look suspicious, I slowed down, pulled over and stuck my head out of the window to ask a question of the tow truck driver, like any curious passer-by might do.

He was leaning against the open door of his cab smoking and taking shelter from the rain.

"What happened?"

"A couple of cars went off the road on the bend there a couple of hours back. The officer here told me they picked up a Ford coupe and a station wagon speeding further south and were in pursuit when they went over the edge."

Jack and whoever he was chasing. I felt nauseous thinking about it and grimaced.

"Any survivors?"

He shook his head.

"Not a chance. It's a sheer drop over a hundred feet down to rocks below."

"I see."

"It'll be light soon and we'll be able to get a line down there. The tide will be out enough to reach the wreckage then.

Most of the accidents out here at night are down to the weather, or a single wreck; some guy falling asleep at the wheel. Funny thing is this happened before the rain came, though. Bad luck, I guess.

Probably out here racing each other and lost control. You know what these young guys are like."

"Yah, I do."

One of them must have been trying to run the other off the road at the bend but they'd both ended up going over.

Just then the patrolman waved me on, and I was more than happy to oblige. I held my hand up to them both as I pulled off, hoping my luck would hold and he hadn't taken my licence plate number. He had no reason to, but you never know.

I didn't hang about and wanted to be home in case the police came around asking awkward questions. Nonetheless, I eased off the gas a bit after the crash site and took it easy on the bends.

My head was reeling as I tried to think things through on the way back to the city. Baker was dead and so were Jack and whoever he had been chasing, which got me around to thinking who that other somebody might be.

It was an even money bet that Baker's partner would turn out to be Kurt Taylor, rumoured to be his partner in crime as well as his one-time partner in policing. A neat fit if you stop to think about it. There was a nagging sensation at the back of my mind that they had something else in common, but not recalling what it was, I had to let it go.

The car lying at the bottom of the ravine would likely be registered to either Baker or his partner or could even be a police department vehicle. Once they reached the wreck, it wouldn't take long to identify who was in it.

There would be some head scratching at headquarters while they tried to figure out what it was doing way down here in Encinitas and even more when Rudy Baker didn't turn up for duty. Eventually they'd wonder why his body hadn't been in the car or brought in with the next tide.

Jack Conlon might be another story though: he might not have been carrying any identification and there was no way of tying the station wagon back to him. They might find weapons and explosives in the car, which would give them something to work with, but the odds were it would take longer to identify him, which might buy me a little time.

He was a fugitive wanted for murder though, and they knew I was looking for him, so would pay me another visit for sure when they worked it out.

For my part, there was nothing much to say I'd ever been in Del Mar. I'd registered at the Fairmont under an assumed name, but even if the police went asking questions, Jack hadn't been staying there. Besides, the owner was a friend of his, so wouldn't be volunteering anything.

One of the gunmen might have identified me and placed a call, but that would have had to have been before events unfolded as they did, so I thought it unlikely. If there had been a third member of their team, that person would have recovered the box, so the odds were against it: it said two-man job to me.

There was little physical evidence back at the Casa Blanca, even assuming anybody went looking for it. If what Jack said about the powerful people who owned and used the place was right, they had an interest in covering things up.

There was no way of tying him back to the place, and they wouldn't be in a hurry to advertise the fact he'd been there. If it came down to it, his presence could be explained away as a break-in and the car as having been stolen. Besides, words could always be had, and pressure brought to bear to see they were kept out of it.

Sometimes the best course of action is to do nothing and

the more I thought about it, the only play that seemed to make sense was to slip back into the city, act normally and see how things played out. I reckoned it might be a day or two at the most before they came around asking questions and when they did, I'd play dumb.

There were a couple of matters I needed to attend to first, though.

I had a priceless gemstone in my pocket and the box in the trunk of my car, neither of which belonged to me, but could bring me a lot of trouble. The box could be traced to Jack and his partner, Eric Jenner, both now late of this parish. Getting caught with it might put me in the frame for murder and that was only with the police, who weren't the only ones looking.

How easy it might have been to head south instead and disappear over the border with the emerald. Easier still to have carried on down to Mexico in the cabin cruiser if it had only entered my head at the time. It would have been a one-way ticket though, what with no passport, a stolen boat and my car left behind at the house - especially if Baker's body was swept into shore.

Still, a lot of wrinkles can be smoothed out when you have got one of the world's largest gemstones in your pocket. I played with the idea without a great deal of conviction as I drove north, knowing myself well enough to recognise it for the fantasy it was. Much as we like to play make-believe or hide from ourselves, we are confronted with who we really are in the end.

There is a truck stop just outside of San Clemente before the 101 divides and I pulled in as the sun was beginning to light the underside of the clouds, to get a coffee from the stand. I was out of luck on that front as there was no sign of life and the board said it wouldn't open until six thirty.

Feeling wretched, I resisted the temptation to take more bennies and breakfasted on a nip of brandy instead, got out to stretch my legs, then sat back in my car. There were a couple of lamp posts in the parking area, which made it light enough for me to see without being easily observed from outside, which suited my purposes.

Since the immediate danger had passed, I slipped the .38 back into its holster and hauled the rucksack over onto my lap to take a proper look inside, as I hadn't had the chance since Jack handed it over. As well as the .45 which I had tossed, there were a few other items which I laid out on the passenger seat one by one to examine them.

First, there was a large manilla envelope addressed to Jack at the apartment, containing the surveillance photo of Kitty and the two boys. On the back of it was an address I didn't recognise but guessed was where he had been meant to deliver the box.

Next came a letter addressed to Kitty, which was sealed and contained a small, hard object of some kind. Then there was a stack of hundred-dollar bills held together with a rubber band. I didn't count them there and then, but it looked to be several thousand dollars' worth.

When I turned it over, there was a piece of paper on the bottom of the bundle. It was a short list scribbled in pencil in Jack's hand and obviously written in haste. There were three names written under each other, which read 'Marty, Agnes, Morgan'.

I guessed the letter to Kitty had been written in advance, sometime over the last week or so when he had been waiting for events to unfold. The hurried note was different though, and since I featured in it, must have been written at some point since yesterday evening. He must have scribbled it back at the house, or even up there on the cliff somewhere: either way, it was one of the last things he did and must have been important to him.

I took it that these were the names he wanted the money to go to. Marty and Agnes, I understood, as people he felt he owed and wanted to help, but why would he want me to have money, other than for giving them theirs? He knew I was already being paid by Kitty, so there had to be more to it.

What was it he had said? That I'd know what to do with what was inside the rucksack and he was trusting me to do the right thing. At the time, I thought he meant with the emerald, but now I realised that it wasn't just that. That was what the photograph meant: he wanted me to investigate and find out who or what was behind it all if he didn't make it.

I'd never had a dead client before, but there's a first time for everything. That had to be what my share of the money was for, although I had my own reasons for wanting to see this thing through now.

There were some heavier items nearer the bottom of the bag, and I pulled two out together. One was a spare clip with what looked like .30-06 rounds, which I took to be for the M1. It wouldn't do to be caught with that, especially if they recovered the rifle from Jack's car, so I'd have to get rid of it somewhere.

The other felt like a loose bullet but turned out to be small silver propelling pencil of antique manufacture. It matched back to the list of names, lending weight to my theory about where and when it had been written.

A small round weight had rolled down into one corner at the bottom of the bag and initially I mistook it for the emerald but realised that was already safely wrapped up in my pocket. My hand closed around something hard and metallic and there was a moment of panic as I pulled it out and recognised what it was: Jack had gifted me a hand grenade.

I didn't know a lot about the things but knew enough to check the pin with the pull ring was still in and the lever attached, which calmed my nerves. The thing was live though, and I put it away gingerly in the glove box, making a little nest for it from some ties I kept in there. I'd have get rid of that too, but how and where? It wasn't the kind of thing that could be tossed in the trash with a clear conscience.

More awake now, I started to formulate a plan. There was a lot of ground to cover, but I reckoned on having a twenty-four-hour head start before the police made the identification on Jack and came looking for me, maybe longer if I was lucky. That was something. I had no way of knowing who else might be looking and what they knew about my involvement, so had to assume the worst.

Kitty was still my client for the time being and I needed to see her, although it felt risky. She needed to know about Jack, and I didn't want her to find that out from the police, even if I wasn't sure what version of events I could tell her. I owed her that much, but another part of me also wanted to see how she took the news. Besides, I had the things to give her from him too.

Having had an idea, there was a particular stop I wanted to make on the way back to the city, so I set off, taking the southern portion of 101 where it runs along the coast. I wanted to find a stretch of shore that was well frequented and not too pristine and stopped at Huntington beach, which fit the bill at the time, although they've cleaned it up since.

Still early, there was nobody about as I went for a stroll along the beach, trying for all the world to look nonchalant, like I was out blowing away the cobwebs. I walked down to the shoreline and further away from the pier with the ocean on my left, with the tide coming in.

I lit a cigarette for cover, all the while looking down at the sand as I went along. To a casual observer I must have looked very like a beachcomber, which in a sense I was, although I was after something specific.

Eventually, I found what I was looking for on a stretch underneath the old oil derricks, where there was a debris field which included a fair amount of old glass. My earlier observations about the emerald had given me an idea and I picked out some pieces roughly the same size and weight as the stone in my pocket.

Turning them over, I selected a particularly attractive one and discarded the others. It was an oval of thick glass, probably from the bottom of a bottle, the edges washed smooth by the action of the sea. It shone bright green when held up to the light of the sun, which was now up.

It looked more like my mental picture of what an emerald should look like than the real thing, and although it wouldn't fool anybody who knew what they were looking at, might work for a while if placed where somebody expected to find one. I grinned childishly at my discovery and at the thought of the deception, wondering if some old Spaniard had used a similar trick to swindle an old Mexican out of the thing, exchanging it for some glass beads way back when.

Slipping the piece of glass into my jacket pocket next to the stone, I was heading back to my car when I remembered the spare magazine for the rifle and walked back down to the edge of the shoreline.

Glancing up like a guilty schoolboy to check I wasn't being watched and timing the gap between the breaking waves, I tossed the clip out into the sea as far as I could, with an action like skimming a stone. I watched it bounce and then sink with a satisfying plop, far enough out I was sure it wouldn't turn up again. It reminded me of the grenade back in my glove box, but I'd have to find a safer way to dispose of that.

Walking back to the Plymouth with less to occupy my mind, it was difficult not to think about Jack going over the barrier and I bid him a silent farewell there on the beach, telling him I would honour my promise and do right by him.

All thoughts of breakfast disappeared as I reached the city and started to flag badly. Concentrating hard, it was all I could do to navigate the morning traffic; never much more than a series of controlled near misses at the best of times.

All I could think of was the sleep I so desperately needed and had been denied back at the Casa Blanca with its luxurious bed. It seemed like that was a century ago and it felt impossible and confusing that it had been only the night before. My apartment lacked the grandeur of the set up there, but I couldn't think of anywhere I'd rather be than my own bed. It might have been safer to avoid the place altogether and book into a hotel somewhere, but the hour was too early for that, and it was too late in another sense.

Eventually I made it home and after parking in front of my apartment block, gathered various bits and pieces together from around the car into the rucksack and made my way round to the trunk to get my Gladstone bag and the box. I thought about leaving the overnight bag behind but needed my wash kit and didn't have the energy for more than one trip.

Feeling conspicuous and struggling with the cumbersome baggage, I made my way the to the door, acutely aware of the vulnerable moment when setting the bags down and fishing out my keys, unsure if I would be able to get to my gun quickly enough if anything happened.

After a repeat of the matinee performance at the door of my own apartment, I relaxed a little once inside, relieved there was nobody there to meet me and that the place hadn't been ransacked. Admittedly I was setting a low bar, but I took it to be a good sign.

It was not long after eight, but I called Kitty straight away and told her I needed to see her. We made an appointment for her to stop by the office at eleven thirty, when the boys would be safely at their schooling. It would also allow me time to get a little rest and a bite to eat, as well as getting my story straight.

Before hitting the hay, I transferred the gemstone and grenade to the small wall safe behind the mirror in my living room. They made for an oddly matched pair sitting in there, each as deadly as the other in its own way.

I left the box by the coffee table in the living room and set the decoy glass emerald down next to my .38 on the nightstand. Not trusting myself to get into bed completely, I took off my jacket and tie, kicked off my shoes and lay down on top of the covers, before setting the alarm for ten.

As sleep came for me, I was wondering about my fate. If I was being watched, they'd know for sure now where I was and that I had the box and whatever it contained. They might come for me, here in my apartment, but I was too tired to worry about that. I'd have to take my chances: let them come if they must.

I had a dark and troubling dream in which a Conquistador was whispering menacingly close to my ear, the same phrase over and over in Spanish, but couldn't make out what he was saying.

17. Bagman

A couple of hours of shuteye was better than nothing, and I felt more normal after my morning routine of shaving and showering followed by steaming hot black coffee, although still tired and jittery from the after-effects of the Benzedrine.

I dressed soberly in a navy-blue lounge suit, black shoes, and understated tie, checked the mirror, and was moderately pleased at the overall effect. I looked every inch like an executive getting ready for a day at the office, albeit one with more scrapes and bruises than normal and carrying a .38.

It was time to do some proper sleuthing rather than running around getting shot at, and there was a lot of ground to cover. I began with a call to my messaging service, grateful there was nothing requiring my immediate attention. The only thing out of the ordinary was that somebody had tried to get hold of me several times without leaving a message, which might have meant something, or nothing.

I'd opened the box earlier and carefully set the substitute piece of glass and the other objects back in the secret drawer. Then I'd fetched the real emerald from the safe and been spooked again by the grenade sitting in there. I found a small box with satin lining my wristwatch had come in and sat the stone neatly in there, wrapped the little package in brown paper tied neatly with string, and addressed it to the person Jack told me to.

Both were items I was keen not to have in my possession if the police were to come calling and I knew better than to hang onto them. The box could tie me back to Jack and the emerald would be difficult to explain under any circumstances.

The weather had worsened, and the rain was coming down hard, so I added a hat and raincoat to my wardrobe, placed the small box in my pocket and headed to Union Station. Having deposited the larger box at the luggage store and exchanged it for a ticket again, I wandered over to the bank of coin lockers on the side wall of the main hall and trying to look casual, left the small package in one and pocketed the key.

Breathing easier, I made for the office, parked up and went to the diner across the street to take in a simple breakfast of eggs over easy, white toast and black coffee, before my appointment with Kitty. Sitting there in a booth, I chased my tail wondering about whether I was or wasn't being watched, which didn't do my digestion any good.

Eventually I gave up thinking about it, settled my tab and headed over to the office. It was just after eleven when I gathered the post from the cubbyhole downstairs and cautiously headed up.

The place had been left pretty much as it was after being ransacked the previous weekend and although I had no right to expect any different, the fact was still an affront to me. Kitty was due at eleven thirty, which gave me a little time to tidy up beforehand.

After files were back in the cabinet, desk drawers relocated, furniture straightened up and the pot plant put back on its stand in the corner, things didn't look so bad. There was still the broken door jamb at the outer door, which I'd have to get seen to, but the rest of the damage was largely superficial.

When everything was done, I sat down and wrote two self-addressed envelopes for mailing later: one for the locker key and the other for the luggage ticket. Then I started work on the other items Jack had given me.

First there was the letter for Kitty, which I smoothed out and placed in the middle of the desk in front of me.

Then the surveillance photograph of her and the children with the address on the back, which I slid into one of the drawers so she wouldn't catch sight of it.

Next came Jack's hastily scribbled note with the bundle of money and the names, including mine. Taking two more envelopes, I wrote 'Marty' on one and 'Agnes' on the other, then counted the money and sat there trying to decide how much Jack wanted them to have. There was six thousand dollars in total.

The easy thing would be two divide it into three lots of two, meaning a handsome payday for yours truly, but I couldn't square things with my conscience that way. If I was going down that road, why not just take it all? Jack had got me mixed up in a whole heap of trouble, but he'd saved my skin at the Casa Blanca and trusted me to do the right thing.

I reasoned that the names had been written down in the order in which they came to him, most likely their order of importance. Mine came at the end because he was paying me to see things through. Not just the disbursements, but to investigate Eric's murder and to check out that address; the one on the photograph now in my desk.

When I stopped to think about it, him being my client wasn't all that strange and I figured I'd be finished working for Kitty shortly, so didn't see why not. In that case, the honest thing to do would be to take an amount for myself as a retainer based on a day rate and likely expenses, like with any other client. I settled on five hundred dollars as a reasonable amount I could justify to myself.

That left five thousand five hundred dollars for the other two. Acting as his de facto executor, I agonised over the decision, weighing out their relative needs and the debt that he might have owed them, trying but failing to summon up the wisdom of Solomon.

In the end, the way I saw it, Marty was first on the list and my judgement was his needs were greatest and his ability to meet them were least, so he should get the most. Agnes would probably lose her job, since with two of the directors dead, the company would likely close, meaning there was a debt to be paid to her also. Balanced against this was the fact she was young and spirited, and struck me as extremely capable, so would find another position with little trouble.

You can never tell with two people, and I speculated whether Jack's relationship with her might have gone further but thought not and decided the nature of the debt he owed to her was from employer to employee.

Acting quickly, I put three thousand five in the envelope for Marty and two thousand in the other, then sealed both and put the one for Agnes away in the wall safe before I could change my mind. Turning back from the safe to my desk, a familiar voice called from the outside lobby, causing my stomach to tighten.

"You know you should do something about your security, Morgan; just about anybody could walk in here off the street."

Kitty came in without knocking and was busying herself shaking out an umbrella and easing herself out of a raincoat. She looked up at me and froze midway through.

"He's dead, isn't he?"

The look on my face must have told her. That and the fact I was stood there awkwardly like an undertaker in my most sombre suit; probably in a subconscious attempt to avoid saying the words. I found myself distractedly turning the letter from Jack over in my hands.

"I believe so, yes. I can't be absolutely certain, but I think the police will be paying you a visit soon."

She stood there inside the door of the office, dripping rainwater, which started to form a pool on the floor. Slowly, she resumed her movements and extricated herself from the raincoat, revealing an exquisitely tailored charcoal grey two-piece.

"What happened?"

Always having preferred sins of omission to outright lying, I opted for a simple version of events and stuck to the facts. Well, some of them, anyway.

"I traced your husband to a place near San Diego, we met up and talked. He was expecting trouble and was there to keep whatever it was away from you and the boys.

He left ahead of me and there was an auto wreck on the way back; a fatal one, which may or may not have been an accident. The car he was driving was one of the vehicles involved. It would have been over very quickly."

Her head was cast down and she was looking up at me from underneath.

"Just before he set off, he gave me this."

Kitty approached the desk and I handed her the letter. She opened it immediately and as she unfolded it, the small object I'd felt inside fell out with a flash of gold, bounced on the desk, and rolled towards me. It was a ring; a wedding band, which I stopped from falling off the edge and handed to her.

"I'm sorry. For what it's worth, I liked your husband. In the few hours we spent together it was clear to me he loved you and the boys very much."

She took a pause.

"I loved him too, just couldn't live with him. I knew something like this would happen one day. The boys are all that matter now."

She looked unbearably beautiful and sad at that moment and her grief seemed very real.

"Listen Mrs. Conlon, it's important the police don't know I found him. They warned me off before and it could spell trouble for me if they do."

"You took a risk bringing me this, Morgan."

"I have a couple of other things. This."

I handed her the antique silver propelling pencil, which had been in my jacket pocket, and she smiled, recognition tinged with sadness.

"I gave him this you know, to make notes when he was with clients."

"There's also quite a large antique box, containing some sort of musical instrument. I don't have it here now, but it might be of some value. It has something to do with his disappearance. Would you happen to know anything about it?"

It wasn't the best time to be asking, but I needed to see her reaction and know what she did about the thing.

Kitty shrugged.

"I don't know anything about an old box or any instrument."

"You'll be wanting it though?"

She shook her head, dismissively.

"There's enough of Jack's junk from the shop lying around the place: if it's got anything to do with all of this, I don't want it."

"What shall I do with it?"

"Why don't you keep it, Morgan."

It obviously meant nothing to her. I nodded.

"Well, okay then, if you're sure.

Mrs. Conlon, I can't say I really know or understand much of what has taken place, but it might be a good idea to take some extra precautions, just in case."

She looked at me levelly.

"Such as?"

"Do you keep a gun in the house?"

"No. I can't stand the things."

"I know a security firm who could send somebody out to keep an eye on the house for the time being."

"There's no need. I'll speak to Daddy. He'll take care of it."

I'd forgotten who her father was, and my suggestion felt foolish and inadequate.

"Yes, of course."

"Thank you, Morgan. For finding him."

It was my turn to shrug. Not sure what use I had been, if any, I offered a lame apology.

"I'm very sorry that things turned out this way."

Unable to be of more tangible help, I went to the stand in the corner, poured us a couple of glasses from the office bottle and handed her one.

"What about the police? Do you think they'll get to the bottom of it?"

"Well, they'll find what they're looking for, as usual. Whether they find what's really there or not is another matter: there can be a world of difference between the two.

Don't be surprised if they come out with some rough stuff about your husband. Remember, they still think he killed Eric Jenner."

"You don't though."

Not a question, but a statement. I shook my head.

"Not a chance, but that won't stop them seeing it that way if they choose to.

What will you do now?"

"Right now, I have an appointment with my father for lunch and it's best not to keep him waiting. After that I'm not sure."

Impressively, she knocked the drink back in one and started to put her coat back on.

"What will you tell your father?"

"He'll know what there is to know as soon as the police do from his contacts at City Hall, especially if it concerns the family."

"I see. Goodbye then Mrs. Conlon, and good luck."

She turned to go but just before she left was distracted,

glancing down at my desk like something had caught her eye there and frowned, paused slightly but carried on.

"So long, Morgan."

This last was delivered over her shoulder as she walked out.

After she'd gone, I stood there feeling empty, replaying the short meeting over in my mind, unsure if it was her loss or mine I was mourning. With nothing much better to do, I turned to the uncharacteristically neat pile of mail, which I'd barely glanced at since bringing it up, and flicked through it distractedly.

One letter stood out as slightly bigger than the others, protruding from the stack and I picked it up. Turning it over, there was an embossed crest on the back, reading 'Stanley Hills Country Club'. Maybe this was what had caught her attention.

It was a short note from Earl Thornton (speak of the devil) or more accurately from his secretary, requesting I meet him at the club the following day at 11:30 am, with a number to call to confirm the appointment. The letter went on to explain that they'd not been able to get through on the telephone, which probably accounted for the missed calls to my messaging service.

I say request, but it was little more than a sparsely worded summons, with nothing by way of explanation. The whole thing smacked of an arrogance and efficiency I instinctively resented. The letterhead was dated the same day and there was no postmark, meaning it must have been hand delivered that morning, probably not long before I'd made it into the office.

She'd said her father didn't like to be kept waiting and whatever it was Thornton wanted, it must have been urgent. Without a valid reason not to meet him, other than my own bloody-mindedness, I picked the phone up from its cradle and made the appointment.

A quick flick through the rest of the mail offered

nothing that couldn't wait, so I pocketed the envelope for Marty, and headed over to his place by the waterfront, figuring I might be able to catch him there. Taking the scenic route and checking for a tail, I drove over to his apartment. If anybody was following me, they were too good for me to notice, so I put the thought to the back of my mind.

At Marty's place, I leant on the buzzer for a while but had no luck: if he was in, he wasn't answering. He might have been sleeping one off in there, or somewhere else, for all I knew. I knocked some doors, trying a couple of the immediate neighbours, to see if they might know where he was, but if they did, they weren't letting on. Maybe they made me for a copper: his wasn't the type of parish where people were keen to snitch on their brethren.

The rain had settled in for the duration, so it being lunchtime by now, I tried the bar on the corner of the block but was disappointed on several fronts. Pleasant enough on the outside, once through the door the interior proved to be filthy and mean looking, which put me off the idea of having a loosener. I asked straight out about Marty instead and the barman said he wasn't welcome there and gave me the evil eye, making it clear I wasn't either.

I beat a hasty retreat, and it not being a day for chasing wild geese, decided against trying my luck at the other local establishments. Eventually I settled on the idea of heading over to Dutch's, the cellar bar where I'd first met him, reckoning on him being a creature of either regular or irregular habit, and showing up there sooner or later.

On descending the staircase into the outer circle of hell, I had a sense of foreboding, mixed with déjà vu. The décor was every bit as other worldly and discombobulating as I remembered and my hand went instinctively to the reassuring presence of the .38 on my hip, recalling what had happened on my last visit.

The clientele was even thinner on the ground than last time, which is to say non-existent. There was nobody in the joint save for me and my guide to the underworld: not Virgil, but Kelly the bartender, polishing a glass and beaming at me.

"Just couldn't stay away, huh? What'll it be?"

"Something to keep the damp away. How about a whisky sour?"

The beer had been good and the glass clean last time, and although it might have been an optimistic request, I needed something a bit more bracing.

"Coming up."

After removing my hat and raincoat and hanging them over the back of a bar stool, I sat down on the next one over, dripping softly as I watched Kelly fix the drink. Expertly, as it happened: things might be looking up.

He made a small jug and poured two glasses, setting one down in front of me and the other off to his right.

"Mind if I join you? It's a little slow and I'm partial to the odd one of these myself."

"Not at all. We'll need a toast though. How about 'to absent friends?"

His shrug told me 'Sure' and that's what we drank to. Me thinking about when Jack had made this same toast to me.

I nodded in appreciation of the drink.

"That's really very good, Kelly. Thank you."

He raised his glass in acknowledgement.

"Nothing hits the spot quite like it, huh?"

"Indeed."

"Say: what happened to your face, Morgan? Those guys from the other night catch up with you?"

I nodded.

"As a matter of fact, they did. We're quite well acquainted now. You seen either of them?"

Kelly shook his head.

"Nah, they haven't been back since. I'd say they've skipped town. Good riddance."

He raised his glass again.

"Yah. Good riddance."

We were quiet for a minute. Two guys just savouring our drinks and comfortable in each other's company. Eventually, I broke the spell.

"Speaking of absent friends, I was looking for Marty: have you seen him around?"

He nodded and eyed the gothic monstrosity behind the bar which served as a timepiece.

"He was in yesterday. It's a bit early for him now though, he usually doesn't show 'til around six. I don't know where he goes before then."

"Aha."

I came to a decision. Entrusting several thousand dollars to a barkeep I hardly knew might seem like a rash move, but I'd been meeting men like Marty and Kelly all my life and knew their sort well enough. In my line of work you get to be a pretty good judge of character and I figured Marty's money would be safer behind the bar with Kelly's twelve gauge than with me.

Besides, surely any man who could mix a whisky sour that well had to have his heart in the right place.

"Say, Kelly. Will you keep this here for Marty? Only give it to him if he's not too loaded though."

I took the envelope from my inside jacket pocket, flipped it over and wrote two words on the back: 'From Jack'.

"Right. Got it."

An envelope full of cash feels pretty much exactly like what it is, and although Kelly must have known what was in it, he didn't say anything, just took it and nodded.

As an afterthought, I fished one of my cards out of my breast pocket and handed it over.

"Would you give him this too? Tell him to look me up sometime."

He studied my card.

"Sure. Say can I have one of these?"

There were still about enough of the things to wallpaper my apartment, even if it might have taken a while, so figured I could spare another.

"What is it, Kelly? You got trouble?"

He shook his head.

"Not right now, but it's never too far away in this job."

With which wise words I left after thanking him, paying for my drink and declining another, somewhat reluctantly. He'd mixed them strong, and I was enjoying the slight buzz, but needed to get off at that stop and keep a clear head, as I had others to see.

I would honour Jack's wishes about the various bequests he wanted made on his behalf but would use my own discretion about their timing. Not bringing the envelope for Agnes was one such judgement call on my part, as I figured with all the bad news about to come out about him, it would have to wait.

She'd struck me as being scrupulously honest and direct, an upright citizen. One who might feel obliged to disclose receiving an envelope full of cash from him, and how she came by it, to the police, which wouldn't do either of us any good.

Especially not me.

18. Franco Mazza

My next move was to see the loan shark Mazza, to try and find out what he knew about Jenner's death. According to Jack, Eric had owed the guy money and they'd been seen together at the Havana, possibly on the night of the murder, if Mikey the barkeep there was right.

Coming out of Dutch's, I found a phone booth on the corner and looked him up in the business pages, giving me a listing for Gianfranco Mazza Finance, which sounded more respectable than I'd counted on. His place of business was at an address behind Union station, just off Main.

When Jack and I had talked long into the night, I'd asked him about Mazza, and on the way over replayed the conversation. Franco Mazza was old school Italian from an immigrant family and his journey through life might be considered a success story by some. He'd come from the streets in Little Italy and ran numbers back in the day, then gone in with Tony Cornero in the offshore gaming ships moored in Santa Monica Bay back in the 1930s, before those were shut down.

Money lending was a natural fit with his gambling interests, and he had a long history of loan sharking to hard working but impecunious citizens, many of whom came from his own community. This was still his main line of work.

His concerns had gradually turned legitimate, and he now owned a couple of card rooms just outside the city limits in Gardena, where licensed poker was permitted. One of the peculiarities of the state of California's strict gaming laws is that poker is allowed as it is considered a game of skill, rather than one of chance. What are the odds on that?

It was slim pickings compared to the action out in Nevada and there was relatively little mob interest; he wasn't one of those guys but must have had dealings and known them well enough. He was small time but tough enough in his own right.

Naturally enough, the gaming businesses were fronted by partners, otherwise they would have compromised his ability to run a legitimate loan company. The two fed off each other, like a snake eating its own tail, but to have an interest in both would be seen as unsporting even here.

Too tired to come up with a better idea, I opted for the direct approach, so headed over there in the rain, which was coming down hard. There was a fair chance Mazza wouldn't see me, but then again maybe he might, if he had nothing to hide or thought he could convince me that was the case.

I parked on Olvera Street and was struck by how much the skyline of this part of the city was dominated by the muscular presence of City Hall, keeping watch over its citizens. Finding a mailbox, I offered an ironic salute to the place as I sent myself the two envelopes with the locker key and the luggage receipt.

His office turned out to be a modest walk-up affair on the first floor of a low-rise block, just along from the old puppet theatre. It must have been one of the last bastions of the once thriving Italian community here, gradually displaced by Chinatown.

Wearily, I stepped in out of the rain, climbed to the first floor and opened the outer door of the standard two room set up. The atmosphere was low key and business-like, with old fashioned, uncomfortable looking chairs arranged around the walls and a coffee table set with newspapers.

A door on the back wall led to what I guessed was the inner sanctum, with the outer office and waiting area presided over by a gatekeeper who might have been Mazza's wife, his mother or possibly his grandmother, I couldn't tell which.

Respectfully removing my hat, I approached the desk, careful not to drip rainwater on this stern looking woman, or in her immediate vicinity.

"My name's Morgan. I'm a private investigator and I'd like to speak with Mr. Mazza about Eric Jenner."

"Do you have an appointment Mr. Morgan?"

"I'm afraid not. When might he be free?"

"I doubt he'll be able to see you."

"Could you ask him, please?"

While this exchange was taking place, a gorilla-sized human being, who had been sitting in a chair over in one corner reading the sports pages, got up and silently walked around to stand uncomfortably close behind my left shoulder. He was just in my peripheral vision if I turned my head slightly, trying to unsettle me.

I reasoned that the security was probably standard operating procedure, it being a moneylending business with cash on the premises, so tolerated his presence. A big guy would be useful when it came to collections: if anybody wouldn't pay up, he could hold them upside down by their ankles and shake them until money rained from their pockets.

The secretary stepped across to the inner office, knocked and went through, closing the door behind her, leaving me standing there awkwardly with the giant breathing down my neck. A waft of cheap aftershave with an undercurrent of garlic sausage came from him and I couldn't make up my mind which made me feel more nauseous. Neither of us said anything.

Thankfully, she came back presently, addressing the man behind me as she did so:

"Aldo, Mr. Mazza will see Mr. Morgan here directly."

It must have been my lucky day.

On cue, the big ape, evidently named Aldo, frisked me

with a surprisingly light and practiced touch, quickly relieving me of my .38, which disappeared into one of his meaty paws.

"House rules, no guns. You got anything else?"

I thought about showing him my badge and carry permit, but realising it would be a futile exercise, shook my head instead.

"You can go in through the door there now Mr. Morgan."

Which wasn't strictly necessary by way of an explanation since there was no other way in or out of the place, but I wasn't going to quibble. As I passed by, her smile had all the warmth of a funeral home chapel.

Franco Mazza turned out to be nothing like I expected. I had a mental picture of some sinister Shylock character, making a cruel living exploiting his fellow man and preying on human frailties. Which may well have been the case, but the thing was he just didn't look the part.

Which just goes to show. Something or other.

Instead, the figure who greeted me was more like a genial uncle, who got up from behind his desk and came to meet me with a broad smile. It was an unexpected gesture of openness and probably calculated, but nonetheless spoke of manners, which I appreciated.

Somewhere in his sixties, short and with more than a bit of excess timber on his small frame, Mazza's roundness suited him, and he seemed comfortable inhabiting it. He was smoking a foul-smelling cigar, which was doing no favours for my growing queasiness in the smallish room. When he spoke, it was around the side of the cigar, which looked like a permanent fixture, wedged into one side of his face.

"Good to meet you, Mr. Morgan."

He stuck out a small hand, not much larger than a child's and we shook.

"You too, Mr. Mazza. You can just call me

Morgan."

"Alright then, I'm Franco. Maria tells me that you want to know about Eric but I'm afraid you're wasting your time. I told it all to the police when they came to see me after he died."

At least they'd followed up the lead.

"You mind telling it again to me, Franco? The boys in blue don't always ask all the right questions."

He laughed, but his twinkling eyes lost a little of their mischief and he was watching me closely, trying to read my intentions, as I was his.

"Ain't it the truth. There's not much to tell really, but I guess there's no harm. What is it you want to know?"

"How long had you known Eric Jenner? How did you meet him?"

He thought about this.

"Let me see. I'd say about six years or so. He was playing cards at a place over in Gardena and we got talking there. I liked him well enough, and in time we got to be friends."

"Did you lend him money?"

The smile left his eyes.

"Sometimes. On favourable terms, you understand, to keep him away from ruthless people".

The way he told it sounded like a fairy tale. He caught my incredulous expression.

"Look Morgan, Eric was a gambler, plain and simple. Nobody was holding a gun to his head when he placed bets."

"Just when they collected on his debts huh?"

He shook his head, testily.

"Wait a minute, that's not fair. Believe it or not, Eric was a friend. I didn't have to see you, Morgan, but I want to explain.

Sure, I lent him money sometimes: it's what I do.

Besides, he had a good job, and the company was doing well, so he mostly paid it back on time."

It all sounded so cosy; people like to gamble, they get into a bit of debt, a line of credit gets extended. All fun and games at the beginning, but it would be very much all business when it came to collecting on the debt. Of course, if you happened to run the gaming establishment *and* the loan business, you were on to a guaranteed winner.

Getting riled wasn't going to get me anywhere, so I made a conscious effort to ease off a bit instead.

"You said *mostly*?"

"Just recently he'd started placing bigger bets, taking more risks trying to cover his losses and his debts elsewhere had started to mount up.

He was drinking more too, which wasn't usually his thing."

"When was this?"

"A couple of months back. I asked him about it, but he shrugged it off, said it was nothing he couldn't handle."

Which fit with the timeframe of the business with the box arriving and the threats.

"I was told he owed you money."

"You heard wrong. His account with me was clear."

"He paid you back?"

"Like I said, his account was settled."

There was something off about the language, the phrase he'd used was overly precise.

"How do you mean? There's something you're not telling me. I'm trying to find out who killed Eric, if he really was your friend, now would be a good time."

I was puzzled.

"Wait, you said 'settled'. Somebody else paid off his debts, is that what you're saying?"

He looked unsettled.

"Well, yes."

"Who was it? How is that possible?"

He talked me through it, like a businessman smoothly explaining the details of a contract, reasonable and familiar with his subject.

"The debt was in promissory notes. To start with we had gentlemen's agreements and IOUs, but as Eric borrowed more, I needed something more formal, you know, in writing. You understand."

I shrugged.

"Makes sense. I've heard of those before somewhere but remind me how they work."

"They're somewhere short of a formal loan contract and with a low interest rate. The thing is they're negotiable, which is to say that they can be traded, bought and sold. Not everywhere mind, but they can in this state."

"Let me get this straight. You *sold* his debt to somebody else? Who?"

Mazza looked distinctly uncomfortable and started digging at an imaginary itch at his neck, like his shirt collar was too tight.

"I don't know."

"What do you mean?"

"I was approached by an intermediary, a respectable attorney here in the city, representing a client, someone with Eric's best interests at heart who wanted to pay off the loan for him, anonymously. The lawyer handled it all."

I was incredulous.

"You say he was a friend, but you sold his debt off to somebody and you don't even know who it was?"

"Relax, it wasn't like that, it was all legitimate. Eric was in a fix, and it was the proverbial gift horse for both of us: what was I supposed to do?"

My mind was racing, trying to figure out what it all

meant. If Mazza really hadn't found out who the client was, there was no way any attorney was going to tell me. Client privilege and all that.

"Am I right in thinking there'd have to be some sort of security put up against these promissory notes in the first place?"

"Right."

"So what did Eric use for collateral, his apartment?"

He shook his head.

"I wouldn't let him use it. A man's got to keep a roof over his head. He made them out against his share of the business at Elegance. He was a director, and it was doing well, so they had value".

While he was speaking, he leant over and extinguished the cigar in a large glass ashtray on the table. There was a short silence as I processed what he'd told me.

"So, whoever took over these promissory notes would have a call on the business, is that right?"

"In theory, yes, but Eric's dead now, so it's probably irrelevant."

"Did you tell this to the police, about the notes and the debt being paid off?"

"They never asked. Mostly they just wanted to know about Jack Conlon and where he was. They seem to think he killed Eric."

"Yah, so Eric's dead and his business partner is wanted for his murder. Speaking of which, how well do you know Conlon? You must have met him."

I was careful to refer to Jack in the present tense.

"Yes, of course. He's Eric's oldest friend and he fell in with us sometimes when we were out. Everybody likes Jack."

"Does he know about this business with the shares?"

"I can't say for sure, but I doubt it. It was a private

arrangement between Eric and me and we didn't see any need to advertise it. Like I say, he used to pay the loans off regular in any case."

"Do *you* think Conlon might have killed Eric?"

Franco Mazza looked thoughtful for a moment; his brow creased in concentration.

"The last time I saw him they were getting on fine."

"At the Havana, wasn't it? The night Eric died. Did anything strike you as unusual about it or off between them?"

"I've thought about that myself.

If anything, it was Jack, not Eric who seemed tense that night. Something had gone wrong at the business, down at the warehouse. There'd been some kind of a mix up and it was causing him a headache. They went off in a huddle to talk about it.

Other than that, it was normal. We all went our separate ways after the show."

Speaking of headaches, I was getting one myself and couldn't think of any more questions to ask Mazza, so thanked him for his time and left him with my business card in case he thought of anything else.

After retrieving my .38 on the way out, I visited a drugstore down the street, bought some painkillers and took a couple before picking up the Plymouth and heading to the office. It was mid-afternoon and the first time I'd had the chance to catch my breath and do some quality thinking: there was a lot to process.

Activity can be a good substitute for progress, providing the illusion that one is achieving goals, instead of merely marking time. Once at my desk, I tried to simulate the rhythm of a normal day and settled into the familiar routine of dealing with the mail. I'd only glanced through it earlier, but unusually, closer inspection revealed two invitations to work on new cases, both requiring a response.

The first was from a lawyer to do some work in a divorce case, which interested me less than the second, investigating theft from a workplace on behalf of the insurance company, one I had worked with before. In all likelihood I'd have to maintain a low profile soon and throwing myself into work would provide a good opportunity to do so.
I needed to be busy, so accepted both cases.

Once calls were placed and the necessary arrangements made, I settled down to the real work of the afternoon. Clearing my desk and taking the largest blank piece of paper I could find, I started to compile a picture of the Conlon case.

Building a timeline was one of the better habits I'd picked up during my time at homicide, a way of rationalising complex events with multiple actors. By mapping out the established facts of who knew and did what, when, it was possible to overlay various scenarios and look for connections. Effectively, trying to establish what was cause and what was effect.

The methodical nature of capturing the details suited my low-functioning mental state, as I attempted to lay out the pieces and make sense of how they might fit together, rather than having them all float around in my head. Once the task was completed, I sat back and admired my handiwork, which wasn't bad for a first attempt and made me feel like a real detective.

I had the sensation of being on more solid ground and my anxiety subsided, so I opened the bar and bought myself a drink from the office bottle, reckoning I'd earned one. Leaning back in my chair with my feet up on the desk, I went through the actors in this little drama one by one, trying to work out what their motives might be.

At some point I must have nodded off and begun dreaming about the case. When I woke up, it was with a start and a strong sense that dark forces were ranged against me. What was it all about? Ostensibly, Kitty had brought me in to find her husband, but it seemed likely I'd been played, but the question was by who? Or by whom if you're the type to be picky about grammar.

As well as the central characters, there would be others doing their bidding. In years of detecting, more often than not I'd had to start with them and work my way back up the food chain. Like those Quebecois, Louis and Al.

Jack told me Eric Jenner brought them in after things turned rough regarding the matter of the box. They were small time, but dangerous enough in their own right and had nearly done for me, but that was only *after* Jenner had been murdered.

To my mind, the case seemed to hinge on his killing. Had they done it? Maybe seen a golden pay day and an opportunity to retire from the enforcement business, so decided to go freelance.

Then there was the corrupt police officer Baker and whoever his partner was. What were they doing mixed up in this? They were after the box and judging by what happened, weren't too fussed about what they did or who they might have to kill to get it.

The business with the surveillance photograph sounded like it might have been them, which reminded me I needed to take a look at the address on that photograph later. Similarly, the ambush, shooting at Jack's car, and the other threats could have been them, meaning they'd been involved earlier on, way before catching up with us down in Del Mar.

Baker was a maverick, but was he really capable of being behind this, and if not, who were they working for? There was something else bothering me about him, nagging away at the back of my mind; I'd lost the connection for now, but it was in there somewhere.

Then there was that Nazi war loot, stolen again and

brought back here piece by piece, bringing me back again to the box and the sensational emerald. Had somebody known their true worth and been watching out for them? Were they out there now, waiting, watching me and planning their next move?

Those things spelled trouble and I had both in my possession, albeit at arm's length. I'd have to do something about that, soon.

What was I to make of the crazy story Jack had told me about his real and assumed identities and the bizarre coincidence of his affair with Janet? I made a mental note to find her later too.

I'd been to see Franco Mazza, but didn't know what to make of him, unable to work out whether he really was Eric's friend, as he had maintained, or was just playing the part. Either way, did I really make him for the killer?

What about the business of Jenner's debts apparently being paid off by a mystery benefactor right before he died: what was I supposed to make of that?

None of it made sense for now, but the wheels were turning, and it was slowly starting to take shape, although my immediate reward for all this detective work was a dull, persistent headache behind the eyes. Eventually the loose strands started to dissolve and swim away from me, like trying to read a message written on the surface of water.

The afternoon passed, and the light outside faded towards early evening. I stood up and stretched, then crossed over to the safe where I locked the product of my labours away, knowing I was sure to add to it in the coming days and hoping my subconscious would get to work on it in the meantime.

Needing a change of scenery, I shut up shop and went to Vincenzo's for a bite to eat, before going home to think things over some more. The plan was to get some rest before freshening up and going to look for Janet at the

Havana. Dinner turned out to be the special of the day, a memorable seafood linguine, which I had reason to be grateful for later.

I'd just got back to my apartment block and was coming through the outer door into the hallway when I ran into my friend and former homicide colleague, Tom Delaney, heading my way.

Tom was on his own, which was a good sign, but the look on his face told me my plans were going to have to wait.

"Hello Tom."

"You're a hard man to find Morgan. About turn, you're coming down to the Glass House with me."

He gestured with a circling motion of his finger for me to turn around, his manner none too friendly. Walking next to me on my right, he held his left hand out, palm up.

"I'll need your guns too. The .38 I can see peeping out at me and any others you might happen to have around."

I handed my piece over and thought for a moment.

"There's a .32 at my office in the desk drawer."

"Okay. We'll stop by and pick that up on the way."

"Say, what's this about, Tom? Do I need to speak to my attorney?"

"Not unless you plan on making a will. Which mightn't be a bad idea, given the company you keep.

Your friend Jack Conlon turned up. Dead. We need to ask you about him and some other people you were on less good terms with."

"Am I under arrest?"

"Did I say that? I came here in person as a favour, Morgan. Take it from me, it'll be the last one you get for a while."

I knew when to stay quiet, and on the ride down to headquarters, did exactly that. There'd been no request to search my apartment, so no warrant, which might mean something, or nothing. It was just as well, given the hand grenade in my safe.

When we stopped at the office, I could tell Tom wasn't really interested and he poked around a little, but only half-heartedly. Maybe he thought I was too savvy to leave anything incriminating lying around.

Since I wasn't under arrest, my best guess was they were still trying to figure out what happened and fancied me for some kind of witness rather than a suspect. Tom had warned me off trying to find Conlon but knew I'd have ignored that and probably had a hunch I had met him, so was taking me on a fishing trip.

I thought about what them taking my guns might mean. Back at the Casa Blanca, I'd fired my .38 wildly into the night in the general direction of the shooter on the hill, but it was a million to one shot, quite literally, that I'd hit anybody or anything. Jack and the others had all been using hardware above my pay grade, .45s and the like, so it was likely they wanted my pea shooters for elimination purposes. Besides, as I reminded myself, there was more than a fair chance they knew nothing about events back there.

It was going to be a long night at the Glass House, and I was grateful for the excellent dinner, which would have to sustain me for some time to come. I was glad it was Tom taking me in too, in as there were others who'd be eager to tie me to a killing.

He'd mentioned people I was on 'less good terms with' and it would be a different story if Baker's body turned up, as we were known to have a longstanding grudge, but it didn't feel like that. Yet.

The best course of action would be to play along, provided things didn't get too rough, as being obstructive would only get their backs up. Instead, I'd frustrate the hell out of them by seeming reasonable and helpful but sticking rigidly to my story. My version of events being that I'd gone to bed with a fever, taken the phone off the hook and not been anywhere or seen anyone for a couple of days.

They'd know I was mixed up in things somehow but lacked anything concrete other than my unhealthy proximity to events. Unless I slipped up and gave something away under questioning of course, which wasn't going to happen, because my parents might have raised pig-headed children, but they hadn't brought up any stupid ones.

As soon as they started in, I could tell they weren't buying what I was telling them, but then again, I wasn't selling it that hard.

The way I saw things, I didn't have to.

19. Earl Thornton

The ride up into the canyons was pleasant, the fresh air giving me the chance to exercise my grey matter, a welcome contrast to being cooped at The Glass House, trying not to think. The interrogation had mainly consisted of going over the same ground time and again, the boys in blue trying to trap me into making a mistake.

There had barely been time to go home, shower and change before keeping my appointment with Thornton, who I'd been warned didn't like to be kept waiting. I'd lost touch with when my last decent night's sleep had been.

I was right about Baker's partner in crime being Kurt Taylor: they'd fished his body out of the wreck at the same time they'd found Jack, who it turned out was carrying a wallet, which was how they identified him. They were looking for Baker too, as Taylor's vehicle was registered to him. He was AWOL, although thankfully they hadn't found him yet.

They didn't have anything on me and knew it. All I'd had to do was sit tight and deny I'd met Conlon or been anywhere outside of the city for the past couple of days. To do otherwise would have been a mistake, so I stuck to my guns. I didn't have an alibi to speak of, but that wasn't a crime as yet.

Speaking of guns, the ballistics came up without anything on mine, so I was in the clear on that score. There were no witnesses I could think of to place me at the scene, other than a patrolman and the tow truck operator, but there had been no mention of them.

In the end they tired of me, and it was clear the investigation had already moved on. Grudgingly, they gave my guns back and let me go, with the usual dark mutterings about my licence, obstructing a police enquiry and so forth.

All of which seemed like ancient history as I pulled into the parking lot of the Stanley Hills Country Club. At the end of a bougainvillea lined drive about a mile long, the place was everything I knew it would be and I hated it, and everything it stood for, from the outset.

It was the kind of place where privileged, white folk came to be with their own kind. No chance of mixing with riff raff, or of getting caught in a socially awkward situation, unless you happened to forget which fork to use for the fish, or some such. People say the cream rises to the top, but experience has taught me that if you look closely, there's often a layer of scum sitting just above it and that's how I felt about this place.

Everything about the white, colonial style building was on a grand scale, designed to impress and intimidate in equal measure. I pulled into a space in the parking lot in the Plymouth wearing my best suit, both of us seeming out of place and underdressed.

A flight of white stone steps led up to the building, dazzling in the autumn sunshine now yesterday's rainstorm had passed. I made my way over to them in a foul mood, despite the beautiful day.

The parking space nearest to the stairs was occupied by a white Rolls Royce Phantom, which wasn't all that big, probably not much more than the length of an average city block. There was one of those little white signs in the flower bed in front of it, designating the space for '*ET, Chairman*', meaning it was Thornton's car, as I knew it must be.

Whatever else he might have been doing, Earl was riding a gravy train. With biscuit wheels. There's money in banks, as they say. I speculated idly whether he would drive the thing himself, or whether he would have somebody do that for him. Either way, it was a preposterous vehicle for one man to be ferried around in.

The guy on reception nearly genuflected when I told him why I was there, then checked an appointments diary next to the main register and pressed a discreet buzzer on the underside of the desk. Evidently, this summoned the lackey who appeared silently at my elbow about thirty seconds later.

He was an ancient retainer, no more than about two hundred years old, dressed in full butler uniform, complete with white gloves and tails, the overall effect somewhere between a tortoise and a mime artist. I couldn't tell if he was looking at me with genuine disdain, or whether it was facial rictus, the result of suffering a stroke, possibly in about the mid-nineteenth century. I wondered what family loyalty made Thornton keep the old boy on.

He conveyed me along a corridor, and we went through an archway into a silent antechamber where he gestured for me to take a seat and offered me tea or coffee while I waited, as I knew I must, to see Thornton. Some minutes later, he returned with a very welcome steaming hot black coffee, although I didn't want to show my gratitude.

When he inquired whether there would be anything else, on a whim, I asked for some Peek Freans cookies. I'd heard tell of the things, but wasn't sure that I had ever had one, liked them, or even knew what they were. It seemed like a suitably awkward request, but if the butler thought so, he wasn't letting on.

He came back some time later with a selection on a platter, marked with the letters P.F. from which I deduced the name was that of the manufacturer, rather than a particular type of cookie. Who knew? I ignored them all on principle, despite mounting hunger on account of having to skip breakfast.

The great man eventually finished with his affairs of state, his game of solitaire, or whatever it was that kept me waiting. The door to his office opened and Earl Thornton stuck his well tonsured head out.

"Mr. Morgan, please come in."

He was back through the door and striding across his vast office before I had a chance to get up or say anything.

He was making for a small but beautifully appointed bar in the corner on the far side of his office and spoke over his shoulder with his back to me, as I closed the door.

"I usually take a gimlet about this time of day if you would care to join me? I hear you like a drink."

I didn't much like the jibe about my fondness for the hooch, or the implication that he had been finding out about me but decided to let it slide. Clearly this was going to be an audience, not a meeting of equals and Thornton wanted me to know it.

There was no offer of a handshake, which I didn't mind, but intriguingly had been extended the courtesy of a drink, which I accepted with good grace. The truth of the matter was I was ready for one after my grilling the night before.

"I'd like that, thank you."

"Have you ever had a gimlet before?"

He narrowed his eyes at me as he asked the question and I wondered if it might be a test of some sort, maybe to do with Jack, or an obscure screening question for the club.

"As a matter of fact, I have."

Accepting the drink turned out to be one of my better decisions that day. I'd only just met Thornton but knew already that I wasn't going to like him. Credit where it's due though, the man knew how to mix a drink. His was an excellent balance of gin, fresh lime juice and sugar, on the sour side and with enough bite to keep things interesting.

Perhaps all rich people went on a course and learned to make the things at Harvard, Yale or wherever. We crossed to his enormous walnut desk, where the Ivy League games continued, with me being relegated to the position of student on a small chair in front, while Thornton played Dean in a massive leather one behind it.

Up close, he was predictably well-groomed, and tennis tanned. My best suit felt shabby next to his, which was cut with effortless grace and spoke of fine tailoring, many pay grades above mine. He was doing his best to project a relaxed air, all business, but I detected an underlying tension.

We sipped our drinks silently and without a toast, for which I was grateful. Thornton would never have sullied his hands with the likes of me unless I could be useful to him, and we both knew it. I waited: he had sent for me, after all.

"You're wondering what I want with you, Mr. Morgan."

He'd read my mind, but it was safer to say little yet and I wasn't going to make it easy for him.

"Yes."

"My contacts at City Hall tell me you're not the overly talkative type, although you ruffled some feathers over there with the things you said when you left the force."

Was he trying to antagonise or dominate me in some way? It was no surprise he was hand in glove with the mayor's office, but I resented the implication he knew things I didn't.

"Whistleblowing, wasn't it? Allegations of corruption against your fellow officers, some of them more senior."

Despite my best efforts, I could feel myself getting riled, when what I needed most was to keep a cool head and think clearly.

"Let's just say I saw things that didn't sit well with me."

"So now you wage your one-man war against injustice, is that it? How quaint. Old fashioned even."

It was either an interesting tactic, or he was so used to having the upper hand, he approached everything with arrogance and condescension. He smiled, at least I think that is what it was meant to be. The overall effect was like a lizard had taken lessons in how to be human, from a snake.

"Why don't you tell me why I'm here?"

"You'll know about this unfortunate business with my son-in-law by now."

Jack was dead, but the way he spat the words out spoke volumes.

Nodding, I sipped my drink and waited.

"The police seem to think you found him."

He obviously had a direct line into headquarters and didn't care who knew it.

"So they kept telling me."

"I know you wouldn't tell them, but if you did find out anything, I'd want you to let me know. For my daughter's sake and for my grandsons. I would consider it a favour."

Everything in Earl Thornton's world was about him and always had been, even the way he talked about his family was defined by their relationship to him.

"You see I wouldn't want anything else embarrassing to come out, for the sake of the family."

"Well, the police seem to think he murdered his business partner and one or maybe two of their officers. I didn't find anything that might be considered more embarrassing than that, although..."

I left this last bit hanging deliberately. He might be reacting to how things had played out now, but by my calculation, Thornton had been trying to get hold of me *before* I met up with Jack in Del Mar. He wasn't the kind who dealt in generalities, meaning there had to be something specific he had in mind.

"Go on."

I was taking a risk, given my denials to the police, but it was time for me to play my hand.

"I did find a box, if that's what you're interested in. I met Jack, and he gave it to me for safekeeping. I offered it to your daughter, but she didn't know anything about it and told me to keep it, so I guess it's mine now."

Despite years of negotiating and bluffing things out, Thornton's hand involuntarily stiffened on his glass when I mentioned the box. It was an instinctive reaction, tension rising to the surface and the tell I'd been watching closely for.

It was all he could do to visibly get himself back under control and utter the next few words, seemingly casually.

"A box, you say?"

He was hooked, but I still had to reel him in. I'd cast myself in the role of a principled but jaded man: one with the courage to stand up to authority, but enough native cunning to exploit an obvious opportunity.

"Yah it's the darndest thing. A big ugly box with a kind of an old piano inside. I couldn't make head nor tail of why it was so important to him. You wouldn't know anything about it would you, Mr. Thornton?"

Smart is dumb and dumb is smart, as they say.

He shook his head slowly, his eyes locked on mine.

"I suppose I ought to take it to the police. They'll probably want to see it."

"Do they know about it, this box?"

"No. Funny thing is, it sort of slipped my mind when I was talking to them, what with all the confusing questions they kept asking me."

"Well then. It's probably best not to bother them with it now, don't you think? They're very busy, after all. Do you have it nearby? Perhaps I could take care of it for you."

His words and manner were casual, but his eyes were anything but.

"You'd really do that for me? I don't have it right now, but it's put away somewhere safe. I can get hold of it in a day or two."

"That's settled then. You'll be compensated, of course."

So, I was to graduate top of the class, 'summa cum laude'.

"Of course. What did you have in mind, Mr. Thornton?"

"Money?"

There wasn't a single thing I wanted from this corrupt man, but had to play my part convincingly for him to believe I had enough edge not to be a pushover, but the common sense to know when to reign it in. When it came down to it, I had to believe I had some of those qualities myself.

Things were getting interesting, and I wanted to see how far he'd go.

"No disrespect, but lots of people have money, Mr. Thornton.

Might there be something else?"

He thought for a minute.
"What is it you desire most, Morgan? A man has got to have a strong sense of what he wants. You tend to get what you focus on in life."

I had no doubt this was true for Thornton, if not for the rest of us.

"I'd have to think about that."

"Here's an idea for you.

Would you like to go back to proper police work? I could arrange a job over at the County Sheriff's office, or even back at LAPD, in time. I could do with a good man over there now."

The way he looked steadily at me as he said this made it clear Baker and Taylor had been working for him. Corrupt men, after that box, who would have killed me in a heartbeat.

We both knew what he was really offering me: to join

his payroll. I didn't want any of it but had to bite my tongue. Appearing insolent would only antagonise him and make a powerful enemy, where maybe I didn't need to.

"I'll think about that, Mr. Thornton."

"Think it over, but don't take too long."

I stood up.

"Thanks for the drink. I need to be going now."

"I'll have Rick attend to you."

He pressed a buzzer on the underside of his desk, and I wondered what else he might be able to summon up on a whim, just sitting there.

"There's really no need, I'll see myself out."

"One more thing, Morgan. I can tell from the way Kitty talks about you that she likes you. Stay away from her."

This was delivered like he was explaining about a part of the golf course at his club that was out of bounds.

Having nothing to say, I said nothing, which made for an awkward silence before the butler came back.

"Rick, please see to it that Mr. Morgan gets lunch. Whatever he wants, on my account."

"There's no need, thank you, I've eaten already."

It was a lie and my traitorous belly was making loud protestations to the contrary, griping on account of the coffee and the liquor. I had dined like a king the evening before, but how quickly the stomach forgets.

The man looked at me like I was clearly a fool not to be filling my boots at Thornton's expense. He was probably right, and I was being unnecessarily stubborn, but I've always had a contrary streak. I'm particular about who picks up my tab and didn't want to be owned by Thornton in any way, no matter how small. Whatever he was offering me, I didn't want it.

"You'll let me know, Morgan."

It was a statement, not a question.

"I shall."

Again, there was no handshake offered and Rick took me back to reception, where he relayed the instructions about lunch to the guy on the desk, then inclined his head very slightly towards me, did a smart about turn and moved off.

As he turned away, I caught the reflection from a gold lapel pin, too small to make out properly but circular, with what looked like a letter 't' or a cross in the middle. Thornton had worn a ring with the same symbol and since Kitty had told me he was big in the masons; I guessed the two men might have a masonic connection.

I told the receptionist lunch wouldn't be necessary and turned to leave. Evidently, my social standing at the club had risen a few notches after the meeting with Thornton, as he insisted that the valet, who was hovering nearby, would bring my car round. I acquiesced, handing over the keys and describing my ride and where it was parked to the fresh-faced young man.

Waiting for him to fetch the Plymouth, I stepped outside into the autumn sunshine and watched a couple of gardeners going about their work, tending to the already overly manicured foliage. Relieved to be out of the place, I speculated about what my meeting with Thornton might mean.

He had wanted the box badly and maybe knew about its contents, but why would it mean so much to a man like him? Had he really been prepared to kill his own son-in-law to get it, or had things got out of hand with Baker and Taylor?

The valet pulled up in my car and stepped out, holding the door open and grinning broadly as I tipped him.

"She's a real beauty, sir. Just my kind of ride. I bet she's really fast."

"None too sluggish."

Stepping into the car, I registered something slightly off

about the club and turned back to him.

"Say, are there no black folks who work here, or no Hispanic types around the place?"

He looked at me earnestly and spoke quietly.

"No sir. That's the way they like it here, Mr. Thornton and the others."

"I see. What about you, are you okay with that?"

He shrugged his shoulders.

"I need the work, sir."

"Take my advice kid and get a different job. Far away from here."

Happy to be leaving, I gunned the motor in a small act of defiance and peeled out of the place double time, with a satisfying screech of tyres. I could clearly see the kid laughing in my rear-view mirror.

20. Lodge Meeting

Call it instinct or what you will, but something made me stop down from the entrance to the club when I spotted the place on the hairpin bend where Jack said he'd been shot at. Driving on a little, so as not to block the road at the part it narrowed, I slew the Plymouth over to a stop and went back to take a look.

He'd been right about it being the perfect spot, carefully chosen, with natural cover from shrubs on the outside of the tight turn. A shooter positioned there would have line of sight for several seconds at any vehicle slowing down to take the corner.

Not knowing what I was looking for, I went along the verge looking straight down and trusting my peripheral vision to scan for objects. There was the usual roadside detritus; rusty cans and the like, but further in there were also a couple of brass shell casings, which I picked up and examined. They looked to be .45s, which may or may not have been from a Thompson, but which fit well enough with Jack's story.

Edging into the bushes, I felt my way in the sandy soil close to the drop, being careful not to lose my footing and made for where the best firing spot would be and crouched down to take a closer look. There were several cigarette butts where somebody had spent time waiting, all the same brand, Kents, and filtered, which was unusual. It also happened to be what Rudi Baker smoked.

As I was getting up from my stoop, but still hidden in the bushes, a vehicle approached and imagining I was the shooter, I put a bead on the car with my fingers like a kid playing cowboys and observed as it slowed to negotiate the bend. There was no way a half competent marksman could miss, meaning it had to have been a warning.

The car was a black Pontiac Silver Streak, which had to be at least twenty years old, and the person driving it was the ancient butler, Rick, who may have had the thing from new. Maybe he had the afternoon off or was on an errand somewhere.

Acting on a whim, or on a hunch (I'm not sure which, or whether there is even a difference between the two) I decided to tail him. His old jalopy was unmissable, and he drove slowly and steadily, making it easy enough work. Instinctively, I hung back, although there was no real need to as he wouldn't have known my car.

A couple of miles down the hill, he took a right fork and we headed further out into the hills. After another mile and a half of winding road, I was momentarily confused coming out of an S-bend to find him no longer in front of me, but quickly realised after overshooting, that there was a small turning on the left into a side canyon, which he must have taken.

Doubling back, I made the turn, onto a dirt road, where dust was still settling back from where his car had disturbed it ahead of mine and slowed down, not wanting to be seen or to run into anybody else. We passed a couple of turnings to the left and the right; big places set back behind gates.

Eventually there was a long sweeping right hand bend at the head of the canyon, where the road circled round in a loop, with a single property set back behind stone pillars. On the other side of these, the landscape opened out, with a gravel drive leading up to a large lodge style building, situated on the other side of a small lake and an expanse of well-manicured lawn.

Not wanting to give myself away, I pulled up before the entrance and watched the Pontiac cross a bridge where the lake narrowed and come to a stop in front of the building, alongside several other cars. The butler got out and went inside.

One of the pillars carried a plaque with the name, '*Oak Apple Lodge*' and the number: he'd saved me a trip as it was the same address on the back of the photograph, where Jack had been told to deliver the box, after being threatened.

It was a secluded setting, with what looked to be only one way in and back out again. I needed a look but didn't like the set-up, or the odds on just waltzing in there, so turned around and slid the Plymouth in under some trees about half a mile back down the sleepy track.

Oak woodland on either side went up to the head of the valley, and my plan was to work my way up through it and skirt around to the back of the building to see if I could get a look. It would take a good while and no little stealth. Every investigator worth their salt owns a decent set of field glasses and I retrieved mine from the trunk and set off, an unlikely looking bird watcher in my best suit, with small but powerful binoculars around my neck.

Grateful that the trees were still in leaf enough to hide me and afford a pleasant breeze on the warm day, my progress was cautious and deliberate. I stayed just below the ridge line at the top of the valley until directly behind the house, then edged down through the trees as far as I dared, hoping to find a vantage point.

There was a substantial stone wall around the place, but from my position in the woods above, I could look down over it into an upstairs room with large windows at the rear of the house and also had a partial view of one of the downstairs rooms. Both of these were over on my right.

To the left, I could make out the top of a large oil tank in one corner of the yard next to the wall, but the rooms over on that side were obscured by trees. There was a door on the ground floor in the middle, next to a fire escape running up to an exit on the first floor, by the room with the big windows.

In the downstairs room, heavy drapes were drawn back,

and the windows partially opened. I could see oak panelling and a large stone fireplace where a fire was set, but not lit, due to the mildness of the day. People were gathered in there but frustratingly, because of the downward angle, I could see legs but not the top halves of their bodies.

The legs belonged to people in suits, standing around in a group. Drinks were being held and every now and then somebody would bend to put one down or retrieve a canape from an occasional table. The mood seemed to be a celebratory, with faint sounds of laughter and conversation drifting my way, although I couldn't make out what was being said.

Unmistakable catering noises of pots and pans being readied were coming from somewhere near the door at the bottom of the fire escape, which I guessed must lead to the kitchen. These caused my stomach to complain loudly as I watched for about ten minutes, hoping in vain to catch sight of a face.

Suddenly the legs, which I calculated belonged to about seven or eight people, filed off out of my field of vision, back into another room inside the house. They left all at the same time, as if summoned, and my watch read one o'clock: they were taking lunch.

I tried to get a vantage point further over to see where they had gone, but without success, so came back and shifted my attention to the upstairs room. There seemed to be less light filtering in here, as if the drapes were parted on this side but not on the far side, at the front of the building.

This room was decked out like a chapel, with banners standing either side of an altarpiece off to the right and the small patch of floor I could see laid with an ornate chequerboard pattern. Never having been in one I didn't have a lot to go on, but it was every bit what I imagined a masonic temple might look like.

I brought the binoculars up for a closer look at those flags, which had strange emblems on them. One depicted a sort of flattened tree, or stylised letter 't', the same symbol I'd seen on Thornton's ring and on the butler's lapel pin. The other had an oval with a cross inside it and words around the outside which I'd seen before too but couldn't recall where.

From my angle, I could read a word on the far side of the oval design, which was '*Deutsches*', which was straightforward enough, but puzzling. Could it be this lodge had some sort of German affiliation?

There was more of the stylised lettering on the nearside of the design, but I couldn't make out the full word. What was visible in the middle read '*-nener-*' and I copied this down diligently in my notebook without any idea what this other word might be.

Feeling hungry and after ten more minutes without finding anything else noteworthy, I decided to call it a day. Whatever was going on here, this group didn't know I was there, although I was trespassing. It would take a good while to work my way down to the car as it wouldn't do to go blundering down the hillside, not knowing who else might be around.

If the party broke up after lunch, I might get an opportunity to observe the men as they left and had time enough to get into a position to do so. Making my way slowly around the property, but staying well back from the wall, eventually I came to a spot with a view of the entrance but far enough under cover for me to stay hidden.

Noting that Thornton's car was now out front, I settled in to wait. Eventually a group of grey-haired men spilled out of the lodge amid joking and laughter and before they got into their cars. They were more animated than before lunch, which had evidently been a good one and my stomach protested again at the injustice.

I didn't see Earl, who must have stayed inside, but when

Rick went to leave, the others went over to his car to shake hands and one held the door open for him. He might have been playing Thornton's butler over at the club, but whoever he was, the body language said he was unmistakably the top dog here.

One of them called out to him and I didn't catch all of it, just a single word and a name:

"...Wiedersehen, Friedrich."

German again. I knew what that meant, alright. He smiled and waved back.

'Friedrich'. Which might become Rick in English.

Although he hadn't spoken a great deal earlier, I'd noticed a slight accent of some sort, but his English was good, and I'd never have known that he was a German speaker. Besides, it didn't mean anything at the time, or at any other time come to that in this melting pot city of ours.

The faces of the other old men didn't ring any bells, but they seemed relaxed and happy in each other's company. Whoever they were, they didn't seem like much of a threat, although I was outnumbered and couldn't afford to be complacent. I thought about waiting for Thornton to show but had pushed my luck enough by staying.

I slipped deeper into cover and waited until they left, then worked my way down to the Plymouth and eased it back along the track. Tired and edgy, I found myself checking the rear-view mirror all the way back to the road, half expecting an ambush that never came.

As I headed back into the city, I tried to figure out what it meant and what my next move should be, other than getting something to eat. The whole business was intriguing with these strange German connections. As I was framing this thought, something else clicked into place.

It was the thing bugging me before, at the back of my mind about Baker and Taylor; what they had in common other than being corrupt police officers. They shared a German heritage that they were both proud of. Rudi Baker was a second-generation immigrant and had looked every inch like what he was with blond hair and blue eyes, although his partner, Kurt Taylor, was less obviously Teutonic in looks.

I figured on doing some desk research and thought those flags with the German writing and strange symbols might shed some light on things, so headed Downtown to the Central Library on West 5th street. The excellent reference facilities there had always served me well.

After parking up nearby, I took in a hasty, late lunch of sandwiches and coffee from a deli, before heading across to the striking building to do a little digging. The solid and secure Egyptian Art Deco interior had an immediate calming effect, and I welcomed the prospect of spending a couple of quiet hours there.

I settled on the theory that the German speaking men at the lodge were all of an age to have come here after the war, and that this might be what they had in common. Factoring in the flags, imagery from the thirties and forties seemed like a logical starting point.

My request sounded odd spoken out loud, but whatever she might have thought, the librarian looked at me neutrally and pointed me in the right direction. Before long, I was leafing through reference materials on one of the most hateful episodes of human history, paying particular attention to pictures of flags and banners.

After looking through many pages of familiar imagery of swastikas, eagles and the like, I happened across a clear photograph of one of the designs from the lodge, the oval with the writing around the outside. What I'd thought was a cross in the middle was a sword and the words around the outside read '*Deutsches*' up one side and '*Ahnenerbe*' down the other, which matched the letters written in my notebook.

Taking a proper look, I realised I'd seen this design before without registering it, faintly stamped on some paperwork accompanying the box. Had the thing been connected with them before? Rick, or Friedrich as I now knew him, had gone straight to the lodge after my meeting with Thornton and been met with a warm reception: was it because they were happy at the prospect of getting it back?

Turning quickly to one of the textbooks, I looked '*Ahnenerbe*' up and couldn't believe what I was reading. They weren't just Germans, they were *Nazis*.

I was stunned. Was it really possible? I caught my breath and must have been holding it for a full minute unawares, before having to take several deep breaths to steady myself.

What I found didn't make for pleasant reading. Within the grim history of the Third Reich, this group's activities made up one of the darkest chapters of all.

The Nazis had risen to power on the back of Hitler's insane personal theories about the existence of an Aryan race, responsible for all of the significant advances throughout human civilisation. He believed that modern Germans were descended from this master race, biologically superior to all others and would become the saviours of mankind, if allowed to fulfil their destiny. As the Fuhrer saw it, inferior elements had been allowed to pollute the gene pool and hold the rest of them back, but he came up with a plan for those, of course.

You couldn't make it up, except he had. The lies sold like hotcakes though, peddled to the German people, a once great nation humiliated after defeat in the first World War and desperate to reclaim its place in the world order.

I read on.

The inconvenient truth was that none of it had any grounding in fact, there being no historical basis for the fraudulent claims naturally enough, since none of it had ever happened. The Reich's leadership became obsessed with finding evidence to bolster their bogus ideology, anything at all to help establish their credentials and justify their homicidal intent towards the rest of us.

That's where *Ahnenerbe* came in. Set up before the war, and operating directly alongside Himmler's SS, the group achieved a cult like status. Their role was to manufacture the proof: to demonstrate that these crackpot ideas about racial purity were somehow rooted in scientific fact.

Scholars were recruited from a wide range of academic disciplines; a small army who spent their time re-imagining the historical record and trying to demonstrate racial superiority through pseudo-science. Their fabricated findings were used by the Reich's propaganda machine to gain support for policies like military expansionism. Ultimately these paved the way for the genocide of the Jews and other groups.

Many were respectable scientists, which was the whole point, and although some may have felt they had no alternative, others were among the most enthusiastic of Nazis. Some of the most depraved activities, like the human experimentation in the camps, was conducted by this very group, supposedly in the name of science.

It was chilling.

My stomach tightened as I read on to see if I might recognise names or faces, but there was little information about the individuals involved. There had been a few show trials, but many of the records were destroyed before the end of the war, allowing them to escape justice or quietly go back to their earlier academic pursuits, without fuss.

The other design I'd seen was there too: the one that Thornton and his butler had been wearing and which had been on the banner at the lodge. The 't' represented variously as a pillar or a tree was an ancient symbol associated with the group, meaning they were Nazis for sure, hiding in plain sight. Comfortable enough in the lodge with its private setting not to worry too much about covering up their activities, but what were they doing here, in our midst?

I thought back to what had happened when the lunch broke up. There had been no clicking of heels or *Sieg Heil* salutes, just handshakes all round. They looked for all the world like businessmen who'd got together for a lodge meeting; old friends together looking relaxed and happy in the California sunshine. Old friends who just happened to be Nazis.

Although they'd looked harmless enough, the men were of an age to have done who knew what in the war. The existence of the lodge with its symbols meant they were still fanatical, which made them dangerous. They would also have younger ones around to do their bidding, as is always the way.

Overcome with exhaustion as the sleepless night at The Glass House caught up with me, I would have happily bedded down there in the library if it had been allowed. With a supreme effort of will, I left the comfortably solid surroundings and guided the Plymouth back to my apartment, deeply troubled but needing sleep.

The sense of foreboding about there being dark forces at work became overwhelming: they didn't come any darker than this.

21. Janet

After a couple of hours of troubled sleep, I woke at around eight that evening and resolved to get rid of the box and the emerald as soon as possible. I'd been given a number to call Thornton's private secretary, day or night, and did so straight away, setting a meeting for the following morning at eleven.

With my hand still resting on the receiver and feeling calmer, I dialled Janet Paris' apartment and again it rang without being picked up. Realising she might be working at or getting ready for a show, I put on a pot of coffee, showered, and toasted some stale bread for dinner. Slim pickings, but there was work to be done and I dressed for the Havana, this time in a lounge suit and the more discreet .32 in its shoulder rig.

I calculated she wouldn't be through at the club until late, after the second show, so had time and needed to head to the office first in any case. The journey was uneventful, and the place was eerily still, with a prevailing sense of calm, all things being relative. I reasoned I was probably safe for the time being, if Thornton and his associates thought they were going to get what they wanted the next day, although the .38 was staying at my side, just in case.

The first job was to retrieve the two letters I'd mailed the previous afternoon outside Mazza's place, which were waiting for me obligingly in the pigeonhole downstairs, together with some other assorted flimflam. Upstairs, I helped myself to a stiff drink from the good bottle (the one for visiting dignitaries and the like) and retrieved from the safe the timeline on the Conlon case I'd started the previous afternoon.

Sitting at my desk, I unfolded it and set about carefully

adding the new information and players uncovered in the last twenty-four hours by my efforts. After I'd finished, I sat there for a while, going over the possibilities, then had an idea and called Tom Delaney.

Somewhat disingenuously, I wanted to see whether he thought the German connection might have a bearing on Baker's disappearance and Taylor's killing and was going to pretend to share my own thinking, when I was really fishing for information. He was out but returned my call about half an hour later, which I took to be a sign that he wasn't still mad at me.

Being a good detective, Tom had picked up on the connection too when he'd run background checks. He told me Rudi Baker's family name had originally been Becker, the spelling having been changed back in the day when they came here in search of a better life.

Similarly, Kurt Taylor's family name had been Schneider, *meaning* tailor, and they'd kept the association but anglicised it at some point. He hadn't known the men personally and wasn't sure whether it meant anything but had asked around the department and spoken with some of their colleagues.

The story he got back was the same one I remembered about them both being proud of their ancestry and boastful about it, even mocking others in the department as mongrels. It didn't seem much at the time but seemed a lot more sinister given what I now knew about who they were working for. Even if it did amount to something, or nothing, he told me that despite any reservations he had, the case was being sat on from further up and was now closed, meaning I was no longer a suspect.

We talked some more about his latest case, a double killing he'd already been assigned over in Lincoln Heights. It looked like a domestic gone wrong: a routine murder-suicide that would keep him busy knocking doors and interviewing witnesses through the night and long into the next day. It seemed like somebody wanted Tom kept busy, away from investigating Baker, Taylor and Jack Conlon.

We said our goodbyes and hung up, him reminding me to watch my step, and me feeling sorry for his workload and the depressing nature of his new case. I felt guilty too, for having lied to one of my few close friends.

Sinister, far-right connections in the case were piling up and I spent time ticking them off. The lodge up in the canyons with the *Ahnenerbe* flags and old Nazis; war loot stolen by the third Reich; a box said to belong to their poster boy Frederick the Great; white supremacist police officers of German extraction acting as enforcers. Then there was Earl Thornton somewhere in the mix, with his butler, who was no such thing, and his whites only country club.

Eric Jenner's death had seemed to be the key to things, but what motive could this group have for wanting him dead? Jack had told me how much his father-in-law liked to own things and manipulate people and he'd offered me money. Paying off the gambling debt seemed like his style, but then he would have had Jenner in his pocket, so why kill him?

I couldn't figure it out. At the point he had control of their business, Thornton would have leverage on Jack, maybe enough to get him to do what he wanted, so why risk that?

Thornton hadn't seemed too concerned about his son-in-law's death; other than the scandal it would bring on the family. There was no love lost between them, but I couldn't imagine the old man having him killed deliberately. Unless something had gone wrong.

Baker and Taylor might have done it, acting on their own, but I doubted it. Thornton had as good as told me that they were on his payroll, and I didn't see them being either smart enough to outwit him or dumb enough to go against his interests. The more I thought it through, my hunch was that they'd been sent to Del Mar to retrieve the box. Maybe they hadn't expected Jack to put up a fight and when he did, things got out of hand.

There were those two heavies, Al and Louis, but I'd seen them in action and didn't reckon on them for Jenner's murder. The manner of the killing was unusual: up close with a small automatic, something like a .25 which didn't seem their style. The ransacking of Jack's apartment seemed more like them, but anybody could have done that, even Jenner himself, before he got iced. Looking for something perhaps.

Maybe I was wrong, and it was personal after all: Jenner was a gambler and owed money, Mazza confirmed that. It might have been Franco himself, for all I knew, or one of a host of other characters. The boys in blue had Jack squarely in the frame for the murder of course, but I wasn't buying that.

I was getting nowhere, going round in circles like a dog chasing its tail and it was time to find Janet, so I returned the updated document to the safe, hoping that if I didn't actively think about it for a while, my subconscious might do some of the heavy lifting and fill in the gaps.

Action would have to substitute for thought, so I locked up and went down and out into the welcome cool of the night. On the drive over to the Strip, I wondered some more about what that group of fascists was doing out here in California. How had they got here?

After a brief period of celebration following the war, the nation had rushed headlong into fighting a new enemy: the scourge of Communism. Was it possible we'd been so busy worrying about the reds, that we'd taken our eye off the fanatics on the far right?

At the Havana again, the whole place fake and tawdry; what little appeal it might have had at first quickly worn off, like cheap veneer. I realised how tiresome it would be to have to work here, day in, day out.

The place was medium busy, and it dawned on me that I'd lost track of the days and it was now Thursday. Mikey, the barman, was on duty again and when he was free, set me up a whiskey sour without being asked. I didn't mind the presumption so much: even less so when I took a sip.

After establishing Janet was performing in the back room, I asked Mikey if he could get a message to her that I wanted to meet her after the show. He said yes, sure he could, then told me how to get backstage to her dressing room later.

He wandered off to fix drinks for a waitress and when he came back, told me one of the guys I'd been asking about before, Franco Mazza, was in, indicating a cubicle over at the side of the bar. Mikey said he'd had some female company earlier but seemed to be on his own now.

I enquired what Mazza was drinking, and he set up a Tom Collins next to my own drink. I paid for both, then made for the booth to brace him.

Sliding in across from Mazza I set the drink in front of his half empty glass and sipped from my own.

"Morgan. I didn't know you came here. What's this, a peace offering?"

"I guess so, Mr. Mazza."

"Something tells me this isn't just social. Let me guess: more questions?"

"Actually, there is something on my mind. A matter arising from the other day. Just one question really."

"Alright, if it's just the one. Let's hear it then."

"It was Earl Thornton who paid Eric Jenner's gambling debts off, wasn't it?"

He shrugged.

"Like I told you, I don't know who it was. It was arranged *anonymously*."

"I got that part, yah, but the lawyer who set things

up. You can tell me that at least. Would that have been a man called Robert Berkeley by any chance?"

I'd done some digging and found out that Berkeley was Thornton's personal lawyer. Franco Mazza shook his head but smiled at me, holding his hands up.

"Uh, uh. I'm not allowed to tell you that, Morgan. Those were the terms."

"Thank you Mr. Mazza, but I think you just did."

I left the booth and paid a visit to the restroom to check my appearance and freshen up, as it was close to eleven, when the show ended. I went back to the bar and asked Mikey to set up a couple more drinks: one for me and one for Janet, then made my way backstage to wait for her. Fifteen minutes must have gone by before she appeared, which was longer than I'd anticipated, and I had to refrain from finishing my drink.

"You're a difficult woman to pin down."

"Well, you've found me now."

She indicated the drink.

"Is that for me? How sweet."

I handed it to her.

"I thought we might talk."

"Give me a minute, will you, Morgan. Well five, actually. To get my makeup off and change out of this dress. Why don't you come back around in a bit?"

"Sure."

I raised my glass to her and wandered off to kill a further five minutes backstage, which is harder than you might think. In the end I went back to the bar for a couple more, returning after what I thought was a decent interval. Juggling the glasses awkwardly into one hand, I knocked on the dressing room door.

"Come in."

"I thought you could use another by now."

I was pleased to be see Janet again. Less so the small automatic she was holding in her lap, a bit too casually for my liking. It was pointing in the general direction of my midriff, a part of me that I happen to be quite fond of.

In the time I'd been away, Janet Paris had removed her stage makeup and changed out of her green satin stage dress into a less showy but elegant black number. She had also taken the time to arm herself with a baby Browning, a compact but particularly lethal little gun.

She was sitting on the dresser with her feet up on a chair, a purse open next to her on the table.

I froze in the open doorway, a drink in each hand by now.

"Just when I thought we were getting along."

"Back up to the door and close it behind you, put the drinks down and don't get any funny ideas, Morgan, or they'll be the last ones you have."

She gestured with the gun.

"Then stand over there in the corner."

I did as she said, with one exception: I put her drink down, but kept my own.

She eyed me levelly as I took a sip, all the while paying close attention to her finger on the trigger of the powerful little .25. Which conjured up an uncomfortable mental picture of those two neat little perforations just below Eric Jenner's ribcage.

Her stance seemed relaxed, but looking closely, there was tension in her hand and a slight adrenaline shake, either of which could get me killed.

"I knew you were trouble the first time we met, Morgan.

You've worked it out, haven't you?"

"Yah. I think so. Pretty much."

"That why you're here?"

"One of the reasons."

"The others?"

"I'll get around to those if you'll let me.

I know now that you killed Eric Jenner, but I'm not sure

why. I've got theories, of course, but I'd like to hear it from you. Care to fill me in?"

Not the best choice of words under the circumstances.

"Why? So you can tell it to the cops?"

I shook my head.

"Uh-uh. I'm not here for that.

They wouldn't be interested in any case. They've got it all neatly worked out: pinned the murder on Jack and they're not looking for anybody else. Of course, he's not around any more to say otherwise."

She looked sad, thinking about Jack and I was relieved to see some of the strain leave her face as she lowered the gun slightly. I tried to work out my chances of rushing her and taking it, or maybe of getting to mine, but she had the drop on me, and the odds on either play weren't good. I'd underestimated her once already and wouldn't be doing it again.

Instead, I began to talk, laying it out for her and playing for time.

"I've been trying to work out who killed Eric and why. There were various suspects, but none of them married up with the way it was done: up close and personal, there in Jack's apartment at the Laguna.

It didn't fit with Jenner's background that he would let his guard down to that extent or not put up a fight. Unless maybe he thought he was there for another reason."

She snapped to and brought the gun up again.

"You said you knew '*now*'. Why now?"

"When I told Jack Eric had been shot with something small like a .25, he frowned; a bit like you're doing now. Only I think his frown was one of recognition: he knew that gun. Jack gave it to you, didn't he?"

She nodded, picked up her bourbon and took a sip.

"A souvenir from the war. He said he'd traded it with some GI, and it was resistance or something. He gave me it when things started to get rough with that box."

"Yah, we'll come onto that thing.

Back to Jenner. I think you lured him to the apartment, then shot him there on the couch, didn't you, Janet? Two little neat holes straight through his heart with that baby Browning pointing at mine right now."

She didn't respond other than to narrow her eyes at me, so I pressed on.

"You tossed the apartment to make it look like something else, locked the door from the inside, then went out the window and lowered yourself off the balcony. It's not that much of a drop, and I'll bet you were a gymnast in high school, weren't you?

Is that about how it happened?"

She took a cigarette from her bag on the dressing table and lit it, squinting at me over the smoke, which was getting in her eyes and narrowing them further. I thought about it, but the gun was level, unwavering. Not the time for a rash move.

"Yes, I shot him, Morgan, but he was a *pig* and he deserved it."

If I'd thought Janet would show remorse, I was wrong. She spat the words out, gesturing nonchalantly with the cigarette and carried on.

"You're right about me tossing the apartment and the bit with the balcony. Lucky guess about the gymnast thing. I didn't lure him there, though, you're wrong about that. It was him who wanted to go there, said he had keys and Jack wasn't around."

"So, why'd you do it?"

She took a sip from her drink and inhaled deeply on the cigarette. Much to my relief, she put the gun down on the desk, probably having decided I was on the level and not there to take her in. She kept it close by, though.

"Jack had known Eric forever: thought he was his best friend. In the end he was blind to what he had become..."

"Which was?"

"A liability. A rat."

She shrugged simply and for a moment I thought that was all I was going to get by way of an explanation.

"So, how'd you do it: get close to him?"

She snorted.

"That was easy. Men are so simple: just a little encouragement is all it takes. Admit it, you fancied your chances with me yourself, didn't you, Morgan?"

She chuckled wickedly as I stood there feeling foolish.

Gesturing to her for permission first, I lit a cigarette to cover my embarrassment and played with the thing as she spoke, not really smoking it.

"I didn't have to go to any special trouble. Eric knew Jack and I were through, I let him take me over to the apartment and left him on the couch, said I was going to fix us a bourbon. Only when I turned back from the counter, I had the gun in my hand, not the drink he was expecting."

I nodded my understanding.

"Up close and personal. That's the how but tell me again about the why. Did he really deserve to die?"

"Don't judge me, Morgan."

I shook my head.

"I'm not in the judging business. I see good people forced to do bad things all the time. Help me understand, that's all."

Looking off to one side at nothing, she began to cry, quietly. I needed her to go on, so said nothing, the silence growing between us.

Eventually she started speaking, matter-of-factly.

"Jack and I were very close once, Morgan. He told me about it all, how Eric stole from the business to cover his gambling debts.

They'd been like brothers and Jack said it was okay, and

they would work things out, but after that he started paying closer attention to the books, keeping an eye on the orders and the shipping manifests and so on.

He spotted some things that didn't add up. Stuff was coming in through the warehouse, and there were these fake deliveries to customers he didn't know existed, although Jack usually took care of that end of things."

"Let me guess: these special clients were all dealt with by Eric?"

She nodded.

"He worked out Eric was importing stolen pieces again, like they'd had to do in the early days, but this time it was behind his back.

Jack couldn't believe it was only about money, and thought there was more to it, so he intercepted one of the shipments to see where it was really going."

I was beginning to understand.

"The box, right? He stirred up a hornet's nest, though, didn't he?"

She nodded.

"Eric was in debt to powerful people. They'd done some dummy runs bringing stuff in, but that box was what they'd really been waiting for. When things got rough, Eric pretended to help hiring those two thugs for protection, but really they were working for him to get the thing back. Jack was a step ahead of him though and knew he was being lied to.

Eric was trying to find Jack through me; he'd guessed I was the one who'd helped him but didn't know whether Jack had the box or had stashed it somewhere. He went to the apartment that night to search it."

He wouldn't have found the left luggage ticket in the letter Jack had sent himself, which I'd come across in his mail.

"He was determined to get what he wanted from me one way or another. He would have double crossed

Jack in the end."

"I guess he might have at that. That's not why you killed him though, is it Janet?"

She shook her head, looking at me, defiantly.

"Eric was the only one who knew Jack's real story: his true identity and what had happened in the war with the other Jack Conlon. My childhood sweetheart.

He didn't know my background though, or that I knew both men. Nobody could have guessed *that*."

She looked at the floor and took a pull on her cigarette before carrying on.

"I couldn't risk what he did know getting back to Jack's wife or his father-in-law. He might never have been able to see the boys again, which would have finished him."

What she said rang true. Jack wasn't by any means a model husband, but he'd loved his wife and worshipped those kids. It would have destroyed him not to see them. If the truth about his marriage to Kitty under an assumed identity had come out, it would be the final nail in the coffin of their relationship.

Thornton wouldn't have been too thrilled either to discover that the father of his grandchildren was really one Jackie Meyer, a Jewish kid from Brooklyn. At that point he might have been in real danger.

"So, you killed Eric to protect Jack?"

She nodded.

"That's about the size of it. I wouldn't expect you to understand, Morgan.
Not unless you've ever really been in love."

I chose to take this as a rhetorical question.

"What happens now? If you're not here to turn me in, why'd you come?"

"I needed to know what happened, but I have something for you from Jack, here in my inside pocket."

Conscious that the gun was still near at hand, I was keen

to avoid a misunderstanding.

"Okay if I reach in and get it?"

She nodded.

I handed over the key to the locker where the emerald was stashed. She examined it.

"What's the key for?"

"The number matches a locker on the back wall of the concourse at Union Station."

"C'mon, don't hold back. What's inside?"

"A small package, about so big."

I made a small box shape with my hands.

"It contains the largest uncut emerald I've ever seen. A fantastic stone, of great value. Even if you only realised a tenth of its real worth, it would keep you in luxury for the rest of your days."

"For real?"

"Scouts honour."

I made the three fingered salute, holding up my right hand.

"Hard to imagine you as a boy scout, Morgan. Is that what this was all about. An emerald?"

I shrugged, not really knowing myself if this was the case.

"I can't say for sure.

Jack and I found it in a secret compartment inside the box on the night he was killed. It was very well hidden, and I don't know if anyone knew it was there."

"Where did it come from?"

"The instrument in the box is supposed to have belonged to Frederick the Great, but my guess is the stone is from much further back. I can't explain properly, but there's something ancient and powerful about it."

She looked at me blankly.

"Anyhow, tomorrow morning I'm handing the box over to that old bastard Thornton, and some particularly unpleasant friends of his. I don't know what, if anything, they know about the emerald, but the keyboard holds some special value for them.

If they do know about it, they're sure to come looking though, which means they'll work their way around to you in the end. Only you'll have a head start."

"Won't they come after you?"

I took a pull on my drink.

"Well, they might, but I'm not so sure. They think I'm on the make, but don't know what I know. I'm playing my hand like they expect me to, and it seems to be working for now. Thornton even offered me a job, the other day."

The memory of it made me wince.

"If they know, they'll watch me for a while: try to work out if I've got it hidden or come into money, but will soon be disappointed on that score. Eventually they'll reckon Jack did something else with it, by which point you'll be long gone."

"Why didn't you keep it for yourself?"

I shook my head.

"Jack's dead and it nearly got me killed too. I don't want any part of it.

If you're looking for the catch, Janet, I think the thing's cursed. Don't hang on to it for longer than you have to."

She nodded.

"How would I go about selling something like that?"

"You'll figure it out. You seem like the resourceful type."

"Why me?"

I shrugged.

"He never said, but I think Jack knew he wouldn't make it. He didn't strike me as the misty-eyed type: I'd say he knew what he was doing. My guess is when I told him about the gun, he figured out you killed Eric, but still felt he owed you.

Maybe he wanted you to have a new life, to make up for the one he took from you and from the other Jack Conlon."

She thought about it for a minute.

"You know, you're not so bad, Morgan. I can see why he trusted you."

Not realising I'd been looking at my shoes for the last while, I looked up to meet her gaze, but having nothing to say, said nothing.

"I'm sorry I teased you earlier. Maybe you might have had a chance after all."

I smiled shyly, unconvinced.

"Where will you go?"

"I'm not sure, maybe..."

My hand was up to stop her.

"On second thoughts, don't answer that. It's better that I don't know where you're headed. It's better that I don't know where you're headed. Don't tell anyone else, either. I mustn't flatter myself: if I can work it out, somebody else could too.

Pack some things and go. Quickly."

I put down my empty glass and was making to leave, my hand already on the door handle, but turned back to her.

"One more thing. You need to lose the gun. If they were ever minded to, the police might tie the slugs back to the ones that killed Eric. Get rid of it: toss it into the ocean somewhere."

"I meant it you know."

I left, hoping that I would never see or hear from Janet Paris again. It was bittersweet, her having just said what she had. I told myself she had been lying for effect only.

And very effective it was too.

22. Proposition

After seeing Janet at the Havana, I'd found a late-night diner near the Strip and refuelled half-heartedly whilst people watching. My mood had been melancholy, and I drank too much coffee then spent a restless night at home. Next morning, I headed up into the canyons again to keep my appointment with Thornton, this time with the box in the trunk of my car.

I'd skipped breakfast and, in no particular hurry, stopped by Union Station in good time for when the left luggage office opened. I took care to check for a tail, but if there was anybody, they were too good for me to spot, which wasn't a reassuring thought.

It was another beautiful morning, and the place looked every bit as pristine as it had the first time, the white stone shimmering in the autumn sunshine. Gardeners were going about their business pruning, or whatever it is they do, the lack of black faces, glaringly obvious now. The thought pulled me up, bringing home the reality of who I was dealing with.

Strengthening my resolve, I gripped the box harder as I carried it up the steps on the way in, where a lackey tried to relieve me of the thing. I declined, telling him that I was to hand it to Mr. Thornton personally, which sent him scuttling off.

I knew that his real first name was Heinrich, but wanted to know the surname of Thornton's butler, Rick, without arousing suspicion. I made a play at the front desk of not being able to recall it and was informed that it was Miller, Rick Miller.

Knowing that aliases adopted by fugitives often have something in common with their real names, as they are easier to remember, meaning less chance of slipping up, I speculated that he might also have taken an Anglicised form of his original surname. In which case, Miller might have been Müller, a common German surname (I have since found out that muller actually translates directly as miller).

Whoever he was, he might have taken a completely new identity of course, but he'd kept a variant of his first name and might have been arrogant enough to keep close to his family name. Meaning that the man now known as Rick Miller might have been called Heinrich Müller in a previous life.

As I was having the thought, the man himself appeared, an icy smile frozen on his face as his eyes went to the box at my side.

"I am to take you directly to meet with Mr. Thornton."

Listening out for it this time, I detected the accent more quickly. It seemed this visit was to be all business, and after Rick had conducted me there and rapped smartly on the door without waiting for a reply, I was ushered into the inner office.

Thornton got up from behind his desk and nodded to me on his way over to the corner bar, as the butler retreated. If there had been any kind of a signal between the two men, I didn't catch it.

"I see you have the box, Morgan. Meaning that you're here to make your deal.

Good man."

I bristled. Although I didn't consider myself good, I didn't need his input, or to think about what it might mean to be considered a 'good man' in his world.

"You'll take a drink."

Again, a statement, not a question, delivered over his shoulder as he poured from a pitcher on the countertop. The gesture seemed studied, rehearsed, like he needed to distract himself. Maybe he didn't want to appear too eager, or this was as close as he got to being nervous.

Much as I didn't want anything from this man, I obliged, needing to play my part.

"Sure."

He handed me another gimlet and his eyes rested briefly on the box at my side. The first sip was sharp and powerful: even if I loathed everything else about him, his ability to fix a drink wasn't in question.

"You've considered my proposal, Morgan. What is it you want in exchange for the box?"

"I'm not after a position on the force Mr. Thornton, although thank you for the offer."

Yes sir, no sir, three bags full sir. I was pitching it as polite, grateful even, but stubborn, with pride enough not to accept his charity. In short, I was pretty much playing me.

He looked at me blankly. This was not what he expected.

"I'm not after money either. Something more valuable."

He was clearly not used to people who didn't want his money and the merest suggestion of a frown crossed his features.

"Something else, then."

I nodded.

"A favour. Not here and now, but things can get awkward in my line of work. I might end up in a tight spot one day and need your help. You have clout at City Hall and elsewhere."

Although I didn't want anything from him, I needed to ask for something and had thought of this ruse on the drive over.

He thought about it.

"I don't like owing people, Morgan. What if it's not within my gift to help you out when the time comes?"

"I'd have to take that chance of course, but I can't

imagine how that would be the case. I'd have to be in a whole heap of trouble."

As he thought it over, I reflected on what Jack had told me about him and how he liked to own people. A peculiar detail struck me, that the difference between owing and owning was just one letter in the English language, but what a difference that one little 'n' makes.

His gaze drifted back down to the box at my side, the deal clincher for him; something he wanted more than anything, and I had it.

He nodded briefly, once.

"Alright then."

I slid the box over towards him with my foot, grateful to be rid of the thing and downed the rest of my drink, figuring that the meeting would be over now that business had been taken care of.

To my surprise, he took my glass and refilled it without asking, then topped his own up. The audience was to be extended and he led us over to a couple of Chesterfields and a vast coffee table cut from a single piece of highly polished burr walnut. The meeting changed gear and it felt like my interview at the Country Club had been successful and I was about to be invited to take up membership. Which in a way, turned out to be the case.

"What do you make of what's happening to this country, Morgan?"

I furrowed my brow, not sure what he meant or where this was going.

"I'm not sure I follow. How do you mean, Mr. Thornton?"

He paused, grappling with the best way to approach his subject, to explain things to the simple man he evidently thought I was.

"We are being overrun; you must be able to see that. People like us will be in the minority before long."

"People like us?"

He nodded enthusiastically.

"That's right, Morgan. Decent white folk are being *replaced*......"

He was warming to his theme now, the white supremacist cause and as he spoke, a dizzy sensation like vertigo came over me, like I was standing on the edge of a precipice. Sickened at what he had seen in me to think I might share his views, I tuned out from what he was saying, before realising he had asked me a question and was waiting for an answer.

"Well, don't you?"

"Err, I'm not sure."

I answered uncertainly.

"This country was a magnificent place, but it could have been so much better for *us* after the war. All I'm saying is that we might have been on the wrong side: did you ever stop to think about that?"

"The wrong side?"

"I know you served your country, but what for? Where did it really get us? If we'd sided with the Germans, we wouldn't have the scourge of Communism in the world today. We'd have been able to halt the spread; caught the cancer early on. Fighting the fascists just left the door open for the Reds."

He had read my doubtful expression.

"I know this isn't how everybody thinks, and it might take some getting used to but I'm talking about patriotism here. True patriotism: the type that takes courage."

He paused to take a sip of his drink and his eyes slid over to the box.

"You're clearly a capable man. I know a group of right-minded people, who love their country and know how to get things done. Men of action like you. I think you would get along with them."

They were right-minded alright: *far-right* minded. I'd

had enough and wanted more than anything in the world to leave.

"Which country would that be exactly, Mr. Thornton?"

"Say what you like about the Nazis, but at least they had vision: a Reich to last a thousand years. This country will have had it before the end of the century.

Think of your own place in history, Morgan. In a hundred years, no one will be alive who remembers you; in a thousand years there will be no record of your existence. If we don't act, all this will be dust."

He spread his arms wide, encompassing the world of privilege and entitlement he had built up around himself. He was deranged. A madman, trying to recruit me with his man of destiny speech and his rose-tinted view of history. In my book, everybody is entitled to their own opinion, but not their own facts.

"World War II. Remind me: broadly speaking that was when one half of the world was trying to kill the other half, wasn't it? You'll forgive me if I don't share your nostalgia for that time. My war wasn't very remarkable, but I distinctly recall being shot at more than once.

So, if you'll excuse me Mr. Thornton."

My manner was as light and breezy as I could make it, brushing off his approach jokily, as I stood to go, not trusting myself to contain my anger.

He wasn't quite done with me though.

"I hope I haven't misjudged you, Morgan."

It felt like a thinly veiled threat.

"All I'm asking is that you think about what I've been saying."

Another thought occurred to him.

"You know, you might be useful to me in other ways. There are times when things need looking into without going through official channels if you get my meaning. Might you be interested in that sort of work?"

I had no interest in being his bagman, official or otherwise, but saw no point in telling him so to his face. He was powerful and dangerous, and mine wasn't the only hide to consider. I forced myself to answer.

"I might at that. It would depend on the circumstances."

This seemed to satisfy whatever mental picture he'd built up of me and my moral compass or lack thereof. He nodded his agreement.

"Good then."

With that I was dismissed. As I left, the butler was making a beeline for Thornton's office, having already been summoned. He didn't look at me or acknowledge my existence in any way and after he'd gone in, I could make out laughter and loud chatter. They were delighted to get their hands on the box and didn't care who knew it.

A cold fury was burning in me, an intense desire to do something about these arrogant people. Jack had charged me with doing the right thing and I had a pretty good idea what he would have wanted. I wasn't as brave as him, but I was for fighting back in whatever small way I could manage.

I would have to bide my time though; there was no way I could take the fight directly to Thornton's network with its powerful connections. Realistically, there was no way I could beat them but sometimes it's not about winning or losing; it's about the difference between fighting or giving up.

A choice we make, that lives somewhere in the stories we tell ourselves about who we are.

23. Aftermath

When the official police department line came out about the whole business, it turned out I pretty much called it right. Their version had Jack killing Eric in his apartment after an argument over money. The company records showed Eric had been stealing from the business, which gave him motive enough. I'd been right about the well-connected owners of the Casa Blanca not wanting to get involved too, as there was no mention of the place.

The station wagon had been pulled out of the canyon with Jack's body in it, which had to be explained though, and according to the police, he'd gone to Del Mar after the murder, stolen it down there and fled to Mexico. He'd told me he'd been there and they had a record of it crossing the border on the return, although no convincing explanation for why he had come back.

LAPD officer Rudy Baker had received a tip off, and acting above and beyond the call of duty, had immediately gone to arrest the murder suspect, assisted by his friend, veteran officer Kurt Taylor of the County Sheriff's department. The police were careful to stress it was an officially sanctioned joint operation; anybody who knew what was what had a good laugh about that one.

Showing great courage, the two officers had confronted the heavily armed Conlon, the resulting gunplay and car chase ending in a crash which killed Taylor and Conlon. The other vehicle involved was Rudy Baker's personal ride, a supercharged V8 '57 Ford Fairlane. His service revolver and other effects were recovered from the car along with Taylor's body, which was in the driving seat. There was no explanation offered for why Baker had been using his own vehicle on police business.

Officer Baker's body had not been recovered from the

crash site, but he was missing, presumed dead. The theory was he had been thrown or jumped clear from the passenger side as the car went over the ravine and his body taken out to sea. As it happens it was far out at sea, albeit some way further south.

In the end, you had to hand it to whoever had cooked up the story: they'd managed to get their ducks all neatly in a row. Eric Jenner's murder was solved, case closed; the murderer had been killed trying to evade capture and two brave officers had lost their lives in the line of duty.

The inconvenient truth of the two men's corrupt and murderous ways would be swept under the carpet and to top it all off, they would be receiving posthumous awards for heroism. The police would come up smelling of roses, reputation intact, to continue their important work, which sometimes included protecting the guilty and punishing the innocent.

It was all complete hooey, of course, neatly wrapped up with a bow for public consumption. A fantasy which served to kill several awkward birds with one stone. If it hadn't been so laughable, it might have been funny.

Naturally, the press played their part in recording the sanitised version for posterity, although the coverage was suspiciously short-lived, the world moving on remarkably quickly. Thornton's influence had evidently ensured that the story was buried, with no more scandal attached to the family than was necessary. The articles I did see played down the Thornton name, stressing that Jack and his wife were estranged. Some even speculated that he must have lost his mind.

My own situation was delicate. The case was officially closed, which meant they weren't looking for anybody else and I wasn't going to get any more immediate heat from that direction, although there was still more than a whiff of suspicion around my name.

There were enough decent policemen around who

wouldn't believe the story, meaning that my card would be marked, and grudges borne. Eventually things would die down, if I could keep my nose clean for long enough, which is exactly what I set about doing.

For the next few weeks my regime was such that, anybody looking from the outside might think I had taken monastic orders. I kept regular hours; went to the office during the day; parked in my usual spot and took my meals in the places I normally frequented. Just a model citizen going about his business, quietly marking time.

I couldn't be sure but assumed here was a fair chance I was being watched and more than once had the sensation of being followed, although there was no evidence this was the case.

There were no instances of breaking and entering or gunplay and suchlike on my part and I was careful not to get into any scrapes or even so much as a parking ticket. In short, nothing much happened and carried on happening, which was fine by me. The routine even did my health and my nerves some good.

In what turned out to be a passable impression of a private investigator, I applied myself to the divorce case and insurance job I'd taken on. I knew my work, could knuckle down to do the job well enough when it suited me and had been sleuthing for quite a few years in one way or another, with frankly variable results. In fairness, a lot of that was down to the fact that the job dealt with human nature and all its splendid unpredictability.

That was the main attraction: unpicking the unholy messes people got themselves into and untangling the endlessly fascinating spectacle of their motivations and desires was what made the job worth getting out of bed for. Or on occasion getting into bed for, if circumstances allowed.

That kind of thing was the exception though; this kind of work paid the bills, but for the most part was dull and uninspiring. I had been a homicide detective in a previous life and in truth missed the job sometimes, but not enough to make me pick up the phone to Earl Thornton.

All the while I was formulating a plan. It would be pointless involving the police, but I'd been thinking about a group who might be able to help and who had the resources and motivation to see the job through. I arranged a meeting at the consul general's office of the Israeli consulate, which I found out covered much of the West Coast from here in the city.

I took care to use a payphone to set up the appointment and to switch cabs on the way to the office, where I met briefly with a junior diplomat. I showed him my credentials, laid out what I had found out about Oak Apple Lodge, the *Ahnenerbe* connection and in particular the Nazi Rick Miller, possible real name Heinrich Müller.

He asked me to wait while he fetched a couple of colleagues, and two bored looking military types took over and questioned me for about half an hour. They didn't introduce themselves and I knew better than to ask who they were.

They asked about my background on the force and as a private investigator, presumably to ascertain I wasn't a crank, or motivated by some sort of grudge. After about ten minutes, they seemed to have satisfied themselves that I could be taken seriously and moved on with more enthusiasm to other matters.

When what little information I could provide them with had been exhausted, they extended their gratitude on behalf of the nation of Israel for my help, which was a first as I've never been thanked by a whole country before. Come to think about it, thanks in any form are pretty thin on the ground in my line of work.

At the end of the meeting, I didn't ask what they were going to do but knew these people had a reputation for acting ruthlessly and getting things done. I warned them not to be at the lodge on the night of November fifteenth, which earned me meaningful looks, but they didn't ask why.

I didn't tell them I was planning another visit to the place myself and had chosen the fifteenth as it was the next full moon; poking around in the woods up there with a flashlight didn't seem like a good idea for what I had in mind.

It might have been useful to take somebody else along, if only to act as lookout, and I had considered Jack's friend, Marty. He'd called the week before to thank me for the money from Jack and ask me what I knew, as he wasn't buying the official police story. I'm sure he would have stayed the right side of sober and made a very able partner, but it was risky to involve him. In the end, I felt it was something I needed to do alone.

The night in question saw me retrace my steps back up into the canyons, certain by now that I wasn't being followed. At the turning up to the lodge, I killed my lights and idled quietly up the track, using the light of the obliging moon to steer by, found the spot under the trees again and slid the Plymouth in out of view. There was less foliage than before, although it was still mild and there was a healthy amount of cover.

My plan was simple. Recalling the oil tank in the yard at the back of the building, I'd brought the hand grenade along, aiming to blow it up and start a fire. I needed to get rid of the thing and couldn't think of a better use for it.

I wasn't sure if the grenade would ignite the oil in the tank or how much fuel there would be but had brought a jerrycan of gasoline with me, confident that would go up. If I was lucky and the tank ruptured, it would spill its contents into the yard and the place and everything in it might go up too.

As before, it was slow going up to the back of the house and I sat there observing the scene through field glasses.

There was no obvious accommodation block, and the rooms were in darkness, with no sign of life. I reasoned that the place was probably used in the day and for functions, but the staff would travel in, rather than live there. Eventually I satisfied myself that the place was deserted.

There might have been a night guard, or a security patrol making checks, but these were risks I would have to take. Any explosion would draw attention, but I reckoned on making good my escape while anybody who came was distracted by the fire I hoped to cause.

Moving down to the back of the lodge and starting at the corner, I walked along the wall towards the back of the building, tipping the entire contents of the jerrycan - five gallons of premium gasoline - over the top of it, hoping the stuff would pool under the oil tank. It was difficult working at full stretch but made a satisfying sloshing sound and the can got easier to handle as I went along the wall until it was empty and the whole place reeked of gasoline.

Working quickly, I placed the empty jerrycan about twenty yards up the hill by a big oak tree I'd picked out earlier, then went back down to the wall. Adrenaline making me shaky and my heart pounding loudly in my ears, I fished the grenade out of my pocket. Although I'd never detonated one before, I had a pretty good idea what to do from the movies.

Not knowing how long the fuse would be set for caused me some anxiety. In the end, having rehearsed my movements to make sure, I pulled the pin, released the clip, and lobbed the thing over the wall directly underneath where I knew the tank to be, then sprinted for all I was worth back up the hill and dived for cover behind the big oak.

As I lay there, my index fingers were jammed in my ears, the right one with the pin from the hand grenade still attached. After a couple of seconds, there was a loud crump as the grenade went off, mingled with the whoosh of gasoline fumes catching, then a bang as the tank went up.

I stayed put and counted to five to avoid getting rained on by debris, then stood up and looked around the tree to admire my handiwork. Satisfying orange flames were lighting up the night at the back of the building, and I wasted no time in hoisting the jerrycan and made a beeline for my car directly down the hill, my way back lit by flames and the full moon.

Lights off, I pointed the Plymouth back down the track and took off as fast as I dared, laughing like a madman through a combination of nerves and exhilaration, fearful of being caught but delighted to have executed my plan. Lights came on in some of the other large properties along the canyon road, but they were set back, and I was gone before anybody came.

There were no police sirens or fire trucks to be heard, other than the usual night-time activity when I reached the city limits. With a conscious effort to cut my speed, I tootled back, just an average citizen on his way home, not a late-night arsonist.

Still buzzing back in my apartment, I poured a celebratory belt and raised a toast to Jack Conlon. It burned all the way down, but eventually the stuff had the desired effect.

I wasn't sure what I was celebrating but had managed to strike a blow in my own small way. Jack would have wanted me to go further, but I wasn't him and I think he would have approved; it felt like my debt to him was settled.

Later, lying in bed, my conscience troubled me as I reflected on the stupidity of my actions and the very real possibility I might have hurt or even killed somebody. Although I believed the lodge had been empty, and didn't care what happened to those fascists, it is not without reason that arson is considered a very serious crime. What if somebody innocent got hurt, like one of the firefighters sent to deal with it?

I rang the fire department early the next morning starting with the fire stations over on Mulholland, figuring one of these would have caught the call out. I got lucky with fire station 108, where I spoke to the duty officer who told me they'd been called out to the Oak Lodge address the previous night.

Using my credentials as a private investigator, I claimed to be working on behalf of the insurance company and enquired whether the loss had been to property only or if anybody had been hurt. I also asked if there might have been anything suspicious about how the fire started.

He told me that by the time they got there, nothing could be done as it was too dangerous to try and save the place, which had burned to the ground. Luckily, there had been nobody staying there, and they managed to contain the fire, which burned itself out without anybody getting hurt.

As far as they were concerned, there was nothing unusual about the cause. It looked like an old oil tank had gone up, probably an electrical fault with the pump or some such, which it turned out was more commonplace than you might think. I thanked him and hung up, mightily relieved.

There was nothing to connect me with the fire and as far as I was aware, no suspicion had fallen on me. Nobody came to see me or followed me, that I knew of. The only follow up of any kind was about ten days later at Thanksgiving, when an anonymous package arrived for me at the office.

It contained a bottle of an aniseed flavoured spirit called 'Arak' and I could make out the country of origin on the label as Israel. There was a card accompanying it with no name but a single word in Hebrew script which I couldn't read, although I had a pretty good idea who it was from and what it meant.

Another was to arrive the following Spring, this time with a sheet from a Tel Aviv newspaper wrapped around it. When I smoothed the page out, there was an article I couldn't read, but the photograph at the top was of Rick Miller, Thornton's butler.

The picture showed him handcuffed to a second man with a crew cut and being led into what looked like a courtroom. Although I couldn't swear to it, the other man in the photo bore a close resemblance to one of those I met with that day at the consulate.

The name in the caption under the picture read Heinrich Müller, and I guessed the rest, though later had the article translated. A wanted SS officer and suspected war criminal, Müller had been living under an assumed identity in the US where he had been identified and followed on a trip to an unspecified Latin American country. Once there, he had been apprehended and taken to Israel to be tried.

Some might consider it rough justice, but to me it was sweet, and I drank a great many toasts that day.

Later, it occurred to me that the case should have made the local papers, but I hadn't read about it. Then I remembered it was Thornton's butler and his network we were talking about and realised the story must have been sat on by his contacts in the press: I wasn't the only one with friends in low places.

24. Farewell

Janet Paris disappeared, and I never heard from her again, although there was a clue to where she might have gone. About six months later I was at the barber's waiting my turn and flicking aimlessly through a magazine, when an article stopped me in my tracks.

What pulled me up in particular was the picture accompanying the story, which was of an emerald, unmistakably the same one and identical in every respect: size, shape and colour. I looked again at the title, which was *'Treasures of the Aztecs'* and read on about a very large gem coming up for sale in a New York auction house.

The long-lost stone had apparently made its way onto the international market, having recently been discovered by a dealer of some repute in Mexico. It had never been cut and was thought to be a sacred item, one which would have held great power and mystical significance for the Aztecs, who prized the things very highly.

The estimate for what it might fetch at auction made me suddenly laugh out loud, earning me a meaningful look from Angelo, who I had startled as he was finishing the tricky bit above the ear of the guy before me.

I never found out whether Thornton and his group knew anything about the stone, or just wanted the box because it had some other hidden value, perhaps the connection with Frederick the Great. Whatever the case, I sincerely hoped it had been destroyed in the fire. Either way, no suspicion fell on me, and things went back to normal after a while.

Although I didn't see Janet, I did see Kitty again about a month after the fire at the lodge, not long before Christmas. It happened like this.

My uncharacteristically busy spell had produced a growing pile of paperwork I had been steadfastly ignoring, added to which I'd never got around to tidying up properly from the time when the office had been ransacked. Not that the files had ever been what you'd call strictly organised in the first place, since I've never been very diligent at that sort of thing.

Anyhow, I was in the office, shuffling paper around without any real sense of purpose and had fallen into reminiscing. I'd just put away the folder of the Maddison case; the one I went back to when there was nothing more pressing, or my conscience got the better of me.

Wise detectives learn to leave their old cases behind; collecting them is unhealthy, but most have one or two they revisit. Ones that are unsolved, unresolved or aren't going away quietly for whatever reason.

The glossy eight by ten print I knew so well slid out of the folder on to the desk in front of me when I was tidying up, guided by some unseen hand. I'd sat there and studied it for what might have been the thousandth time, which got me nowhere, as usual.

I decided to keep the photograph close to hand rather than put it back in the folder, knowing I would look at it again soon and put it in the desk drawer. It sat next to the hand grenade pin from the night of the fire, which I'd kept as a memento.

Seeing it reminded me about the Conlon case and everybody connected with it, and as I was standing there, Kitty breezed into my office. It had seemed uncanny, although it might not have been such a coincidence, as she was in my thoughts a lot at that time.

"Still no security in this place, I see Morgan. You need to fire your decorator too."

She looked around in mock distaste. Wearing a black suit jacket with matching pencil skirt and a large-brimmed fedora hat with a black satin band, she somehow managed to look both every inch the widow and absolutely fantastic at the same time.

Like performing a magic trick, she produced a bundle of money about the size of a house brick out of her bag and dropped it on my desk. The notes were hundred-dollar bills and there must have been thousands there.

"What's that for?"

"It's yours, Morgan. Jack had life insurance and I think he would have wanted you to have some of it. Besides, you earned it."

Unsure what she meant, I went to speak, but she put a hand up to stop me.

"I've got enough."

Which indeed she had.

"You know he paid me already."

"Take it. Please."

I was taught that when people give you money, provided you know what it is for, you should accept it and say thank you. I wasn't sure exactly what this for and pride made me want to give it back, but it was the proverbial gift horse, and my empty pockets were telling me otherwise.

A dark thought occurred to me, causing me to frown.

"It's Jack's money you say? Not from your father?"

"My father? He likes you well enough, but it's got nothing to do with him. Why would he...?"

Kitty was shaking her head, looking confused.

"No reason. Just an idea I had."

She brushed this aside.

"I'm going to Europe in the new year, Morgan. Taking the boys and making a fresh start. Daddy has contacts there."

I was sure he had.

"I think he'd like to set me up with some rich aristocrat."

"A new father for the boys?"

"Maybe. They need one, you know."

Kitty was looking at me directly and I crossed around to the front of the desk on impulse and drew her towards me. I kissed her, which she didn't seem to mind, so I kissed here some more, which she seemed to mind even less.

"What did you do that for, Morgan? You auditioning for the part?"

"I wanted to know what it would be like. I've been wondering since the first time we met."

"Why'd you stop? Not to your liking?"

"Quite the opposite. We both know it could never work between us, though Kitty."

"So, why'd you start?"

"I wanted to know what I would be missing out on. Besides, you look good in black."

She pushed me backwards gently and looked at me closely.

"Why do I get the feeling there's something in your past?

It can be a good place to visit, but you can't live there, you know."

"So I'm told."

Freeing herself, she picked up her purse, turned and left, as abruptly as she had come in, with nothing else by way of a goodbye.

I sat heavily, looking at the pile of banknotes, usure what to do next. Having money gives you options, and the thought occurred to me to take a vacation somewhere far away from the city. It would buy me time to think things through.

Deciding the bar was open, I got the office bottle, set up a good hit of the Morgan family inheritance and went about the business of having a good long think. The springs on my captain's chair complained loudly as I put both feet up on the desk and leaned back to sip my drink, which is harder to do than it sounds, as you'll know if you've ever tried. As luck would have it, I've had a fair bit of practice.

I got to wondering about what had just happened and relationships in general, about whether any of us are ever actually in love, or just in love with the idea of being in love. Deep down, I found my own answer for that one, but didn't much care for it.

Somebody else was in my thoughts and about halfway through the second drink, acting with rare decisiveness, I dragged the telephone awkwardly towards me. Rummaging through the desk drawer, I pulled out a card and dialled her number. I let the phone ring for longer than might be considered decent, until a woman's voice answered warily at the other end.

"Hello?"

"Hello Agnes, is that you? It's Morgan here, you remember me, don't you?"

"Sure. The regular guy. What is it you want?"

I'd heard that Elegance was being wound up when I bumped into Franco Mazza again, who turned out to be more on the level than I'd given him credit for.

"I heard the business is closing. Do you mind my asking if you have a job to go to?"

"No. We've pretty much wrapped everything up there now and I won't be going back after Thanksgiving. I was thinking of going back to Lanegans you know, the department store, to get my old job back. Somebody from Earl Thornton's country club got in touch about a position over there too."

I couldn't let that happen and acting on impulse, heard myself saying:

"How would you feel about maybe working for me?"

"For you? Doing what?"

She sounded dubious. I realised I hadn't really thought it through but looking around the messy office gave me an idea.

"Well, I don't know exactly. I'm very disorganised and you seem to have everything all buttoned up. I'm tired of dealing with everything on my own and I think you could help me out."

"I dunno. It sounds fishy. Are you sure you can afford to hire me?"

I eyed the windfall on my desk.

"Oh yes. That's one thing I am sure of."

She was thinking it through on the other end of the line.

"So, what next?"

"If you're not busy, why don't you stop by my office tomorrow at about eleven and we'll work the details out and draw up a proper contract. That can be your first job."

"You want me to write my own contract?"

"Well, I can't do it. I can pay you from next Monday, but I don't actually want you to start for a couple of weeks."

"Why not?"

"I'm taking a vacation, just a short one. It's been a long time since I've been away. Sometimes I think I've never really been anywhere."

She was easy to talk to and I surprised myself as the words came out.

"They say travel broadens the mind, don't they, Agnes?"

"Yes, but it sure slims down the old purse."

We began at the same time:

"Every silver lining...."

".... has a cloud."

We both started laughing. Suddenly, I had a good feeling about this.

"You say that too, huh. I thought it was just me."

"Where will you go?"

"I don't know. Somewhere quiet, by the ocean. I was thinking Mexico maybe; I hear there are some fantastic places and things to see down there, Aztec temples and the like."

It seemed to make sense. I was tired of the city and of playing my part in other people's troubles.

"You'll stop by tomorrow at eleven then?"

"Okay, I will."

She took the address, and we said our goodbyes and hung up.

My original intention in calling was to arrange to give her the money from Jack, which I still had in an envelope in the safe. I figured she could use it and the dust had settled enough by then.

The more I thought about it, this new plan seemed good and I sat, sipping whisky for quite a while. As I did, I thought about the Conlon case and all the people in it and in particular about Jack and Janet's story.

In a strange way, it seemed to make sense there had been two Jack Conlons, as one hadn't been enough to go around. I hoped he wouldn't have minded me kissing his wife, but figured he probably had bigger fish to fry. Or no fish to fry at all. Who knows how that all works?

The one I knew had killed two men, albeit bad ones, and I had helped him, although it had been them or us. Not to mention all the other law breaking I'd got up to. Sometimes good people are forced to do bad things and good things happen to bad people. I couldn't be sure which I was anymore, or if anybody was really keeping score.

When it comes down to it, we are all cast adrift, left to follow our own moral compass. As much as any of us might reasonably hope to achieve are some small acts of kindness in the face of a world which somehow contrives to be both relentless and indifferent.

Printed in Great Britain
by Amazon